SECRETS
IN THE
DARK

HEATHER GRAHAM
SECRETS IN THE DARK

mira

ISBN-13: 978-0-7783-6936-3

Secrets in the Dark

Mira
22 Adelaide St. West, 41st Floor
Toronto, Ontario M5H 4E3, Canada
BookClubbish.com

Printed in U.S.A.

For my daughter-in-law, Kari, co-grands, Gayle and Kelly Stewart, son Jason, and of course—Sebastian!

CAST OF CHARACTERS

The Krewe of Hunters—
a specialized FBI unit that uses its members' "unique abilities"
to bring justice to strange or unorthodox cases

Adam Harrison—
philanthropist founder of the Krewe of Hunters

Jackson Crow—
Supervisory Field Agent, Adam's chosen leader for the team

Angela Hawkins Crow—
original Krewe member, exceptional in the field
and on research

Philip Law—
criminal psychiatrist and Krewe Special Agent, home office

The Euro Special Assistance Team or "Blackbird"—
a newly formed group created to extend the Krewe's reach into Europe to
assist with crimes abroad

Della Hamilton—
late twenties, five-eight, light brown hair, green eyes,
with the Krewe almost a year

Mason Carter—
six-five, dark hair, blue eyes, FBI for six years, joined the Krewe starting with
the "vampire" murders

Jon Wilhelm—
early fifties, experienced law enforcement with Norway's National Police
Directorate, speaks English with an American accent because he studied at
Yale (working in Norway)

Edmund Taylor—
early forties, London's Metropolitan Police Detective
Chief Inspector

Jeanne Lapierre—
fifties, tall and solid, long-time Parisian detective,
excellent at his work

François Bisset—
forty-five, light blue eyes, friendly and professional manner,
their Interpol liaison

Sean Johnstone—
Detective Inspector working in the Whitechapel and
Spitalfields neighborhoods

Trey Harper—
officer with the London Metropolitan Police

Ripper—
determined to be the best and most renowned "Ripper" ever

Stephan Dante/the King of the Vampires—
organized serial killer, globe-trotting to bring his "kingship"
from country to country

Gary Hudson—
bartender at Ye Olde Pub on Whitechapel Road

Dr. Lucretia Mayberry—
forensic anthropologist

Professor Arnold Goodridge—
archeologist from Colorado State

Stacey Kerry—
head of the makeup department on the film
Darkness and the Vampire

Abigail Scott—
Victorian journalist and advocate, died 1895

PROLOGUE

The king was dead.

Or, rather, at this time in history, incarcerated.

Of course, the "king" believed that he would "rise" again—after all, a vampire was immortal.

But the Vampire King had taught Ripper well. Just as the world was filled with different countries, presidents, kings, queens and prime ministers—and, of course, great dictators—the world should equally be filled with kings of the underworld.

And with learning, a man could rise to greatness, become king of his own domain.

Ripper smiled to himself, watching the world go by around him. He wasn't lurking in the shadows. He was sitting amongst the neon lights of the busy bars in Brixton, watching.

Just watching.

He'd learned from his master to watch, and to listen. And there was a lot to watch. Of course, the area was popular amongst all age groups, but it attracted the young and the beautiful.

He'd learned as well to mimic a variety of accents. If someone was fascinated by Scots, he could roll his *R*'s like no one else. Irish was an easy one to slip into. Welsh a bit harder, and then, of course, there was proper British and such twists as those made famous by rock bands, like a Liverpool bit.

He was anything anyone wanted him to be. He could even imitate Americans—from a hard-toned New Yorker to a fellow with a Southern drawl or even a man with a Western twang.

All in a day's work.

Well, of course, there was work, too. Which meant he could only watch so late on certain nights. But tonight…

Ah, but tonight was his. And he learned from experience—from watching the master at work as well.

He'd learned how to play the game, how to maneuver, what to do and what not to do.

In short, his reign was just beginning.

And that all-important lesson he'd learned?

Not to get caught! After all, he would be king in his own right. And the man history knew as "Jack the Ripper" had never been caught—though every few years, there was a new theory, a new belief that forensic measures might not have given the world the truth.

But that would never happen. And like that Jack, this Ripper would never let himself be caught.

No, he would never let an obsession rule him. Emotion would never come into the picture. He had learned all the tricks of the trade, including the one he'd learned all on his own. Never let anything but cold, cool calculation rule his actions, never…

Never, never! But then, he'd known deep in his heart from the beginning that he was his own man, with his own plan and agenda. He'd made a start before he'd met the vampire. But back then...

Well, he had feared the slightest rustle of sound. He hadn't had the confidence he had now, hadn't mastered his craft, so to say. Now...

He had been a good student. The best student. And he was smart enough to utilize all that he had learned, including the fact that he must not make mistakes, that mistakes and obsession could lead to behavior that wasn't the most calculated and smart.

And now...he had such a dream, such an agenda!

Maybe he'd always coveted the idea of being king.

King of the Rippers!

Three stunning young women were walking by his table. Laughing, chatting about coming to Europe to find a prince.

He pretended to look at his watch, as if he were waiting for someone. And as they came nearer, he started to rise, almost knocking into one of them.

"Oh, I'm ever so bloody sorry!" he said.

"No, no, it's all right!" the closest girl in the trio said, smiling. She was an attractive blonde, perfectly configured with wickedly long legs, generous breasts and, best of all, a trusting smile.

"Sorry, me mate just had to stand me up and I'd figured..." He paused, shrugging and indicating the table where he'd been seated. "Well, unless you'd like to join me!"

Three might be a challenge, but...

"Sorry! I'm Brad Terry. And this..." He paused again, in-

dicating the environs of Brixton. "This is my home ground
if I can give you any pointers. You are American."

"We are, straight out of Kansas," the blonde said. "I'm
Shelly McNamara and these are my friends Ginger Cannon and Tess Garcia."

"Nice to meet you. And thank you," one of her friends,
the brunette introduced as Ginger, said. She glanced at the
blonde, Shelly, and said, "we'll leave you to get pointers
for us. Tess and I will try the place right across the street if
you want to join us."

Ripper smiled. He'd listened and watched enough to
know that Shelly McNamara's friends were giving her leeway to flirt with him and decide if she wanted a bit of a
British fling or not. They were leaving her alone but offering her a safety net.

Pity for her and them that it wouldn't be enough.

The two friends waved and started off. Ripper looked
at the young woman, Shelly, and gave her his most innocent, charming smile.

"What will you have?" he asked her.

Whatever it was, she'd have more.

So much more...

As she sat down, smiling, eager and adventurous, he
thought that his night was going to go beautifully.

Yes, the king was dead—incarcerated.

But then again...

Long live the king!

CHAPTER ONE

Della Hamilton looked out the window as they drove from Heathrow Airport to the center of London, Detective Edmund Taylor driving and her partner, Mason Carter, seated behind her.

She took a moment to close her eyes and imagine that they were there for a fun vacation, to enjoy the sights.

She loved the city of London. A history buff, she'd been fascinated as a teenager to visit with her parents, to roam the halls of the Tower of London and ride over London Bridge, visit the remaining Roman sites, stare at the legendary Big Ben and marvel at the beauty and the stories to be discovered within the hallowed ground of Westminster Cathedral.

She hadn't been back since she'd been a college student, and on that trip, she'd revisited a few of her favorite historic sites, but she'd also spent time in Chelsea, Covent Gardens and other areas for the nightlife and fun with friends.

Now...

Now, she was Special Agent Della Hamilton and part

of a unique unit within the FBI. She and Mason had been assigned to a new "assistance" force, and thus they headed to Europe when the need arose. They had started out on a case in which a killer had skipped from country to country, his method of killing unique. They'd been able to trick him into being captured when he'd returned to the United States and, through his taunting, they had learned that he had more followers—doing some of the killings attributed to him—than they had previously expected.

And so now...

London. A city of over eight million people, busy with their day-to-day lives, most good citizens, hard-working human beings. And yet, like anywhere in the world, there were those among humanity who were not quite so decent. In fact, they might be described as purely evil.

"We've had some bloody whack jobs in this city," Edmund Taylor said, his eyes on the road, his head shaking as he stared hard ahead. "Just in the last decade we had a man who killed his victims, chopped them up—and ate their brains. And other body parts, I believe. He was incarcerated, released and killed again, once again chopping up his victim and eating their brains until he was rearrested. We have no death penalty and he was sentenced to a secure mental facility, but..." He paused, shaking his head, and Della had to wonder if he wasn't wishing that, in certain cases when a killer escaped to kill and kill again, there might be a death penalty in Great Britain.

But Edmund just shook his head and continued with, "All throughout its history, there have been incidents that defy anything resembling normality. Going all the way back to Jack the Ripper. Latest case in point, our so-called Vampire King—a man I am entirely grateful to see incarcerated and behind bars, thanks, of course, to Blackbird and the two of you."

From the back seat, Mason leaned forward to speak. "Blackbird! We're a team. And working as a team, we got Dante. But the man is claiming that he didn't do the killing in London—and when he made those claims, he didn't know that Della was in contact with all of us and that his words were recorded. But those victims he was referring to were killed by his method—the victims were drugged, carefully exsanguinated, and left as sleeping beauties."

Edmund nodded. "We don't know just how many killers there may be—but we've gone through every bit of evidence we have, which is sadly not much. Dante was good about teaching his people that forensics are at a point these days where a single hair can identify a killer. And he also made a point of leaving bodies where they'd be discovered but not before the elements around them had compromised whatever might be found. He isn't saying more, right?"

"One of our agents who is also a criminal psychiatrist has been working with him," Mason said. "And, so far, he knows what we surmised. You were with us in the bayou. He said he killed in France, but not all the victims in Norway—or in London. Dante was great at finding those people who were seeking something in life that they didn't have. Some looking for any excuse to kill and some believing in whatever ridiculous story he told them. Hopefully, any of the true idiots he had among his followers never got to the point of murder—and are scared to death now that he has been taken and, in the United States, may well face lethal injection. Of course, every country where he killed wants a crack at him, but..."

"But?" Edmund asked.

"I think even the most peace-loving countries in the world want a man like him removed with no possibility of parole or escape," Della provided flatly.

Edmund didn't respond, but watching him, she knew that he might agree.

"I'm always conflicted," she told him. "There is no undoing an execution if it's later proven that someone was innocent. But sometimes, when evidence is overwhelming, and a killer does get out and kill and kill again… I guess we wouldn't be human if we didn't wish it could be stopped."

"Of course," Edmund murmured.

She turned and glanced at Mason. He was serious, a thoughtful frown creasing his forehead. She was glad that he was her partner for so many reasons. She had been hesitant about him at first—before they'd met on a case, he'd been working solo for a year because his partner had been killed in the line of duty. That did something to any law enforcement officer. But while he hated to kill, he was a crack shot and an excellent judge of when deadly force was necessary and when a suspect could be talked down. He had an extreme sense of justice. It also helped that he stood an intimidating six foot five, was incredibly fit and blessed with ink-dark hair and eyes so dark a blue they could appear almost black in shadows.

And it helped, of course, that in the Krewe, it was all right to fall for one's partner. Krewe members were simply different—some said special, others said cursed—and for their work, it was important that they shared that difference.

They were simply a minute portion of the population.

Like many others—in law enforcement in general—she and Mason had also made the most of all their off-time. There was always a fine line that had to be observed. They cared. They cared deeply for the victims, for ending violence that was humanly possible to end. They also knew that they had to stop and smell the proverbial flowers when they could—they needed that space to stay sane and as prepared as humanly possible as well.

It was natural that she couldn't help but wish it was a vacation.

But it wasn't. And since it wasn't, she was grateful that she was with Mason—and Detective Edmund Taylor. They were becoming their own "special" unit, unofficially termed Blackbird, while they were officially the Euro Special Assistance Team.

Edmund Taylor was, in Della's mind, a top-notch detective. They'd met in Norway, on their hunt for the "vampire" who had struck in England and France before turning to the Scandinavian nation. While the FBI had long had liaison offices across the world, they were unique in their ability to join in on an investigation—when asked, of course. Interpol had provided them with François Bisset, their go-between for all countries, and they worked with the detectives involved in each case. While this was a new case, it was also an old one.

Because no one knew what magic or hypnotism the confessed killer Stephan Dante had used on others or just how many other killers he had created and/or trained.

Edmund knew the case. He was somewhere in his early forties, but he had worked long and hard with Scotland Yard to earn his position with homicide and in this case, what they were calling "special services." He was solid and serious most of the time, just an inch or so shorter than Mason and a man who evidently worked his frustrations out at the gym and could still smile and find humor upon occasion, letting his guard down when he was among friends. He was a handsome man with a headful of light brown hair and eyes so soft a brown they might have been almost amber.

"Yeah, us!" he said lightly then. "We caught the killer—who let us know that we didn't catch all the killers we need to catch. But…we're on it. We've been on it. Night is coming, so…did you two want to get to the hotel and get some sleep, or—"

Laughing, Della interrupted him. "No, we're ready to hit the ground running. That's the plan with us having our own pilot and private plane. Of course, poor Gene, our pilot, needs to be ready to fly at the drop of a hat, but he gets lots of downtime, too. And he wants to see the sights, so…anyway, no! We had plenty of sleep on the plane. Do you have any ideas? I'd assumed we'd go over files—"

"Which we will, tomorrow. Two of our victims—supposedly taken by the *vampire* killer—were last seen in the Brixton nightlife area. I thought you might need a pint or two as well after your long journey."

Della glanced back at Mason. "We just flew in from Bucharest, so hardly a long journey. Since Dante had insinuated that we might find clues at Castle Bran, we went to the castle, and, called you—as you know—so…"

"Yes, indeed. We need to find possible suspects—and then, as you suggested, discover if any of them lost a wife or loved one to a suicide—as suggested by our quickie trip to Transylvania and discoveries regarding Vlad Dracul. A suicide they just might blame on themselves. But we're struggling to find suspects, going back over all the paperwork… Anyway, I'm not going to feel sorry for you for a long journey since…" He paused to grin. "Since you did get something of a holiday in there, and the castle is beautiful and the Romanian countryside even more so. But we can have a relaxing drink and dinner—and perhaps spot something or at the very least, chat with a bartender or two."

"I think we can function well with a pint," Mason said. "Has anything happened since we made our way here?"

Edmund shook his head. "But I was there when Dante was taken down in the Louisiana bayou—I heard what he said. The victims killed *already* have families, and—"

"Don't worry. We understand. The victims deserve justice, and truth in that justice. And we need to make sure there aren't more victims," Mason said quietly.

"Exactly," Edmund murmured. "And if there is someone out there—something we all believe—we have to stop him before he starts on his own *reign* of whatever kind of terror he's planning."

"Yes," Della said quietly. "So, a pint it is!"

They'd headed out from Bucharest in the midafternoon. But even though the flight was short, time at the airports and driving was turning day into night. A fog was sweeping in, as one so commonly did in England, and the sun was dying in the western sky.

It was beautiful and eerie.

But not so eerie in the Brixton section. Restaurants and pubs blazed with lights. Visitors and locals were hurrying about. The night was temperate and pleasant and many were dining at outside cafés or sipping drinks at sidewalk tables.

Edmund luckily managed to park right on the street. They all exited the car and for a minute, stood looking around at the many lights.

Couples and groups walked about, laughing, teasing,

chatting, some arm in arm, all out for a good time, for ca-
maraderie with old friends and new.

"Hopefully, the news about Stephan Dante has kept
women from casually hooking up in bars."

"Men and women have been casually hooking up in pubs
since forever," Edmund said. "I've wanted to do a press
conference, but the powers that be... Well, no one wants a
panic. And at this time, all we have is what Dante is saying
and we have no proof and... Well, no press conference. But
thankfully, they still think I should be part of this special
force and that we should continue to investigate."

"The sad thing is that something is going to happen before the powers that be decide a warning is in order—and
that's probably the way in every western country, not just
England," Mason told him. "Hey, we get on it, and we
move fast."

"All right, well. Welcome to England! So...would you
have a dark ale or light?" he asked. "Oh, let's head there,
to Bixby's—great bar food and wonderful taps."

"It's a plan. It's also where one victim was last seen,
right?" Della asked.

Edmund nodded. "Aye, but... Hey! I'm not lying. Great
bar food and clean, clear taps!"

Bixby's was a large establishment with plenty of inside
seating and even more on a large courtyard just outside.
Those tables offered views of both the interior and exte-
rior of the restaurant with a bar central in the courtyard,
with still more tables spilling out onto the sidewalk and
the street.

"Great table!" Mason assured Edmund as they were
seated.

It was a great table just inside where they could see what

was going on where they were—and out the door to the street. They could watch the flow of humanity around them, couples, groups and the occasional loner.

Della found herself studying the couples as Edmund and Mason ordered after she had waved a hand, indicating she'd be happy with anything they chose.

There was a young couple near them, both smiling, holding hands now and then, sharing their food, either new lovers or old who were very much in love! They were speaking French, she thought, overhearing a bit of the conversation.

She didn't believe that the killer they were seeking was French.

He was American or British.

Another couple intrigued her at first; they were joined by an older couple, and it appeared that they were young newlyweds out with the wife's parents.

"Fish and chips. Better here than at home," Mason said. "Or, maybe I just think that they're better because we are in jolly old England."

"No. Fish and chips are better here," Edmund said lightly. "Hey, no insult. Creole cooking is it in Louisiana, and when not in Cuba, Cuban coffee is best in Miami."

"Ah, we all lay claim to our culinary delights," Della murmured. They were having dinner. There was no guarantee that anything was going to happen here tonight.

Here—or anywhere.

"The biggest problem we have is that, of course, everyone assumed that there was just one killer—that's why they had me and our Interpol liaison Bisset and Jeanne Lapierre from France joining you two and Detective Wilhelm in Norway. We don't have a list of possible suspects, though tomorrow, we'll go back through the files. Within them now, we may just find those we cleared at the time because Dante was here and working and they could twist the truth…all the witnesses had alibis that seemed truthful, and then when the murders started in Norway, well…"

Della was half listening and half watching people as they came and went. A group moved and she noticed one of the courtyard tables closest to the sidewalk. A pretty blonde sat there, laughing as she chatted with a young man who appeared to be in his early thirties. He had slightly shaggy light brown hair and an easy smile. She wasn't sure why, but she didn't think that they'd known one another forever—they had the look of two young people flirting and enjoying the get-to-know-you part of a relationship.

And they most likely were just a young couple getting to know one another.

"Excuse me!" she murmured.

She stood and pretended to head out and look down the sidewalk as if she were trying to see if a friend might be arriving.

But as she passed by the table, she heard their conversation.

The girl spoke with an American accent; she probably hailed from somewhere in the Midwest.

The man spoke with an English accent, as if he'd been born and bred in London.

"Well, we could meet up with your friends, or…" the young man said.

The blonde giggled and ran her fingers over the back of his hand. "My friends are genuinely nice, and I think that you would enjoy them. Then again…how quickly we could move, so much we could see and do if we were alone!"

Della wasn't sure why, but alarms rang loudly in her

head. She wasn't sure that she thought anything out, she just hurried back to the table and picked up her pint of ale.

She meant to explain, but just as she picked up the glass, she saw the couple rising. She hurried back, weaving through tables, anxious to reach them before they could leave the restaurant.

She pretended to look elsewhere and slammed into the young woman, making sure that her ale flew into the air… and fell due to the force of gravity, soaking the pretty young blonde.

"Oh! I am so sorry!" Della cried. "I am truly sorry, I've ruined your night, oh…!"

The man stared at her for a split second. "I'll go get something," he said quickly, stepping around her and heading for the bar in the center of the courtyard.

By then, Edmund and Mason had come up and Edmund quickly did the speaking. "Hello, miss, we are so sorry, but forgive me—" he paused to flash his badge "—do you know the gentleman you were with, or did you just meet?"

"Uh," she said, frowning, staring at the badge. "I—uh—did I do something wrong? If so, I'm deeply sorry, I'm loving being here, this trip has been a dream—"

"You haven't done anything wrong," Mason quickly assured her. "We're just—"

He broke off. He had twisted around to watch for her companion. "He's not getting a bar rag—he's gone," he said. "I'm going after him."

"Oh, my God, what did he do?" the young woman whispered.

"Maybe nothing, maybe nothing at all!" Della said quickly. "But we're advising young women against being alone with men they've just met. There have been unusual murders in the last year and—"

"They caught the guy! It's all over the news everywhere. They caught the Vampire King!" the girl said.

"He had followers," Edmund said quietly. "And if we've ruined your trip in any way, we're heartily sorry, and yet—"

"You really are a detective. I'm not being pranked or anything?" she asked. "Did my friends put you up to this? I mean…you," she said, looking at Della. "You're American. This is England. You can't have any authority here—"

"I am an American. FBI, on special assignment because we don't know that the *Vampire King* was the only one doing the killing," Della explained quickly. "And if you're disturbed, we are sorry, but in my mind, disturbing you—"

"I'm not just disturbed. I'm wearing beer," the girl said.

"And again, I am sorry. I'll be happy to pay for your dry cleaning—"

The girl suddenly shuddered. "No, no, I'm sorry, I'm being ugly and I don't mean to be, it's just that he seemed like such a nice guy and…"

"I think if he was just a nice guy, he'd have gotten the rag and come back," Edmund said. He reached into his pocket and gave her one of his cards. "I swear, I am with Scotland Yard. And please, I'd greatly appreciate a call if anyone does anything suspicious near you—"

"He didn't come back!" the girl whispered. "He—he didn't get a rag and come back!"

"You have friends here in London with you," Della said. "Do you know where they are? May we walk you to wherever they are?"

The girl looked at them and swallowed nervously. Then

she nodded. "I'm Shelly McNamara. My first trip with college friends. That man... I..."

"You're young, beautiful, on your first European trip, and it seemed you met a great British guy and there's usually no reason for that to be anything but fine," Della assured her quickly. "Again, I'm sorry that the world has come to this, but...please, don't go with strangers alone. Make sure that if you're going to be with anyone, that someone knows exactly who you are with and where you're going to be. Please. For your own safety."

"Walk me across the street?" the girl asked.

"Of course," Edmund said.

Edmund lifted an arm, indicating that he would follow her. Della paused briefly, looking for Mason. But he hadn't returned.

She felt a chill, wondering if her intuition had been right in any way.

The young man had seen her, and surely Mason and Edmund, and he had disappeared. He'd been charming the girl—until they might have attracted the attention of others...

Mason was good. He could move quickly. But the man had apparently found a back way out. Brixton was brimming with its night crowd. There were people, restaurants and pubs everywhere.

She should have gone with him. But she had been the one who had splashed the girl with ale. And Edmund had the proper credentials for this country and...

Maybe the man had just been a student with a warrant out on a petty drug charge or the like and had simply needed to escape any brush with the authorities.

Mason would find them.

She hurried after Shelly McNamara and Edmund. Shelly's

friends were inside the pub, sitting at the bar, listening to a tale from the young woman who was serving drinks there. They smiled, curious when Shelly arrived with her friends.

"You're wearing beer!" one of the girls said.

"My fault—I ran into her," Della explained quickly.

"And he's a cop—a copper here, right? Or a bobby?" Shelly asked, looking at Edmund.

He smiled and said dramatically, "They call me Mr. Detective—Detective Inspector Edmund Taylor. And, of course, ladies, we're all at your service."

"What happened to lover boy?" one of her friends asked.

"That's Ginger. Ginger Cannon and my other friend here is Tess Garcia," Shelly said in way of introduction. "Oh! And you must see this lady's badge! She's Special Agent Della Hamilton, FBI."

"In England?" Tess said.

"Attached to a case," Della said briefly.

"Vampire King!" the pretty bartender, who had gone silent in the middle of her story when they'd arrived, spoke up.

"He's been caught, right? The news went on and on about him. Well, of course. Creepy and scary as hell. So, what about lover boy?" Tess persisted.

"Gone. And I'm starting to like myself in good British ale. You can get me another," Shelly said.

"Well, I think I could do that. Nice to have met you all and please, enjoy London, but take care," Edmund said.

"Whoa!"

They were all startled when the pretty bartender, who had turned to the television just as a soccer match was interrupted by a newscaster cutting in with "breaking news."

Every London paper had received a letter—claiming that Jack the Ripper was back in the city.

They all paused to listen.

"Naturally, the police were informed immediately and many believe this to be a hoax, but just an hour ago the station received an anonymous letter, a single type-written page, mailed to the station from nearby warning, Jack is Back. We don't know how serious this threat to be, but with recent murders in and around our great country, we felt that it was only right that our populace and our tourists be warned immediately."

She went on speaking, describing the recent capture of Stephan Dante and warning that everyone, especially young women, needed to be careful.

Watching the screen, Edmund shook his head. "Jack is back. Great." He seemed to forget Shelly McNamara and her friends. "Of course—"

"It could be a hoax," Della said. "And I'm sure that it's with the police and a forensic crew by now, and maybe they'll find out that it is a hoax, or, at the very least, discover something about whoever sent it."

"A hoax by an idiot, or a warning from a protégé!" Edmund said. He realized that the three girls at the bar were watching him, but he no longer seemed to need to project a cordial image for his city.

"Please! Be careful," he said.

He started out of the pub and Della was quick to follow, turning back to the three young women with a smile. "So sorry about the beer. Do be careful!"

Close on Edmund's heels, she saw that Mason had found them. He was shaking his head with disgust.

"Never even got to follow him—he raced out through

the kitchen. He was gone when I hit the alley, but I tried both directions and… It may be nothing," he said.

"Probably nothing," Della said. "Just a guy with a petty crime behind him afraid of authority."

"But something about him bothered you," Mason said.

Della shrugged. "Yes. But… Hey. Intuition can be wrong."

Edmund was watching her. "I saw him so briefly," he said. "But… I don't know. I got the feeling I had seen him before and I don't know in what context."

"We can keep looking," Della said.

"We can. But…"

"He's gone. Wherever he hides out, he's there. He's gone. We're not going to get him tonight. Damn. We have a tab open across the street!"

"Paid it," Mason assured him. "Well—"

He frowned, breaking off as his phone buzzed faintly. "Philip," he said, glancing at his caller ID.

Della and Edmund watched him, frowning, as he listened to the caller.

"Philip is—"

"I know. I was there, in Louisiana, remember?" Edmund reminded him. "Special agent with the Krewe, psychiatrist working with Dante."

If they'd been alone, Mason would have put the call on speaker, Della knew.

But they were standing in the street surrounded by Brixton nightlife.

He ended the call and looked at them. "We must take a quick hop home. Edmund, you're free to come, or work the case from here. Philip has gotten a lot from Dante— including the fact that he did kill women in unsolved crimes where the officers came to suspect that they were his *practice* killings. He had details, so… Anyway, Philip thinks that we might get a great deal more on a suspect if he observes Dante talking to Della."

"Private jet with sleeping quarters there and back?" Edmund said. "I'm with you. Unless, of course, you two want to be alone? I guess that—"

"We'll be fine with you in the plane," Della assured him quickly, looking at Mason and laughing. "We're to be at the airport by seven a.m. The pilot has been informed."

"So…let me get you to your hotel. I guess we all need some sleep," Edmund said.

There was nothing else to do that night. There really hadn't been much that they could have done, except…

Della couldn't help but feel that something had happened.

And as they hurried back to Edmund's car, they could hear people talking about the emergency news broadcast.

Jack's back.

"You may have saved a life tonight!" Mason told her softly. She smiled and nodded.

Maybe. And yet…

It also felt as if they had just missed something.

They reached the hotel and there, they showered and fell into bed. Without words, Della turned into Mason, anxious that night to make love.

To see the beauty in the world.

In his arms, she slept.

But in her dreams, she suddenly saw the man's face again, and in her mind's eye, he smiled and whispered, "Jack's back!"

She woke with a start, but Mason pulled her back into his arms.

"We will find this man, too. Get some sleep. Tomorrow, you face Dante again."

She was tough, she assured herself. She was a good agent, trained, savvy and she knew it.

But it still felt good to pull his arms more tightly around her, knowing that there was support, in the field or in their minds, that only they could provide for one another.

It would all become much harder because…

She knew in her heart that it was no hoax. Jack was back.

CHAPTER TWO

"There is nothing like the taste of blood. Nothing."

Licking his lips salaciously, Stephan Dante spoke the words before leaning forward to continue with, "You must understand. It came to me, a force, telling me that I was the king of the vampires. Blood. You feel the very sweetest flow of energy as you swallow, as you consume what was the life force of another. And as it fills you, the body comes alive with heat, with the promise of eternity. And there is a power that sweeps into every limb and across the mind and soul. There is nothing—nothing—like the exhilaration and power and..."

Perhaps the most disturbing and frightening aspect of the man speaking was the fact that he looked like the proverbial boy next door. He was tall, had a great smile and was leanly muscled—Della remembered thinking that he could be a linebacker when she had first met him as a friendly local bartender. He was a clean-shaven man, with wavy brown hair and a way of smiling that might be taken as boyishly charming, but that smile also hinted mischievously of something just a bit on the edge. It was fun and harmless—unless you wanted more.

And, of course, he was beyond doubt a sociopath. He'd had his agenda, his method of killing, and his "signature" as the forensic crews and profilers said. But he had no problem dispatching anyone who got in his way by any means possible.

Thankfully, he was incarcerated now, and handcuffs held him firmly to an iron bar set in the table. The interrogation room where Della Hamilton now faced him was engineered for discussions with the most dangerous prisoners. And no matter the boyish charm he possessed, from law enforcement to the guards, everyone knew he was extremely dangerous.

Della knew that even better than most. She and Mason were the two members of law enforcement who had managed at last to lure him into something of a trap, and thus he was now a prisoner. They'd had backup the whole way but catching him had been like trying to get a get a grip on an eel in an ocean of slime. He'd become obsessed with her—thinking that she'd join him!

If not, of course, he'd have been happy to drink her blood.

She was eternally wary of the man, and aware he was still trying to bait her.

So, she waited.

Della remained expressionless as his voiced trailed and he waited for her response.

She finally shrugged and said, "In other words, you get your rocks off killing people." Her tone was flat and she made a point of looking away, bored with his dramatics. "Sad."

He shook his head. "You don't begin to understand," he told her. "And I'm disappointed. *You're* sad! I believed in you. I thought you were a cut above the others. We could have been the most amazing team!"

"You know, I am a team player, but I just never saw myself on any team you might be leading," she assured him. She leaned forward herself. "Okay, you know that you're looking at the death penalty."

He shook his head, smiling. "Trust me. I will live forever."

"Great. You enjoy whatever eternal life you find after your lethal injections."

"Europe doesn't have the death penalty."

"Well, I'm not a lawyer, but you're in Louisiana right now. The state does have the death penalty. And even our federal government offers the death penalty in certain cases."

"It will never happen," he assured her.

"I need a name," she said flatly.

"A name?" he queried, amused. "You probably need several names."

"Well, then, give me several names."

Dante lifted his hand in a vague motion. "Seriously? Even if I wanted to, I probably couldn't give you any names. I meet people who long for something better. A name is just that—a label. And my friends like to consider every aspect of what they need in life. And I tell them how to get it. I don't do background checks."

"You made sure you could connect them with people who could create false identities and passports for them."

He shrugged. "Maybe. Maybe my friends are nationalists!"

"So. Tell me about England."

"Northern European country. Together with Wales and Scotland and Northern Ireland, it's called Great Britain. Produced the Beatles and other great rock groups. What about it?"

"Who killed with you as a *vampire* in England?"

He shrugged. "I don't do names, I told you. But, hey, the guy in England was fairly good, but he'll never be me. Maybe he'll segue. Whatever. I don't even remember. Thing is, with any of my followers, they'll know that the king of the vampires is dead. They'll…choose their own kingdoms!"

King of the Rippers?

"You do know what people look like, right?"

"Looks are like names. They can all be changed."

"Yes, but there's only one look that's real. You know, like you look now."

He shrugged. "Who knows what I saw. Again, I'm resting now."

"You're incarcerated awaiting trial."

"Right. Taking a little rest." He gave her his most charming smile. "But I'll rest and get my strength back and…"

He paused, leaning as close to her as the cuffs would allow.

"I will let you have fun before I drink your blood, and for me, it will be so delicious, I will drink, and drink, and drink, and lick my lips!"

"Yeah. Whatever. You do remember people. You could have forensic artists do sketches."

"Ah, but you know that we're all chameleons!"

"But there is that one look. I saw a guy. Is this one of your friends?"

She'd given her best memory of the man with the young blond woman in Brixton to one of the Krewe's best artists and she was sure she had a good likeness.

She pressed it toward him on the table and watched his reaction.

Did his lips tighten just a bit?

He stared at the picture and shrugged. "Could be anybody."

"You know him."

"Hey, I know nothing!"

"All right, let's try this. Who provides you all your false passports?"

Dante started to laugh. "Seriously? What do you think? They go by their real names? They report their earnings to the IRS?"

She smiled sweetly. "All right. Well," she said, starting to rise, "you haven't cooperated with anyone—"

"I have cooperated. I gave that psychiatrist dude all kinds of helpful information."

"Not enough. And you haven't helped me in the least. Have a nice afterlife."

"You don't listen. They won't get me. And that's it? You're not going to sit here and try harder? I mean, hmm, you really don't know half of it, though I guess you... I told you! I have helped. I talked to that other guy. Well, in truth, he's not bad. That special agent who is a psychiatrist or whatever who comes in here is all right and I look at him sometimes and think that he's reading my mind—"

"Special Agent—and Doctor—Philip Law, and yes, he's read a lot in your mind. He told me that you honestly believe that whether as a criminal or creature, you do see yourself as the king of vampires—or the ultimate in talent for vampire killing, and thus, until you magically free yourself—such killings have ended."

Dante leaned back, smiling broadly. "Ah, the king is dead, long live the king! Yet each king is different, and each claims different prowess, and different ways to rise to power. No. There will never be another me, and I will reign again one day, mark my words. Poetry! The vampire rests, yet other nobility will come to the tests, for each man will rise to the beat of his own drum."

"Ah, but that's the future. We know one thing. As you suggested, we visited Bram Castle. I believe that you suckered in a co-killer in England by finding a man who had lost his wife to suicide—perhaps she did the unthinkable rather than face life with him, as Vlad the Impaler's wife supposedly did when the Ottomans under Radu attacked. You do like to give clues. But sometimes, I think you're telling the truth. You just don't have the answers."

"Well, stay near me, my lovely. You could have ruled with me. Now, of course, when I make my way out of here, well… I'm sure your blood is going to be delicious—hot and spicy." He finished speaking and laughed. "He's going crazy out there, beyond the glass, right? He is with you, I know. Good old Special Agent Mason Carter. Watching. Wishing he could come in and shoot me."

"Hmm. No, in truth, Mason doesn't like killing—he only kills if he has no choice when it comes to saving an innocent life. But you wouldn't begin to understand that, so… Well, it's been dull and tedious, but gotta go."

She stood, aware that he would do something, say something, to draw her back.

"That's it? Oh, come on."

"Well, I think I've got all you're going to give me," she

said, leaning on the table for just a minute and smiling at him. "When we find our suspects, we're going to be looking for someone who lost someone they loved to suicide. And, when we go through the files, he could be someone police have interviewed already. And each king reigns on his own. Jack is back, eh?"

He stared at her, frowning for a minute.

"Oh, come on! You do see news here," she told him.

Dante leaned back, smiling again as he shrugged. "Good old Jack is back. He'll never be as talented as me. But... he'll have his fun! And letters to the newspapers! Just like the original."

"Well, according to most profilers, detectives, psychiatrists and historians through the years, every one of the letters was a hoax."

"Not true! He sent a piece of a victim's kidney to some dude with a letter!"

"Right. But forensics at the time couldn't even prove if it was human—or animal."

"A human is an animal."

"A human or a different animal. Anyway, I guess your friend who would be king of the Rippers didn't study all the files on the case. But, hey, whatever."

He leaned forward. "But no one knows for sure, do they? There are still several suspects that scholars argue over. Maybe the kidney was human and maybe the letter was written by Jack the Ripper. Since the world is going on theory, so can the king of the Rippers!"

"All right, so...one of your followers *does* have his sights on becoming the next Jack the Ripper," Della said.

"Maybe."

"Okay. Thanks."

She stood to leave again.

"You can't go yet!"

"Why not?"

"You've barely been here."

"Right. But I have what I need. Unless you want to give me a name."

"Jack the Ripper."

"Bye-bye!"

"I'll make him watch me drink your blood!" Dante cried angrily.

She didn't reply. She tapped on the door and the guard opened it to let her out. "Glad that guy is cuffed and chained," he said, shaking his head.

Della smiled and nodded.

Dante was yelling about his prowess and how she would regret not realizing his power, slamming his fists against the table.

"Let him burn some of it out, that's my suggestion," she said, "and thank you."

Mason, Edmund and Philip Law were just coming out of the observation room as she left the guard.

"He was right about one thing—we arrested him, but if I'd been forced to shoot him, well, hmm, I don't think I would have lost sleep over it!" Mason said.

"I may ask you to pop in there next," Philip said. "He still thinks he'll get his hands on Della. But you really infuriate him. And angry people spout out things, so..."

"I do my best to apprehend those who need apprehending," Mason said. "I, like Della and many of our ranks, feel mixed on the question of life imprisonment and the death penalty. But, hey, I'm human and sure, I want to throttle the bastard when he starts at Della, but..."

"We need him to talk," Della said.

Mason looked away for a minute.

Sometimes, it was hard for him, for them both.

But they'd managed to make it work. She was trained, as she had reminded herself last night. She was an agent. It was still natural for him to want to protect her. But they'd managed a great relationship—personally and professionally.

"He's sending us through hoops, but we may still need him alive," she said. She looked at Philip and grimaced. "At least I think we were right—he did find a follower who had lost a wife to suicide."

After Dante's arrest, he had gone on about Bram Castle—and it had seemed that there just might be something there to discover. While Vlad the Impaler hadn't really spent much time there, it was believed that his first wife had jumped to her death.

Dante still seemed to want to convince everyone that he was a vampire—in one way or another.

He was, she thought, simply a cold-blooded killer.

But his little bits and pieces could help them. She and Mason had gone to Bram Castle before heading to England, and she believed that he was so arrogant and sure of himself that he did throw out real clues—that needed to be followed.

"Hey, he likes you," she told Philip. "And you have gotten a lot out of him."

Philip Law was one of triplets, married to one agent with the Krewe and brother to another. They were handsome siblings, all "gifted" with seeing the dead who remained, and especially gifted in other areas. Each had used those gifts in different directions. For Philip, he'd wanted law enforcement along with wanting to know what made the

human mind tick, so he had gone through years of school-
ing, receiving his doctorate in psychiatry while minoring
in psychology.

He couldn't exactly read minds—or all minds. But he
could often untangle and discover what a person was twist-
ing or hiding.

"I've gotten a fair amount of information out of him,
yes. At least we know what happened in several instances
in the United States. But listening as he tried to keep you
going, I believe that he knew that someone he was *training*
was fascinated with Jack the Ripper before this all hit the
news. I hope, of course, that I pulled you back here for a
good reason and I think that maybe we did get it."

"Has he heard what's been all over on British media—
Jack's back?"

"Of course, he heard it. Whether people think it's a
hoax or not, something like that spreads and it's all over
the news and social media. But here's the thing, or what I
think we may have gotten from today. Yes, he knows who
is doing it—he recognized the sketch you showed him.
And whatever made you wary of the man, your intuition
was right on."

Mason let out a grown of disgust. "We had him!"

Philip lifted a hand. "What? If you had caught him, you
couldn't have held him. There's no law against picking up
a pretty—willing—girl in a bar or pub. You'd have had
nothing."

"If he follows Dante's lead, he'll change his look. If I had
been fast enough, we'd have—"

"Hey, Mason, I was there, too," Edmund reminded him
quietly. "And we had absolutely nothing on him. British
law—we couldn't have arrested him, we couldn't have de-

tained him. Same here, there wouldn't have been a thing that could have been done. Okay. So—"

"So," Philip continued, "like I said, I learned from working with Dante that he was the killer on a few of our unsolved murders. They were his *practice* murders—law enforcement here had put them together but hadn't been sure because things had been just a bit different, because, of course, he was practicing for getting his vampire ritual right. Between my talks with him and what I observed here today, I believe that you're going to need to start looking in an earlier direction. Anything that remotely matches the killings that Jack the Ripper carried out—"

"We have slit throats," Edmund said. "But not the kind of mutilation that was practiced in the past."

"Because that's the key word—*practice*. Like Dante, this killer is perfecting his method. It's possible he's quickly strangling or suffocating his victims—something past detectives thought the Ripper might have done to silence them—and then slitting their throats. But most psychiatrists and profilers believe that even *Jack* had his practice sessions. The killing wasn't the turn-on for him. The mutilation was. The first thing that needs to be learned to carry out murders like that is to shut the victim up as quickly as possible. This current killer has probably learned that lesson. But the world is different today. Forensic science has come a long—long—way. But, for now, you need to look through the British Isles. Places the killer can easily reach. Few people have the talent for fake IDs and passports that Dante managed. But he learned from other inmates when he was incarcerated earlier in his life. He gained money from learning where stashes had been hidden by robbers that knew they were never getting out. That's how Dante funded himself and moved like the wind—he could pay. He used the system to his advantage. I doubt that this killer is going to hop from country to country with the speed that Dante managed. But I do believe that he's going to be just as obsessed with being the best there is. The king of the Rippers, if you will."

"You know, we do have something," Mason said.

Della frowned, looking at him. "What?"

He shrugged. "Me."

"What?"

"Sorry. It occurred me just as we were speaking here. Della, you went to the table where our suspect was sitting with Shelly, the blond tourist. Our suspect decided to disappear. But as he did, he touched my jacket. He did so trying to get by me as quickly as possible. We need to get my jacket to forensics. We might just get a fingerprint or skin cell...and while it's a long shot, I think we need whatever shots we can get, long or short."

"He may not be in any system, but hell, yes, go for it!" Philip said.

"We're on it," Edmund assured him.

"Local office, all speed," Della said. "I'm sure we can find you another jacket. Thank God you're all into leather."

"Hey, that didn't sound right!" Mason teased.

"I'm not touching that comment with a ten-foot pole," Philip said. "But Dante is still in there slamming his chains around. The guard is letting him wear himself out. I realize you have been wearing it, but Mason, slip out of that jacket. We'll try for prints. I'd like to see Dante's reaction to you, since he probably assumes you're together and he has such a thing for Della."

Della looked at Mason. He shrugged and nodded, turning to Philip. "Whatever you think. You are the mind man. He's not obsessed with me, though, as he is with Della."

"No. He just really hates you," Philip said cheerfully. "Want to head on in?"

"All right."

Della watched as Mason tapped for the guard and was let through the door to the hall of interrogation rooms and then through to Stephan Dante.

Dante had been creating all the noise and havoc he could with his cuffs and chains.

Seeing Mason, he went dead still.

"You!" he snapped venomously. "Of course, I knew you were here."

"It's my job. You're not going to tell me anything, but hey, I'm here. Bored out of my skull, but they asked me to come in and so…here I am."

"Right. If I was going to tell anyone anything—"

"You would have told Della. Hey, yeah. So, you really think that you're getting out?"

"I know that I'm getting out. A good lawyer… You have no proof against me."

"Well, there's your confessions," Mason pointed out. He'd slid into the chair across the table from Dante by then and was almost sprawled out in his seat—displaying boredom.

"A good lawyer? And we have no proof? You're dreaming, man. Your confession was recorded."

Dante waved a hand in the air. "You know, Della was just talking about the fact that as far as most so-called learned men think, all the letters received by the police and the newspapers in the Ripper days were hoaxes. So, maybe I'm just a crazy hoaxer."

"Well, I'm not arguing that you're crazy."

"I say brilliant."

"Brilliant—crazy. There's a fine line sometimes that gets blurred," Mason told him. "Anyway, I'm not sure. They do a study of that case in a lot of the profiling classes they have for us at the Bureau. I'm not sure that all the letters were hoaxes. They couldn't test. Maybe the Dear Boss letter that was signed Jack the Ripper wasn't a hoax. Anyway, until then, the killings were called the Whitechapel murders. Then, there's what they call the From Hell letter or the Lusk letter. See, I disagree. I guess Della and I have watched different documentaries. I think that the piece of the kidney sent to Lusk with the letter did belong to Catherine Eddowes. The medical examiner back then believed that it was part of a human kidney, left side, and that the person had suffered from Bright's disease, something called nephritis now, and a catchall for autoimmune situations and others—like alcoholism. Anyway, what does it matter? You're in here. And he's out there…" Mason paused, smiling sadistically, and leaned toward Dante. "He's out there, and he's going to outdo you all over the place!"

If Stephan Dante hadn't been secured to the table, Della—watching the exchange intensely along with Philip and Edmund—believed that he would have leaped over the table to attack Mason with fists flying and teeth gnashing.

But he was secured by his cuffs and the chains, and while he tried to bolt up, he was forced back, slamming down to his chair.

"Sometimes, he goes by John Smith," Dante spat out. "Then there's David Jones. But I tell them at the get-go, never give anyone your real name, not even a partner!"

"Hey, wow, thanks, that's something!" Mason said. He

stood. "Well, hey, enjoy. Oh, and I hope you get that good lawyer. It will cost you a fortune before you get the death penalty."

As Mason tapped for the guard and left the room, Dante went into a rage again. "I will be out and you will be sorry. I will make you watch. You will watch every single thing I do to her and with her and you will watch me drink her blood before you die!"

Mason ignored him and rejoined the others, arching his brow and looking from Philip to Della.

"Anything?" he asked Philip.

"Well, he gave you two of the most common names in the English-speaking world, but yes, the man who would be the Ripper King goes by those names. He may change up. But—"

"It's something," Edmund said quietly. He was carefully holding Mason's leather jacket. "Should we head into forensics now?"

"We should. Philip?" Della asked.

"Thank you for coming all the way here. I think that you did get what you could—"

"And it is something," Edmund said quietly. "So, if we're all in agreement, I think we need to get moving. And I think we need to head back right away."

"You're good. I think it will be good, too, that Dante has been agitated and it will be an honest thing when I tell him that Della is already gone and you don't even want to bother with him. He could want to throw out more bits of info to me to make me call Della to bring her home again, hop back and forth across the Atlantic," Philip said. "Hey, will this all get…tricky?"

"What all?" Mason asked him.

"Well, it makes sense for you to get that leather jacket right to Forensics. But that will be FBI Forensics in the US and—"

"It won't matter. Although we have nothing to arrest him for, it will give us something. Unless, of course, we can trace prints to a previous event and even then…if we can find him, we can get prints again. It's hope—that's what it is," Edmund said.

"And on that note…thank you, Philip. Keep at him!" Della said.

"Thank you for pond-hopping back for this," Philip said.

"Hey, what's a pond or two?" Mason said lightly.

They headed out, stopping for their weapons, returning to the car. Mason drove. Edmund, in the back seat, heard his phone ring and excusing himself, he answered it.

Della turned back to see him. He winced and ended the call.

"We have a victim, a *Ripper* victim. And this time…"

"This time?"

"Well, I guess his practice has made…perfect. Maria Monty, a tourist from Seattle, Washington. She was staying right across the Thames and had taken one of the Ripper tours several times. She was discovered just an hour ago… two deep slashes to the throat and her body, her body… ripped from the neck to the groin."

CHAPTER THREE

Another victim.

Well, they had known that this kind of killer wouldn't stop. He was, in fact, just beginning, certain that his "reign" would be the best.

He knew he had to let go of believing that they'd had a killer—and let him get away. He had to remember that they were on the side of the law, and by law, there would have been nothing they could have done even if they'd stopped the man. There were no laws in England or America against having a drink at a bar and flirting with a pretty girl. He couldn't concentrate on what couldn't have been done; they had to move in a forward direction as quickly as possible.

"We've all feared there would be another victim—even before we got back, but I think that the trip to see Stephan Dante was important," Mason said quietly as they navigated the London streets by car. "Philip knows his stuff. The man we saw is a good suspect, and we will figure out who he is. What do you have on the victim so far?" he asked Edmund.

"Well, go figure," Edmund said. "She was found in Whitechapel. An area that's gotten way better with time—and Ripper tours and tourists. Forty-three, an American schoolteacher on holiday. Maria Monty. She was found at six a.m. in an alley—insides out. We'll see her at the morgue—I've assured them that we're on the way back."

Mason felt his face was tightening. This man was going to play the game. He was going to try to replicate Jack the Ripper, going by the five murders most profiling experts and "Ripperologists" claimed to have belonged to the one killer.

"We will drop this jacket with local Forensics and Della," Mason said, "at the airport—"

"Calling the pilot," she assured him.

Edmund was shaking his head. "Say we'd gotten that bloke in Brixton. What could we have done? Asked him why he was trying to pick up a pretty girl in a bar? We couldn't have done a damned thing. And it might not be him."

"Well, I can't help wishing we'd gotten him. At the least, we'd know him—" Mason began.

"No. We wouldn't," Della said. "He's a pupil of Dante, remember? He'll have fake ID. But more than that—Dante would have taught him about wigs and makeup and prosthetics. And he'll be able to change his appearance."

"Yes, and we're *all* pretty sure that Dante recognized that sketch you showed him. And I know the law and I know we couldn't have held him on anything. But, hey. I can't help it. I know that was the guy and that he slipped right through our fingers—easily," Mason said.

"At least you thought to go after him," Edmund said.

"So, we won't recognize him if we see him again," Mason

said. "And now, he's struck. In Whitechapel. He'll be looking for four more victims—with the last being killed inside and mutilated beyond recognition, just like Mary Kelly."

"Mason, the man in the bar may have just been someone who didn't like police!"

He drove quickly, knowing the area well. They reached the local offices. Thankfully, Mason had worked with the NOLA office a few times and when he explained what they needed, his jacket was quickly taken and the paperwork was done. A member of the forensics team came out to speak with him, dead serious since he knew what it was about and telling Mason that he couldn't promise him anything but he would do everything in his power to find something that might help them.

"Heading back to England now with Detective Inspector Taylor," Mason told him. "But if you get anything, I'd appreciate you telling Field Director Jackson Crow—he will know how to reach us wherever we may be."

"Including over the Atlantic!" Edmund added cheerfully.

They headed out. Mason's phone was ringing; it was Gene. He was ready when they were and as soon as air traffic control gave them the clearance.

"Seriously, we're damned lucky. We can make it back to the airport in another thirty minutes, another thirty for clearance from the tower, and in five or six hours, we'll hit the ground," Mason said.

"Well, you know, land safely and deplane," Della said dryly.

"With awesome speed!" Edmund said. He was looking at his phone.

The sound of his voice changed. "Ah, bloody hell!" he exclaimed.

"What?" Della asked.

"They've gotten another note. The newspaper received it—I guess our guy doesn't feel that he should dare take a chance with sharing this on his own, he wants to send things to the paper just like the original. This one is...a dilly. So bad that..."

He handed his phone to Della.

She looked down at the message he had received and read aloud.

"Jack is back, this time no hack,
    there are so many he adores, but seriously, bloke,
they are all just whores.
    He will clean the streets, no matter the coppers on
the beats,
    for Jack is back and he's got the knack!"

"Hoax—or the real killer?" Della asked softly.

"This time, the real killer, I believe. He thinks he's a great poet," Mason murmured. He offered them a grimace. "It's going to be up to us and our team and every law enforcement officer out there to teach him that he'll have plenty of time behind bars to become the *killer* king of poets."

"But he does have something the original *Jack* didn't have," Della said, frowning. "Social media. He will consider himself greater for that alone, for the terror he invokes. And he's basically stated that all women are whores, so..."

"Social media, something he has. Phenomenal forensic teams across the world, something we have. Della, we are going to get this guy," Mason promised. "There's the airport—we're already on our way. Oh, and something else he didn't count on."

"What's that?" Della asked him.

"Us," Mason said flatly, and Edmund nodded seriously in agreement.

They were *damned* lucky with the private plane Adam Harrison had provided for them. Flying across the "pond" was easy. They could sleep.

Edmund and Della did sleep.

Mason couldn't.

He'd stopped blaming himself for letting the man they'd seen escape. He believed that Della's instincts had kicked in and they had probably stopped him from killing that night.

But he'd found another victim. And if they didn't get him fast, he'd find more.

"Hey!"

Della had been sleeping in the back but she came up and slid into the seat next to him.

"Hey," he said quietly.

"You haven't slept at all," she admonished.

"I've dozed right here." He smiled. "I never knew such luxurious accommodations before—I learned to just doze in a chair when the need arose."

"You're not a good liar. Mason, you must get it through your head that *you* didn't lose a suspect. We were worried about the young woman and… Mason! You at least thought to go after him."

He nodded. "And I'm comparatively young, strong and fast—and he eluded me."

"All right, let's think about this. It could have been worse if we'd stopped him. Then, if we had something to go on and had a chance of getting to him, he could have started screaming about police harassment, he could have brought in lawyers...and walked away."

He nodded, taking her hand, and offering her a grin. "I'm going to be okay. I can't help but feel that... Never mind. I'm going to be okay. I promise."

"Of course. Because we will get him," she said determinedly.

The pilot announced that they were about to land at Heathrow and Edmund Taylor came from the back to take one of the seats across from them.

"I hope I prove useful and become the permanent British bloke in this alliance thing we've been working. This is the most amazing travel I've ever had."

Mason laughed. "I was just thinking the same thing. I was feeling guilty at first. I thought we were taking the plane from the US agents. But we're not. I'm not sure if you know about Krewe history, but—"

"Ghostbusters," Edmund said.

"We often get the weird," Mason said.

"You know, weird cases, occult cases—vampire cases," Della explained dryly.

Edmund waved a hand in the air. "A team versed in the unusual and ready to deal with ghosts, goblins, whatever—I read up about them. *Krewe* because the first case the American unit worked was in New Orleans and they have all their Mardi Gras krewes there, *krewe* being an organization that stages parades or floats for carnival. And Adam Harrison had been putting some of the right people together for different strange cases before he talked to friends in the government and the FBI to form his unit. He also happens to be an incredibly rich guy who would rather help the world than play golf. Heard he lost his son—some people would have gotten bitter. I hope to meet the man one day."

"I'm sure you will."

Mason glanced at Della, smiling. Adam Harrison *was* an amazing man. His son had been "gifted" and when he'd died, he'd someone passed his special senses through to a friend. And working a strange death with that friend, he'd learned that there were more "gifted" people in the world.

Adam hadn't been able to see or speak with the dead himself—until several years after his son's death. Knowing that the man had then come to be able to see his teenaged son was something that gave Mason a lot of faith. There was more—he already knew that. But he felt as well that Adam's amazing gift for charity and caring for others had been the thing that had allowed him to see his only child, even in death. But now they were a new section of that team. One that could prove to be a little bit…hmm.

Awkward.

Because if Edmund or Jeanne Lapierre—the French detective they'd worked with on the vampire case, or François Bisset—their Interpol liaison—saw or spoke with the dead, they hadn't shared that information with Mason or Della.

Philip, with his medical degree, had explained it the best he could. Like all things with human beings—the good, the bad and the ugly—heredity appeared to be the main factor. One percent of one percent of all people had a predisposition for the connection. Oddly enough, one percent of one percent on the world stage wasn't that small a number.

"Adam is just a wonderful, kind and giving person. He's spent his life giving," Mason said. "In all honesty, I haven't known him that long, but the people who have love and admire the man. And the first agent he recruited was Jackson Crow, an unbelievable field supervisor and between them—and the rest of the Krewe—you couldn't ask for better coworkers. So, well, yes. Good travel. And—"

"As always," Della said, "we get to hit the ground running!"

"We don't have to run," Edmund said dryly. "I left my car at the airport. We've been set up at New Scotland Yard with offices and we'll head there. François was home, but he's taking the Chunnel over and he'll be with us by tonight. Wilhelm is tying things up in Norway and will join us as well, and Jeanne Lapierre plans on arriving by this evening. Or whatever it is—morning here, right? Still getting accustomed to the puddle-jumping!"

"Hey, yeah, it's a trick, but a fun doable one, in a way!" Della said. "And…well, you, Wilhelm, Jeanne and François are great to work with and…hmm. And, England is easy enough for us—nice that our cohorts speak our language."

"You blokes kind of speak English!" Edmund teased.

"Or," Della teased in return, "you might say that we perfected English."

Edmund groaned.

"Hey, you know a smattering of several languages," Mason reminded Della.

She nodded. "A smattering! Hey, I can buy coffee in several languages! And, of course, find the restrooms."

"Why do you think they call them restrooms?" Edmund asked, grinning. "I mean you don't go there to rest."

They all laughed. Mason suggested, "Well, let's see, in lots of countries, say France, they are much more specific! *Toilets!*"

"Then we have men's room and ladies' room," Della reminded them.

"And facilities," Mason said. "Hmm, but facilities…that could mean many things!"

"Speaking of creature comforts," Della said. "Mason, you don't have a jacket now. England. Remember? It can be very wet and chilly!" Della reminded him.

"Not to worry. The world is full of stores. I'll find something."

Edmund laughed. "For you? At your height. Sleeves long enough?"

"Hey, not to worry," Mason repeated. "Sales make the world go around. We'll find something somewhere."

"Yes, and we're putting you to bed on the plane and you are going to sleep!" Della told him, her tone light, her eyes serious.

He shook his head. "I'm honestly not tired. Della, you and Edmund should read up on our victim."

"And what are you doing if not sleeping?" Della asked him.

"Reading up on the first victim—the original Jack the Ripper's first victim," he said. "And it is a different world. Edmund, of course they're on this at Scotland Yard already, I imagine, but I'd like us to have immediate video surveillance from anywhere near the murder scene."

"Of course. But he's going to have his face down—" Della began.

"I'm assuming he'll be wearing a deerstalker cap, and we'll have our forensic people at Scotland Yard determine the man's height and size. Not every small store and pub has surveillance cameras, but several will and we'll get something on our suspect."

Mason left the two of them seated across from one another at the front of the plane. He'd remembered to download a few books—searching hard to find what he thought would be the most factual among the many, many written on the killer. And it was time to predict their killer's next move.

He might as well make Della happy and lie down in one of the cots in the back of the plane as he did so.

The women considered to be the five canonical victims were Mary Ann Nichols, Annie Chapman, Elizabeth Stride, Catherine Eddowes and Mary Jane Kelly. The pattern of "stalking" or "choosing" appeared to be the same—the killer sought down-and-out women, alcoholics, usually, prostitutes, in Whitechapel, an area where at the time migrants struggled with overflowing living quarters and the poor from across the British Isles congregated.

Murder was not unusual in Whitechapel then.

These murders were so heinous and brutal they would be unusual in any place at any time.

First... Mary Ann "Polly" Nichols. And her life, before the Ripper ended it so abruptly, had certainly not been all wine and roses. She'd been married and had five children. Her husband claimed she left him, her father claimed that her husband left her. Alcohol had surely fueled the couples' constant fights and marital woes. They separated. A very strange law asserted that if a wife was making money in any illicit way, the husband did not have to pay support. So as her life drifted from workhouse to charity and prostitution, her husband ceased to pay her anything and on the night of her murder, she'd been ejected from her doss-house for not having the fourpence necessary for a bed. She was rumored to have asked them to save her one. Polly had earned the money several times during the day but spent it on alcohol. She was reputed to have said, "I'll be back soon enough. See what a jolly bonnet I've got now!"

She was last seen by friends, staggering away with her "jaunty bonnet" in the wee hours of the morning. She was next seen by two men who didn't know if she was drunk or sleeping or dead. They went in search of policemen— *after* pulling down her skirt.

At the scene, what the doctor saw was that her throat had been so brutally slashed that her head was barely connected to her body.

It was only later, during the autopsy, that it was discovered she had also been slashed from her groin on up to her breastbone. Because she was a prostitute, her murder was linked to the murders of Emma Elizabeth Smith and Martha Tabram and they quickly became known as the Whitechapel murders. The moniker of Jack the Ripper was yet to come.

Mason studied the map of the area where she had been found, at the gated stable entrance in Buck's Row.

He looked at the email they had received regarding the victim so recently discovered.

Not Buck's Row.

But in a back alley about a block and a half away.

He felt his brow furrow. He was convinced that if the original Ripper murders would have occurred today, the Ripper would have been found. Just from the get-go, the preliminary investigation by a medical director would have been much more thorough. But today they had DNA and fingerprints, facial recognition software and so much more.

And yet here they were, in the twenty-first century, desperate to stop this killer before he struck again. The body was now at the morgue; they would visit when they landed, just as they would visit the scene and speak with the forensics team.

Scotland Yard would already be pulling any surveillance film from the area, along with any security cameras.

But this killer—heading out on his personal "reign"— had been trained by one of the best. He would know about forensics. He would wear gloves. He would avoid cameras. He would know that he might even be traced through epithelial cells. And he would be careful.

Mason saw that Della was coming down the aisle to perch at the foot of the cot.

"Sleeping, huh?" she teased.

"Resting."

"Ah, but you should be resting your mind, too!"

"Hey, it is restful to sort out a disordered mind."

She grinned at that. "Disordered?"

He groaned. "No, I was going over the past—because I believe our new Ripper is going to try to do a complete repeat of the *canonical* victims of the original Ripper." He shrugged. "And who knows—despite every armchair detective, every actual detective, scholar and profiler out there, they might have been wrong. But..." He paused and shrugged. "Here's where this killer is so different— something he's saying in his letters—he may have killed his victim in Whitechapel, but the area isn't the same anymore. Hipsters have moved in. It's still a melting pot, but it's generally considered as safe as anywhere else to walk around at night—well, until now. But it's a very popular place to live—central with easy access to the Tube. It's just not the same."

"Nor are his victims."

"Right. What I was saying about his letters—this killer

just hates all women. Being female apparently makes one a whore."

Della nodded gravely. "And I can't quite figure. The young lady we met was so nice, just a tourist, and…she was probably excited and flattered to be an American in London with a handsome young man ready to show her a few sights. And, I'm afraid, we'll discover that our victim now is the same. Mason, do you think he'll strike again right away?"

Mason shook his head. "No, he'll want the attention first. He'll relish the news. He'll be glued to everything he can hear about the new *Ripper.*"

Della nodded. "Edward seems to believe that we'll have a bit of time." She sighed softly. "I've done my reading, too. Rereading," she told him, grimacing. "I had a profiling class with a teacher who was obsessed with the case."

Mason grinned. "Yep—Special Agent Mike Smith. I had him, too."

"Okay, so, Mary Ann or Polly Nichols was killed in the early morning hours of August 31 in 1888. His next victim, Annie Chapman, was found at about six a.m. on September 8. Just over a week later. And, of course, that time—"

"The body was mutilated to an even more horrific degree," Mason said. "But again, the throat so severely slashed that the head was barely attached to the body."

Della nodded thoughtfully. "Many believe that he strangled his victims first to keep them from crying out. I'm not sure if that's any better, but it's horrible to think of how they must have suffered."

"Small mercy, according to what we know, the mutilations were carried out after death."

"Small mercy," Edward said, joining them and taking a seat on the opposite cot. "We're almost there. But not that

I've been eavesdropping...the third victim was Elizabeth Stride on the night of the *double event*. She wasn't mutilated, but her throat received the same treatment. It was right after her body was found that they discovered the body of Catherine or *Kate* Conway. Her intestines were pulled out of her body and left over her shoulder and at what we consider the end, he found Mary Kelly in her little apartment or room and what he did to her..." He paused, shaking his head.

"Hey. We're not going to let this guy get to number five," Mason said determinedly.

"There were bits of her flesh everywhere. Her face was unrecognizable, he'd stripped the skin from it and other parts of her body. I guess he felt safe and that he had plenty of time he was in a room," Edward said quietly.

Mason sat up, reaching across the aisle to take him by the shoulder. "Edward—"

Edward straightened, nodding, and smiled grimly. "Bloody hell, yeah, we will get him! Anyway, I think we'll be landing soon and...we'll hit the ground running?"

"Or," Della said, "land safely and smoothly and drive right where we need to be in your car!"

"That works, too," Mason said, grinning, but he added, "Edmund, I promise you, we won't stop, and you know—"

"I do know. Hey, every officer in the city is on this, too. We will stop this would-be king. We'll let him be king of the prison system," Edmund said.

And as he had suggested, the pilot said they were landing soon. They headed to their seats and buckled in.

This killer was truly a disciple of Stephan Dante.

The thought drilled through Della's mind as she stood

with Mason and Edmund, listening as the medical examiner explained her findings, seeing the ripped shreds of the new "Ripper's" victim.

He had known that there were cameras. He'd learned all about DNA and trace. And with heightened security prowling the streets of Whitechapel, he had still found a place, near the scene of the 1888 crime, where he was unlikely to run into resistance.

They hadn't been to the crime scene yet but Edmund had known where it was and they would visit when they left the morgue. Whereas time always kept things changing, much of the architecture of the area was the same as it had been for the last hundred and fifty years or so.

The alley was directly behind an old bar that had stood there for ages, only the names of the owners changing. It was one of just a few such alleys. While the bar had surveillance cameras inside and at the front, there were none that covered the little bit of back alley that was shared with two clothing stores, a coffee shop that closed at six o'clock and, ironically, a souvenir shop that carried Jack the Ripper T-shirts and other paraphernalia.

But the victim...

They learned that agents couldn't become too personally involved. Nor could they become cold. Cold would have been the least of her problems at the moment.

Pain streaked through her. It was maddening to know that they had been expecting this—and that they hadn't been able to stop it.

"Maria Monty, a teacher from Seattle, Washington," the medical examiner, Dr. Elizabeth Woodward, said, her tone even. But she looked across the body at Della and Della knew that they were feeling the same depth of dismay. And the ME said so aloud.

"I've seen a lot. I've been at this for twenty years. But the way that this woman was torn apart... Thankfully, I can tell—due to nonreactive tissue—that the ripping came after death. Bruising there—" she indicated the woman's neck with the deep slashes "—indicates that she was strangled quickly and effectively, then the slashes were made, one from each side, and, as you can see, the head barely remains attached to the body."

"And she was forty-three years old," Edmund said flatly, his eyes on the corpse as well. "The same age as Mary Ann Polly Nichols."

"Which is quite amazing," Mason said. "I believe that he stalks his victims—"

"Did the original Jack the Ripper stalk them?" Edmund wondered aloud.

"Depends on whose theory you go by, maybe," Della said. "If you go by the Royal Conspiracy theory, either Prince Albert Victor or Sir William Gull, the royal physician, chose the victims to rid the world of anyone who knew about Annie Crook and her illegitimate child. Personally, from everything I've read, Sir William Gull was an exceptionally good man. And other members of the royalty have had illegitimate children without killing everyone around them. Of course, back then, that kind of behavior by a possible heir to the throne... Anyway, I believe it was one of the other suspects, and that, no, he didn't stalk them. But as I said—"

"Choose your theory," Mason finished for her. "Doctor, is there anything else you can tell us? Hairs, fibers, anything?"

"Well, I have cat hair, according to trace," Dr. Woodward said. "The alley has several cats—fed by the bar and the coffee shop, so…"

"We haven't been to the scene yet," Mason said. "And we should go now."

"I don't get it," Dr. Woodward said. "Talk about your theories. The original Ripper was supposedly *down on whores*. This woman was a schoolteacher!"

"This Ripper thinks all women are whores," Edmund said. "But for his first, he did find someone the same age as the original victim. Coincidence? Or did he do his homework? And if so, how did he know that he could find this woman, the right age, at a bar when he wanted her there?"

"We need to know if she'd been there before," Della said quietly. "It's time we move on. We can't help her any now. We need to—"

"Right. Find him, stop him," Edmund said.

"Please!" Dr. Woodward whispered.

They thanked her and headed out. Edmund's car was parked close and they were soon in it.

"Imagine, I have spent my life believing in modern techniques and science—now mixed with reason and logic and maybe a little instinct and intuition. But this bastard has managed this!"

"He will slip up," Mason said. "Not to mention the fact that I think that we know who he is."

"We know what he looked like—once," Edmund said.

"I have a feeling we'll know him again," Mason said firmly.

Della glanced back at him. She wondered if he was convinced himself, or if he was trying to convince Edmund that it would be so.

"We'll hope," Edmund said. "And, I take it, you've both been here before?" he asked.

"And taken the Ripper tour," Della said quietly. She loved London and she had loved visiting here—even this area. She'd been here first as a college student, even before she'd almost been the victim of a serial killer herself, learned she could see the dead, and decided that yes, beyond a doubt, she would learn everything that she could and use whatever strange "talent" she had in law enforcement.

"Well, he couldn't leave her exactly where he probably wanted—there are cameras in the street there for the bar and for an ATM across the street. Bank in the box, as my little sister called them. We can park in the alley—they still have the crime scene tape, though Forensics have been through. They waited for us. We can bring the car up to the bar area," Edmund said, turning into what appeared to be a tiny side street.

They passed by garbage and recycling bins in the narrow area and several feet before a line of crime scene tape, Edmund drew the car to a stop.

They exited.

Numbered markers around the crime scene showed them where the victim had lain.

A massive spray of red showed where she had bled out.

Before they could exit the car, Mason's phone rang. He glanced at the caller ID and murmured, "Jackson! Go ahead. I'll catch up."

Della followed Edmund, carefully moving under the tape as Edmund briefly introduced her to the cop watching over the scene—and keeping sensationalists, journalists and others from crowding to stare or to create more of a media whirl.

It was an alley. Wide enough for one car—Edmund was

going to need to back out. There were bins for glass, plastic and waste lined up against the wall.

There were cigarette butts around the back door that led to the alley. Patrons came out to smoke.

This "Jack" hadn't been observed by any smokers.

Surveying the place and the circumstances, Della thought that the killer had to have struck quickly. Strangling, slicing and gutting his victim. He'd probably fantasized about it time and time again, and then practiced what he was going to do in his mind, and, in fact, maybe in person, judging how long it took to get to the back of the bar—and how long it would take to escape from the alley into the streets beyond.

He had to be on camera somewhere. They needed to study footage taken from every security and traffic cam to be found.

She heard footsteps; Mason was coming up behind her.

"You're not going to believe this!"

"What?" Della demanded.

"We may not know where he is now, but we know who he is—at least, we know the name of the man we saw with the young woman in Brixton. And with the crimes he's suspected of committing, I'm more than certain that we know the real name of the man we're looking for!"

CHAPTER FOUR

"Modern forensics!" Mason said, glancing from Edmund to Della. "They were able to lift a print from the jacket."

"I guess it really is a good thing that you're so into leather," Edmund said dryly.

"Hey!" Mason protested. "Well, I'm glad I was into leather that night. Anyway, they got a hit off AFIS. Jesse Miller. Dual citizenship—his father was an American and his mother was born in London. He was born in London himself, and imagine this," he added, his mouth tightening in a grimace, "he spent time between the two countries, and when he was in the States, the family lived with his paternal grandfather—a shrimper living just outside New Orleans."

"So, he didn't just know Stephan Dante from England—he knew him as he was growing up?" Della asked. "Now that, I didn't figure! But, how—"

"His fingerprints are on file because of an assault charge because he attacked a man with a pool stick at a bar on

Bourbon Street, NOLA," Mason went on to explain. "That's it on his record. Apparently, he's never broken any laws in the United Kingdom. But it was enough for his fingerprints to be on file."

"The only thing is," Della reminded them, "we don't know if the man we saw was this new killer or not. I had a hunch about him—that's all. And we saw him in Brixton. He killed in Whitechapel. We saw him with a young woman and he killed someone Mary Ann Nichol's exact age."

"True," Edmund agreed. "But what a coincidence, huh? Stephan Dante grew up in Louisiana and so did this bloke, half the time at any rate."

"I'm just saying that we need to be cautious and not jump to hunches," Della said.

"They're tracing his credit cards," Mason said. "And, of course, Philip is going to go back in and have a chat with Stephan Dante. He'll bring up the name Jesse Miller and see what reaction he gets—in his most amazing Philip Law–way, of course."

"Now I'm wishing we were still there—and here."

Mason grinned at her. "We haven't managed human cloning or time travel yet—not that anyone has shared with any of us, anyway."

"Ah, conspiracy theory!" Edmund said.

"No, not really," Mason said.

"Just kidding."

"Better be!" Mason said with a grin before growing serious. "I think it's important that we're here. If this killer is trying to play off the Jack the Ripper legend and become the king of all Rippers, I believe that he'll wait for his next kill. Of course, he's stalking his next victim now."

"How is he doing this?" Della asked, shaking her head, and looking around the alley. "He chose this place. He knew that the smokers at the bar came out back to smoke. But…he must have even timed the servers and bartenders taking out the trash!" Frowning, she looked at Edmund. "Our victim was a smoker?"

"Yes," Edmund said.

"So, either he was inside watching her, or he knew she was in there." She studied the numbered markers that showed them where the body had lain. "He caught her right as she came out the back door." She moved to the door as if stepping out of it, nodding to Mason. He frowned and walked over to her and knew that she wanted to act it out.

"He'd have been there, right against the wall and…" She positioned Mason and continued, "And he grabbed her the second she stepped out, and, as the doctor suggested from the bruising at her throat, he caught her quickly and strangled her quickly."

Mason feigned the attack the killer must have made—a swift attack with no hesitation.

Looking up at him, Della said, "And he laid her right down on the ground, ripped up her dress and very quickly did his slashing before disappearing down the alley and out…out into the nightlife."

"Judging by the marks on the ground and the crime scene photos, I think that's exactly the way it went down. He's timing his every move, but then at the time of the original Ripper killings, the killer knew his timing, too—he killed a few women in the brief time between patrols on the streets."

"He knew his timing," Della agreed.

"And no cameras back here. Still," Mason said, "he had to leave the alley."

"Area surveillance," Edmund said. As Della had done, he looked around the alley. "All right, the forensic team picked up every cigarette butt and they bagged the trash and bottles. They'll pull DNA in the hopes that somewhere along the line, we'll be able to do some comparisons. Then again…it's a popular bar and there will be dozens upon dozens of prints and even more DNA and… Anyway, let's get back, meet up with our Jeanne Lapierre and François Bisset. Both should be at our headquarters soon if they're not there now."

"Let me grab a few photos of my own," Della said. "And then, yes, we'll be far more useful back at headquarters." She was quiet a minute. "We can't stop what happened here now."

"They're collecting all the surveillance now for us?" Mason asked Edmund.

"Yes, our people are on it," Edmund murmured.

They had all seen the crime scene photos. They'd all had them in their email and had studied them already on their phones or tablets.

But Mason understood Della's feeling. Photos taken from different angles. He believed that she was right; the killer had seized her just outside the door. He had strangled her quickly and gotten her down. The blood pools and spills suggested that he'd made the first slice as he lowered her to the ground; the second, even deeper, once he had her down.

When she finished snapping her shots, she looked at him and Edmund and they started out. But as they reached the car, they were met by a tall man, probably in his early thirties, with light brown hair, serious dark eyes and wearing a casual jacket and jeans.

"Johnstone," Edmund said, greeting the arrival.

"Edmund," the man said, nodding and looking at Mason and Della.

"This is your—"

"Yeah," the man named Johnstone said. "First on the case," he added.

Edmund turned to Mason and Della. "Detective Inspector Sean Johnstone," he said to them by way of introduction. "Sean, Special Agents Della Hamilton and Mason Carter."

They shook hands and the newcomer smiled grimly. "This was…too much like what we know of the past. Except that when the barman came out after last call, he knew that she wasn't sleeping right away and called the cops. Two uniformed officers cordoned off the area, but I was here within thirty minutes of the call. The officers were good; they kept everyone out. I was here and the forensic crew were here almost immediately. Our belief—confirmed by the coroner's preliminary report—was that she was killed within forty-five minutes of the last call, or else someone else would have headed back here for a cigarette. And no matter what the hell someone might have been drinking, they'd have noticed her where she was lying."

"You're with—Scotland Yard?" Della asked, and, of course, Mason knew why.

The man's accent seemed far more American than English.

Sean Johnstone smiled. "I was born in Yorkshire, moved as a child to Chicago for my father's work, came back for college and now, here I am. Sometimes I sound English and sometimes I sound American."

"Got it," Della said, smiling. "At any rate, Inspector Detective, we're glad to meet you and we're here to help, of course, not to—"

"Don't worry. I'm not proprietorial," he said. "Edmund has been on all this from the start, and I'm up to par with what's gone on with Stephan Dante—as soon as I found that this was my case, I read everything possible in your notes and so on. I know that Dante trained whoever our killer may be now. I'm grateful to have a team on this—not that every cop in the British Isles isn't ready to step in with assistance in any way possible."

"We have a possible suspect," Mason told him. "A man behaving strangely at a bar in Brixton the other night. We have an ID on him, too, and the more help we have on hours of surveillance tape will be great. While there are no cameras in the alley, there are plenty on the streets."

"And being thoroughly collected to be ready for us at our temporary office headquarters," Johnstone assured them.

"Then let's do this," Mason said. "Time for the movies."

"We're going to need lots of popcorn," Della murmured. She hesitated, frowning and looking at Sean Johnstone. "I take it that there's going to be double security around here everywhere, right?"

He nodded. "We had the streets flooded already." He shook his head. "Thing is that the killer had to be bloody. How the hell did he walk back on the street wearing a ton of blood? The original Ripper might have been a butcher, and sure, in 1888, walking around with a bloody apron might be par for the course. But not today."

"He was trained by the best. He has something to go over his clothing. He's wearing gloves. He knows all the tricks except—" Mason began.

"Except?" Sean Johnstone asked.

"Everyone makes a mistake. He will make a mistake. But that's it—we can't wait for that to happen. We must stop him before he commits another murder—before he gets his chance to make a mistake. We can head back—"

"Wait," Della said suddenly.

They all paused to look at her.

"I'd like to walk around for a minute. Get a feel for these streets again. If you want to go back, I can grab a ride—"

"Might not hurt the visiting Americans to take a walk," Mason said.

"I'll walk with you," Edmund said.

"Not a bad idea, if you don't mind," Mason said.

"This murder was *near* the place where the canonical first victim was found—I'd like to walk to and around the area where the second victim was found," Della said. "Because, if our friend goes by what appears to be his agenda, that's where he will strike next."

"Hanbury Street, Spitalfields, now a trendy section of East London," Sean Johnstone provided.

"Near the Ten Bells Pub, where the next victim, Annie Chapman *might* have had her last drink," Edmund added. "Very trendy now as well—until someone starts killing again, the ghosts of crimes long past can be big business. Trust me, ghost hunters clog these streets as well. I think every paranormal show known to man has done an episode in these *haunts.*"

"Ten Bells, hmm?" Mason said. "Maybe not a bad place for us to *haunt* ourselves tonight."

"Thinking the same. Except, not so much together. If Jesse Miller is our killer, he already knows the three of us. Then again, we could take a page from his playbook."

"And that is?" Sean asked her.

"We can turn into chameleons—change up our look. I'm not suggesting prosthetics or getting ridiculously costumed—"

"I'm all into costumes, no problem!" Sean said.

"Well, all right then. We'll look at the now-trendy area, and come back to find a few spirits tonight," Edmund said.

"It's a plan," Della assured them. As they started for the car, Mason happened to look back down the alley.

He paused, frowning.

A woman was standing there, watching them from a distance. Not that he knew his fashion that well, but she appeared to be dressed as a nineteenth-century schoolteacher.

Were people sick enough to be dressing up in period wear for the new Ripper?

Or, he realized, smiling, was she a remnant of that long-ago day when a maniacal killer had first roamed the streets to bring the area to infamy.

She stared back at him strangely, frowning as well, then appearing surprised. She lifted a hand to him, frowning still.

He lifted a hand in return.

Everyone was heading to Edmund's car, other than Sean Johnstone who was walking to his own.

"Um, hey, I need just one more minute here," Mason said, "going to check that side of the alley one more time." He shrugged. "I think that there's a method to my madness—never really sure."

He glanced at Della. She knew what he was doing.

He hurried on down the length of the alley, one of the

few remaining winding back streets in an area that had come of age after the Jack the Ripper slayings.

At the end of the alley, he saw that his Victorian-age ghost had turned around the side of the corner building, as if she recognized that it would be awkward to appear to be talking to the air. He was afraid for a brief moment that she had gone. Some spirits remained—but feared the living, just as the living might fear ghosts.

But she was waiting for him. She was a small woman, perhaps in her early thirties when she had passed from mortal life. Her hair was neatly smoothed back into a bun and her blouse, buttoned high to her throat, was covered by a small blue vest that matched her long blue skirt.

She hadn't been a victim, he was certain. Not of the man history had come to know as Jack the Ripper. She was too well dressed and coiffed to have ever "plied the trade" in Whitechapel.

"Hello," Mason said, "I'm Mason Carter, with a special task force."

"American?" she murmured. "Well, some thought that he did move on across the water. Some thought that he might well be an American. No one wants to believe that one of their own might be such a heinous killer. And yet it happens again!" she said softly.

"Did you see anything? Is there anything—"

"No, I am so sorry. I should have thought of the pub here, and the alley…and I did not. I do not mean to be so rude. I am Mrs. Abigail Scott, and…"

Her voice trailed for a minute.

"Mrs. Scott, were you a victim of such a killer?"

She smiled, shaking her head. "No, but as the years go by, I realize that I was ahead of my time. I was an advocate for these poor wretches, trying to make change. My husband had been a barrister. He passed away quite young from a wretched debilitating disease. I had two small children to feed and was extremely lucky that my uncle was a newspaper man and allowed me to become a journalist. I wrote about the state of the poor people crowded here back then, I wrote about the plight of the people here, I advocated for change and social reform."

"My sincere admiration," Mason told her.

"I wish I had seen something. Though I feared that if I had, I would not have been able to do much with the information, but now… The woman down there—she sees me, too."

"My partner," Mason said.

"Partner?" she asked, raising a perfect brow. "Is that what you young people call it these days?"

Mason smiled. "My partner, Special Agent Della Hamilton. She is one of the most amazing law enforcement officers with whom I have ever had the pleasure to work. She is also more—I have never loved anyone as I love her. So…yes. Partner in everything. We are Blackbird—a new team connected to a specialized unit of the FBI. Our members all have the gift of seeing those such as yourself—who choose to be seen."

"Oh." She paused, seeming taken aback for a minute, but then amused. "Well, I shall be glad to speak with her as well. But to my great sorrow, I have nothing to tell you."

"We're going to head to the Ten Bells tonight, to watch that area. If you're of a mind—"

"I will see you later, Mr. Carter."

He nodded. He never expected to be formally addressed

and he wasn't about to correct this wonderful spirit who just might, in time, prove a wonderful asset.

She could go where they could not—without being seen.

He bowed politely, about to turn and head back, when Della came around the corner.

"Ah, my dear lady, we were just speaking about you!" Abigail Scott said.

"Without being too obvious lest they lock us away," Mason said, "it would be my most sincere pleasure to introduce the two of you. Mrs. Abigail Scott, please meet Della Hamilton, Special Agent Della Hamilton. Della, Mrs. Scott was quite the progressive in her day and she's willing to assist us, having witnessed such horrors before."

"Thank you, and a pleasure to meet you," Della told her.

"She was a journalist and advocated for social change," Mason said.

"Amazing and wonderful," Della said.

"No, it will be amazing and wonderful if I can help you now," the ghost replied, and she smiled. "And the world has gone on, decade after decade. Please call me Abigail. And I shall have no problem referring to the two of you as Mason and Della."

"Agreed!" Della said. "Abigail, I'd so love to talk to you now, but Mason—"

"She'll find us tonight," Mason told her.

"Thank you," Della said. "We're supposed to be meeting up with others and searching through video footage. While the killer might have been hidden in the alley, he had to leave it."

"Yes, of course. There are cameras now," Abigail said. She smiled. "I will watch, and watch. And do everything that I can."

"Thank you," Mason said.

Della nodded and added a soft refrain of "Thank you."

Together, they turned and hurried back to the waiting cars.

Could they be right?

Della didn't know what it had been about the man in the bar—Jesse Miller—that had caused her to make sure that he didn't leave with the young woman.

And maybe it was true that he had taken off because he was afraid of the police, or—

No. They knew his name. And that he had a record.

And they knew, too, that there were no known warrants out against him. He hadn't, however, proven to have a known address in the United Kingdom. His last listed residence had been in Northern Ireland and authorities there had assured them that he hadn't been living at the residence since his parents had died four years ago.

They knew who he was—they had nothing on him. All they had was his prints.

But the killer wasn't leaving prints.

There were, of course, those people who just didn't like the police or law enforcement of any kind. And maybe his past experiences had made him think that no woman was worthy of being picked up for a night if she brought along questions from the authorities.

Maybe they had help now. She lowered her head and smiled, thinking that Mrs. Abigail Scott might well be the catalyst they needed to discover the truth. While death didn't change the fact that a person could only be in one place at a time, they could be in that place without being seen.

And while Abigail wouldn't be able to knock out a would-be killer, she could find them—and send them in the right direction.

It was all coming together...

And yet there were still so many simple questions.

Questions kept flooding her mind as she sat in front of her computer at headquarters. It had been good to meet up with François Bisset and Jeanne Lapierre—both men had been professional and warm—doggedly determined to pursue justice, truth, and human kindness as well.

"Blackbird is back," Mason had whispered to her, which had allowed her a smile. Technically, she and Mason were the only members of their dedicated European Krewe team. But if all the top brass from the countries involved agreed, they'd be great members of a permanent team.

She didn't want to be technical. She didn't care what any officials from any country wanted to call them—they all made a hell of a team. Blackbird was back, or would be once Wilhelm arrived from Norway, the country where she and Mason had begun their hunt for the vampire killer, though he'd struck before arriving on Norse shores. Bisset and Lapierre, in contrast to Edmund Taylor who was only in his early thirties, were in their forties and fifties, respectively, men who had long been involved with law enforcement. While Lapierre was still a detective in Paris, Bisset had started as a patrolman in that same city before going on to become a key part of Interpol. He could reach almost anyone at any time and was an incredible asset, having a comprehensive knowledge of Europe, its different countries and their laws.

Jeanne Lapierre was just one damned good detective.

She was reflecting on their team as she went through the various footage they had received from local businesses, banks and traffic cams.

And in spite of the fact that they'd been happy to be back together—Frenchmen greeting Americans, Edmund and Sean Johnstone, who was now with them as well— the large conference room that had been dedicated to them was oddly silent.

They were all focused on the screens in front of them.

She wasn't sure just how long she'd been staring at her screen, concentrating on the streets where the alley began and ended, when she noted someone turning out of the alley. Glancing at the traffic cam's time stamp, she saw that the time had been just about 2:30 a.m.

"My God!" she breathed, sitting back.

"What?"

Della wasn't sure how many people said the word, but it was a chorus from around the room.

She looked up, freezing the image on her screen.

She shook her head. "You can't see his face, but this is one cocky and arrogant killer. I'm throwing it up on the big screen," she said, hitting another key on her computer to send the moment she had captured onto the large screen suspended at the far end of the room.

"Arrogant, surely," Mason murmured.

"He's wearing a deerstalker hat! The bloody nerve!" Edmund declared.

"And he waves at the camera," Jeanne Lapierre said, shaking his head. "It's as if he's saying, I'm right here, you're impotent and I'll show you."

"Where was he heading?" Mason asked.

"Let's see…"

Della hit a key on the computer again and the video continued to run. "There, heading toward the main street—and ducking behind a group of cars and then…"

They all watched.

It was as if the man had disappeared.

"He knows where the cameras are," Mason said flatly. "He knows not to leave prints, to be careful not to get any cuts himself lest he leave his own blood at the scene. He has planned this all out—I imagine, from the time that Stephan Dante was picked up in New Orleans, he's been laying out his plans."

"Competition among killers," François Bisset said with disgust. "If you are ready to head back to the streets, I'll continue here with the video. Edmund and Sean have seen to it that every business owner in the area knows that if they want to keep their business brisk, they'll add their own security and cameras."

"Scotland Yard is truly on this all the way," Sean assured them. "My partner was out on holiday, but he's back working with the ground patrol in the area."

"What is our plan?" Edmund asked, looking at Della and Mason. "Yours should be to get to your hotel room at last and get some rest, this side of the pond. We have you at a great place in Westminster not far—"

Della interrupted him, laughing. "First, you must be as tired as we are since you were on the plane with us. And, if possible, I'm thinking that we should find lodging in Whitechapel."

"An excellent idea," Sean Johnstone said. "There are several places that belong to those agencies that rent homes. Being right there…"

"On it," François Bisset said. "Give me five minutes and I'll get the right people to cancel what we have and change things over. Jeanne—"

"Find us a house or lodgings somewhere small but where we can also come and go at odd hours," Jeanne said.

"*Pardonnez moi!*" François exclaimed, smiling. "I will be there, too, thus you can guarantee, I will seek what will work best."

They all laughed together, and it was a good moment.

"But we're going out tonight!" Della reminded them.

"Of course. And because it is a stop for Ripper tours, due to being a great pub that has been there since the 1700s, we will start at the Ten Bells. Historic, and still serving excellent fare and fine stouts and ales," Edmund said.

"Onward to Commercial Street!" Edmund said.

They rose and gathered their things, but as they headed out, Sean's phone began to ring. He paused, excusing himself as he listened while nodding to friends in the department as they left the building.

Outside, he paused on the sidewalk.

He listened and replied. "We'll be there shortly."

He ended the call and looked at the others. "One of our patrolmen was just stopped by a woman in the street. She claims she saw the murderer last night."

"And we're going to her?"

Sean shrugged and grimaced. "She stopped the officer right in front of Christ's Church on Hanover Street—and across from Ten Bells."

"Then we're going to her. Now. So much for going anywhere in disguise tonight," Mason said.

"If Jesse Miller is the killer, he knows you, me and Della,"

Edmund said. "He doesn't know Jeanne or Sean. We can keep our distance from them and…"

"My new best bloke!" Sean teased Jeanne, who groaned in protest.

"Fine. We can be a father and son out for a night!"

"But the witness is waiting—"

"The policeman she approached is a friend," Sean told them. He has her waiting by the church—she didn't want to come into the station. Listen, this may be nothing. This woman might be a total flake—she didn't want to come into a police station anywhere to give her statement—she believes that it might have been a royal conspiracy back in the day, and, of course, politics can still be corrupt…better just to talk to us."

"Did the patrolman suggest that she might be on something?" Della asked.

Sean shrugged. "No. But…"

"Hey, a possible witness? Let's go!" Della said.

Sean left his car; Edmund did the driving. As they traveled down the street, drawing close to the pub, Della saw the rise of Christ Church.

"Beautiful," Della murmured.

"Historic churches tend to be beautiful," Sean said. "St. Botolph's—known by some in the 1800s as the prostitutes' church is equally as beautiful, rebuilt and repaired through the years, stands right at Aldgate, or what was the eastern edge of the old Roman Londinium. In the Ripper's day, it was illegal for the prostitutes to stand and solicit so they would walk around and around the block." He shook his head. "It was all sad back then—many of the women tried to work and did work at what they called workhouses and some spent time as maids, but too many wound up as prostitutes. And who knows? Were they alcoholics whose drinking habits caused their problems, or did their problems leave them nothing but the solace of alcohol?"

"The whole thing is tragic," Della murmured, looking around as Edmund found the parking Sean had indicated and they exited the car.

"Around back," Sean told them. "We recently had surveillance going on a drug sting. We have facilities that were used for that and the patrolman has our witness there."

They followed him as he walked around the beautiful church to a nearby townhouse. Sean keyed in a code and they entered the tiny yard before heading up steps to the little place.

The house was still set up for surveillance with cameras angled out to the street. The place itself looked like a poster ad for private accommodations companies—the windows were handsomely draped, helping to hide the police equipment. A well-appointed dining area adjoined a parlor with warm furnishing in crimson and brown.

The patrolman who had alerted Sean and a young woman were sitting in the parlor area, evidently just waiting, both looking uncomfortable and nervous.

The young patrolman stood quickly as they entered, obviously relieved that they had arrived. Sean quickly introduced him as Marty Townsend and in turn, Townsend quickly introduced them to the young woman, Sarah McDonald. She appeared to be in her early twenties, a pretty, young woman with dark brown eyes and hair. She had also jumped to her feet when they'd come in and after the intros, Della spoke up quickly, placing a gentle hand on her shoulder, thanking her and asking her to sit again.

"Forgive me!" the girl said quickly. "I felt that I had to help if I could, but I'm so scared, so, so scared! I mean, what if it was a conspiracy back then, and… I'm grateful to Officer Townsend—he didn't make me do anything, he brought me here, he called you. I couldn't—I could not—go to a police station. *He* might see me. *He* might know!"

"It's okay, it's okay," Della assured her, glancing quickly at Mason. The girl was American, her accent midwestern. "We're here, we're fine, you're fine. And you are very brave, trying to help us. We'll see to it that you have protection." She glanced at Edmund and Sean, hoping her words were true.

Both gave her small nods.

"Please, tell us what you know," Della said, pulling up a chair close to the young woman. Mason and the others chose seats as well, trying to make her feel more comfortable.

"First, I wasn't drunk, I swear it. Yes, I was at a bar, I was drinking, but I wasn't drunk. I was out with friends and when we left, I'd assured them I could get back okay—my hotel was just a few blocks away. I wasn't drunk—"

"It's okay, please, we believe you," Della said.

The girl let out a long breath.

"So, I wound up a little lost. I turned down the wrong street, and that's when I saw him coming out of the alley."

"What time was this?"

"I think about twelve thirty. Some of the bars don't stay open that late, but most at eleven and maybe twelve on weekends."

"You made the wrong turn, and then you saw him coming out of the alley?"

Sarah McDonald nodded.

"And can you describe him?"

"I know exactly who he is!" Sarah exclaimed.

"Who?"

"Jack the Ripper! He is back. It was Jack the Ripper!"

CHAPTER FIVE

Great, Mason thought.

They'd found a witness who was unstable, paranoid and…

Crazy. Perhaps. But Della was speaking to her gently again—*not* jumping to conclusions.

"You mean, of course, that he looked like the images of Jack the Ripper as reported by witnesses back in the day?" Della asked.

The young woman nodded seriously.

"I wouldn't have known what you called that kind of a cap, but they've been inundating the news and internet with the old cases…because it's happening again. I heard him described as a man with *shabby genteel* clothing or the like. And wearing a deerstalker cap. The man I saw was in a suit jacket, decent but worn, and he was wearing a deerstalker hat."

Della glanced over at Mason. Her words of description matched the man they'd seen coming out of the alley on the surveillance tapes.

Mason gave Annie an imperceptible nod.

"What age do you think he was? Any idea on how tall?" Della asked her.

Sarah McDonald grimaced and looked helpless for a minute. "The second I saw him, I was terrified. There was a billboard in the street—you know, one of those standing billboards advertising something or another. I was so scared. And I don't know why—"

"Was he covered in blood? Carrying a knife?" Della asked.

"I don't know. I saw him come around the alley and I guess that we'd just been so inundated with information on the past—and present—that I froze behind the billboard. Thankfully, there were still other people on the street and he hurried out to the main road and quickly blended in with others—he was moving fast. I did see that. And I don't think that he was old, but I couldn't say if he was thirty-five or forty. And he was maybe five-eleven or six-one in height, I just... Average build. He kept his head low so I don't... I mean, I hadn't even known that anything had happened then! The world had heard about the letter sent to the news and there was so much repeating and repeating... I was terrified. Then, of course, when he was gone, I felt a little ridiculous, and I went on back to my lodging and nothing happened at all except..."

"Except?" Della pressed.

The girl shook her head, looking pained and baffled. "I don't know. I guess that paranoia had set in. I kept fearing that I was being followed. But I got back and...nothing. I'm at a chain hotel. There was one clerk at the desk and she waved to me and I went on up and I was glad that it was just a room—I checked my closet and the bathroom and the shower and under the bed and there was no one there and I began to feel silly again. Then I heard something, and I was scared all over again because I'll probably never know if the killer saw me or not and if…" she paused again, wincing "…I should leave the country. But I'm here for a medical conference and it's important and… I guess my life is more important, but I'm afraid, so afraid! You said that you would protect me, right?"

"We're going to see to it that we know your schedule, that we have patrolmen aware at all times where you are—" Sean began.

"Oh, my God! They had patrolmen all over the night that poor woman was murdered! Oh, my God, that's not… You don't understand! This guy is good!" Sarah said.

"Well, honestly, we don't suck ourselves," Sean said. But he looked around at Edmund, Jeanne, Officer Townsend, Della and Mason. "You must understand that we are vigilant, that every officer in London, in England, in all of the British Isles is aware of this situation, is on heightened security—and that we are good, we can stretch, but we do have limited resources—"

"Wait, please," Mason said. "If English law enforcement can see to Miss McDonald's safety for the next six hours or so, I know that our assistant director can arrange for security for her."

Edmund smiled and nodded. "Nice to have a rich boss!"

"Nice that he's a guy who will spend it on the right things," Mason said. "I know that we can set something up, and believe me, it will be with someone we trust implicitly. Are you okay?"

Sarah McDonald looked from Della to him and nodded. "Your boss won't just say something like send that scaredy-cat home?"

"Not Adam," Della said quietly.

Mason realized that Della was looking at him, her eyes implying her approval. And he realized something else.

More than just being cautious, in this strange case, Sarah McDonald just might be right. If this "Jack" had seen her, she just might be in trouble.

And if they were with her, along with keeping her alive, they might find their man.

Marty Townsend spoke up quickly. "I can watch out for the next five hours. I could only sit in here like this because my shift ended. I have hours left in which I can watch out for Sarah. She was too scared to sleep. I'll go with her and keep guard at her door." He looked at Sean and Edmund and said, "Not to worry. No overtime. I was just going to go home to go to sleep."

"That's great," Mason said.

"And so good of you!" Sarah said.

"Fine. Then we're good to go. I'll get ahold of Adam," Mason said.

He rose and the others did as well.

"Well, we shall leave you two, then," Edmund said. "And get out on the streets. We're going to do a little pub-crawling."

Mason grinned. "Barhopping for the Americans present."

"Same thing either way," Jeanne Lapierre supplied dryly.

"And so it is," Edmund agreed.

"Jeanne and Sean need to head off alone," Della reminded them. "If Jesse Miller is our killer and stalking victims, we'll be recognized. We never did change our appearances any."

"Off you go, then. We'll follow at a more leisurely rate. Officer Townsend, Miss McDonald, please listen for my call—I will let you know as soon as I've heard from Jackson," Mason told them.

"Thank you!" Sarah McDonald breathed.

"Right now, I'll let her get some sleep," Marty Townsend said. He was grim and serious, and Mason believed that he was a dedicated officer and the woman was going to be safe in his hands. Townsend was a tall, well-muscled man in his late twenties.

This "Jack" didn't want to fight a big man. He wanted to take women by surprise and kill them so quickly they didn't know what hit them.

As Sean and Jeanne Lapierre moved ahead, Mason and Della followed at a more leisurely pace.

Mason immediately put a call through to Jackson Crow and explained the situation.

"They are throwing all that they can on this, but our witness is frightened silly. I was hoping that Adam would deem her important enough to hire a security—"

"Not to worry. I'll have someone on a plane as soon as possible," Jackson promised. "We've got people out around the country as usual, but I'm going to send an agent in. I'll connect with Angela as soon as we finish this call and I'll let you know who is coming."

"The plane is here, but going backward and forward—"

"Leave it to me. We do have another plane," Jackson reminded him. "Let me talk to Angela and find out who we can move the fastest."

Mason thanked him and ended the call. He caught up with Edmund and Della who were walking just a few feet ahead.

"Jackson is sending someone," he informed her. "Not sure who yet, but he'll have someone here by tonight, if I know Jackson."

Della nodded, looking at Edmund. "Trust me, Mason is right. If Jackson says we have someone, we do."

"That's great. I mean, maybe she doesn't need any security—"

"And maybe she does. And having another Krewe agent here won't be a bad thing at all," Mason said.

"All the help we can get," Edmund assured him.

Mason smiled and linked arms with Della. "Looks like we're heading straight ahead. Beautiful view of the church from the outdoor seats!"

"We'll grab those," Edmund said. "I think we can see who is coming and going and those who are inside through the windows if we can get to that table right there."

They were able to grab the table they wanted. Edmund ordered for them, determined that they all sip at one of his recommended English brews.

As they sat, Della leaned forward. "I think we're going to need to always keep in mind that this man is claiming to repeat the past but creating his own version of it. Of course, the general perception is that the women killed were prostitutes. They were—but their lives were so tragic. I saw a picture of Annie Chapman with her husband before her life went to hell—before the hell of her death. It was all so sad! Three children—one died at the age of twelve and one was born disabled. We see things now that are so similar. Some horrible tragedy in life occurs and we're fragile human beings. Also! There are many who still believe that Martha Tabram or Turner was Jack's first victim. The mutilation was different, but she was stabbed thirty-nine times."

"I think her killer was enraged, but the differences..." Edmund said, shaking his head. "When she was killed, though, people took little notice. The East End was horrible at the time. Seventy-eight thousand people crowded into a small area—either immigrants or the poorest of the poor in London. Oh! So, back in the day of the potato famine in Ireland, you had hundreds of thousands of Irish moving to London, not to mention," he added, "that caused a huge immigration to the US, too. Then, people could be ghastly—anti-Semitism ran high and about ninety percent of the Jewish population lived in the East End. So, imagine, a horribly overcrowded place where people were constantly rioting and the police could barely keep up—where alcoholism was often the only escape from the horror of life and fights and violence were the way of their world. Martha was killed, and then Mary Ann or Polly was killed, and that's when people took notice and became aware of the Whitechapel Murders."

"The first mention of Jack the Ripper was in the From Hell letter," Della murmured. "And, of course, you wound up with the Metropolitan Police and the City of London Police—"

"And graffiti evidence on a wall was erased by Sir Charles Warren because he feared it would cause riots in the streets. The writing was found after the double event, or the night in which Liz Stride and Catherine Eddowes were both murdered. But! Was it evidence, or just graffiti? They didn't know then and they don't know now. Charles Warren received such condemnation that he resigned his commission and...hmm. There were those who like to stir unrest. And, of course, *Juwes* might have referred to Jubela, Jubelo and Jubelum—the men who killed Hiram Abiff, a figure in Freemasonry, an allegory story, but the murder of the man was quite violent."

"'The Juwes are the men not to be blamed for nothing,'" Mason said, quoting the words that had been written in graffiti after a Ripper murder—and immediately erased for fear of anti-Semitism rising in the area. "But I'm doubting that our Jack was a Freemason. There were those who thought that it was written by someone—having nothing to do with the murders, since there was often graffiti found on the area walls—just to cause more racial unrest. At any rate, I have a feeling our killer is going to stick to notes to the newspaper or media. The killer of the past didn't need to know much about forensics—this killer is well aware of them."

"Do you think that it might be Jesse Miller—the man we saw in Brixton?" Edmund asked.

"Something about him bothered me. But that may mean little," Della said.

"Well, he took off the minute he saw us," Edmund said. "That might mean something."

"Which might mean he's guilty of something. And, of course, it doesn't help that we can't find any kind of an address for him or any record of him using credit cards anywhere," Mason said.

"But, of course, he could just be a common thief," Della reminded them.

Mason could see that Sean and Jeanne Lapierre were seated at the bar, chatting with the bartender.

Della was watching the bar, the patrons and the street, and he knew she was hoping, as he was, that if something was happening, they'd see or even sense something first. Of course, if this killer was following the Ripper, he wouldn't kill again so quickly.

"I'm going to stretch my legs for just a second!" she said suddenly.

He almost protested; it was difficult not to. But she smiled at him. "I'll be right there, on the street," she said.

"Right," he said.

She left the table. Edmund spoke as they kept their vigilance. "Some of the conspiracy theories that have gone around are pretty crazy to me. Like the royal connection—and not because I'm a major monarchist or anything, but just because it makes no sense. Here's the idea on that one—Prince Albert—known as Eddie—secretly married a commoner and had a child with her. Mary Kelly witnessed the union. So, either Prince Albert or his physician—or both—had to get rid of Mary Kelly because she had a great blackmailing scheme devised. And, if you go by that theory, the women knew each other. And Liz Stride wasn't left unmutilated because a killer had been interrupted, but because the killers had the wrong woman. So, if they were just getting rid of people, why the overkill?"

Mason shook his head. "Instrumental murder, they say, is murder just to kill. Beyond a doubt, the killings were, in my mind, expressive murders. Massive overkill. What, exactly, he was expressing, it's hard to tell these days. No one knows if the letters were real or hoaxes."

He spoke casually to Edmund but watched Della a distance away on the walk where the outside pub tables were set.

She was pretending to speak on the phone.

But she was really speaking with the ghost of Abigail Scott.

He almost stood to join her. He knew that Della would tell him anything that was said and if they gained new knowledge, they'd devise a way to share it with the others.

"I think he was crazy and just got crazier as he went

along. Some suggest that it was Herman Mudgett, or H.H. Holmes, the American serial killer. But Mudgett was a poster boy for being an organized killer. He devised his *castle*, or his hotel for murder, devised ways to get rid of the bodies… I don't see them as being the same in any way. Some think he was Montague Druitt—even his family members supposedly thought it was him and his body was found in the Thames soon after Mary Kelly was killed. That's a more logical suspect to me, or, for that matter, George Chapman—aka Seweryn Kłosowski, who was imprisoned and executed, but he was a poisoner—there is a difference between poisoning someone and ripping their body to shreds and removing flesh and organs, and he wasn't imprisoned or executed until several years after the Ripper killing stopped. There you go—hmm. My money is back on Montague Druitt. After he supposedly kills himself after the horror of the Mary Kelly killing, the Ripper killings stop."

Mason smiled briefly. "From what I understand, through the years, every English law enforcement agency known to man has tried to discern the truth. Still, no one knows. I've heard that the FBI and the CIA have also tried to figure out the truth. No dice. I guess we'll all have our theories, but none of us knows the truth."

"Even the best profilers are stymied—with their own theories, of course," Edmund said.

Mason was listening, but as he watched Della out on the street, he saw that she was being approached by a man. The ghost of Abigail Scott was still by Della's side.

But she was a ghost.

Not an armed officer or agent—or sumo wrestler.

She was a beautiful woman and it wasn't a surprise that a man might be interested in speaking with her.

Except that any man who wanted to speak with her might be a killer.

"You think?" Edmund murmured, watching as well. "Early thirties, I'd say. Handsome enough bloke but looks strong enough to quickly strangle a lass."

"Not that lass, trust me, but I think we might move slowly and approach from either direction," Mason said.

He stood, pretending to do so casually. Edmund did the same. They nodded briefly to one another, and then approached the couple—and the ghost—standing on the walk from opposite ends.

"Hey, there," Edmund said, as if greeting a friend.

Mason was ready.

He expected the man who had approached Della to run. The man did not.

He stared at Edmund and then turned to see Mason approaching.

"Friends of yours?" he asked Della.

"Yes, as a matter of fact. We're all on the same tour. Edmund and Mason. Edmund, Mason, this is Trey Harper—he's from Liverpool. Just like the Beatles!"

"Liverpool, eh?" Edmund said.

The man was watching them as warily as they were watching him.

Mason was glad that Edmund asked flat out, "Trying to pick up a young American woman right out on the street, are you?" he asked.

"I was suggesting that she *not* be out on the street alone."

"She's in full view of the pub," Mason said politely.

The man ignored Mason and turned to Della. "You really know these two? Well?" he asked.

"Yes, quite well, as a matter of fact," Della said.

The man nodded and turned to face Mason, studying his size and his face. "Then keep an eye on your friend. We're living in dangerous times and you should know that—the news has been all around the world."

"Oh, we are looking out for each other," Mason said. Adding, "That, of course, is why we came right out here when we saw her talking to a strange man. Do you have ID on you?"

"You want my ID?" he asked.

"I do," Mason said.

"I'll show you mine, you show me yours," he said.

"You first," Mason said. "I asked politely."

"You did. Sure."

Trey Harper reached into his pocket. To Mason's surprise, he produced a badge along with his identification.

His name really was Trey Harper.

He was with the Metropolitan Police.

In turn, Mason produced his identification and Edmund did the same.

Della lowered her head, trying not to smile.

"How do I not know you?" Edmund asked, smiling.

"I was working undercover for the last two years. A drug sting that got wrapped up just a few weeks ago, and since then, I've been on holiday. Back just in time to head back out to the streets, plainclothes, watching out for what's going on," Trey Harper explained.

"Well, that makes sense. This just all fell into my lap when the vampire murders started up. Good to meet you," Edmund said.

"And good to see that you're on the streets," Mason told him.

"And you?" Trey said, turning to Della.

Della grimaced and produced her badge.

"Leave it to me," Edmund said. "I'm sorry. I was trying to make sure—"

"Don't be sorry for trying to save lives," Della said. "And we're glad to know that you're out here—"

"Honestly. We are in force on this, I promise you," Trey said. He grinned. "Well, all seems quiet enough here. I'll head on to the next place." He shrugged and grimaced. "Well, supposedly, Mary Kelly was seen at the Ten Bells before her murder, and she was heard singing an Irish lullaby that night. And whoever he was—after all the other murders—she must have let the killer into her room. Astonishing. That's why... Well, when I saw Special Agent Hamilton here, I just wanted to make sure that she wasn't running around the streets of Whitechapel alone. Though I take it that our modern-day would-be king of the Rippers might take on far more than he bargained for with Special Agent Hamilton."

"Well, I hope so, too," Della said. "But we like to think that we aren't working alone."

"Never alone," Trey Harper said seriously. He pointed into the pub. "I see that Sean Johnstone is in there. Good man. And he's carefully working with...?"

Della smiled at him. "Jeanne Lapierre, French detective."

"Oh?"

"We've been working a number of murders together," Edmund said. "It's an all-out effort."

"As it should be. Well, I'm off, great to meet you. All of you."

When he was gone, Della turned to Mason and Edmund. Abigail Scott was still there, of course, silent as she watched the men.

"Hey, we need to figure something out," she said.

"All right," Mason told her.

"I was starting to figure that Trey Harper just might be law enforcement. And I don't want to give away any of our undercover officers or agents. So, in the future, if there is any sense at all that I'm getting in trouble, I'll give you a sign."

"Quite right!" Abigail said softly.

"What kind of a sign?" Edmund asked.

"I'll flip my hair back. If you see me do that, get out here as fast as possible."

"All right," Edmund said.

Della looked at Mason. He nodded slowly. "All right. Of course, if we see you walking down the street with anyone toward a dark alley..."

She laughed softly. "Yes, then you follow."

By the time she finished speaking, Sean and Jeanne had come out to the street.

"I just saw Trey Harper walking away," Sean said.

"They were afraid he might be the new Ripper," Della explained.

"Trey?" Sean said, amused. "Sorry—he and I have worked together before. He is one solid citizen."

"Any single man—" Della began

"Wait," Edmund said, frowning. "You know, there are those who believe that all the letters were hoaxes, and that *Jack* the Ripper might have been *Jill* the Ripper."

Della shook her head. "I don't believe so. In the past, the ways that the bodies were mutilated indicate that it was someone who truly hated women—"

"You don't think that women hate women sometimes?" Jeanne Lapierre asked dryly.

"Yes, of course. Anyone can be hateful. But some of the mutilations took a fair amount of strength, and our killer has indicated that in his mind, all women are prostitutes. I could be wrong, but here are the things that I believe—one, our killer is a man, and a man trained by our vampire killer, Stephan Dante. I also believe that he might have been in love once and whoever he loved committed suicide, either blaming him or leaving him believing it was his fault. Perhaps he cheated on her and the fact that another woman—professional or just someone he knew or met even briefly—cheated with him gave him this passionate belief that he couldn't have been at fault, that the woman, like all women, was a whore, as he so delicately puts it," Della said.

"I don't know about the past. I know that the police were inundated with letters and tips, hoaxes and what may have been true," Mason said. "But I believe that the taunts the media has been receiving now are from the real killer."

"What about the other bloke?" Sean asked. "Sorry, I didn't mean to sidetrack there!"

"The other bloke?" Edmund asked.

"You didn't see him?" Jeanne Lapierre asked. "No, wait, of course, you couldn't have seen him. He was inside, concealed by the placards for this place."

"If he was inside—" Mason began frowning.

"Well, he came out, of course," Sean said. "But...hmm. I guess he took the other door while we were watching you, ready to hop up if there was trouble. Then, of course, as you were all talking, I saw that it was Trey Harper."

"What about the other man?" Mason asked.

"He appeared to be about six feet tall or maybe a little taller. He was wearing a hoodie and hunched over in the corner. Looked to me to be about thirty-ish," Jeanne said. "Sean, what do you think?"

"I think he was staring at Della, but then, lots of men in and around the pub noticed Della, but...most of them appreciated her appearance and went on with their nights," Sean said. "But I thought that he was watching you, Della, when you were alone on the street. And then we saw Trey approach you and when I looked again, he was gone. He could have just been a loner out for a drink. Man, it's frustrating when you don't know much of anything!"

"You've seen the pictures we have of Jesse Miller. Could it have been him?" Mason asked.

Sean looked at Jeanne Lapierre.

Jeanne shook his head. "I don't know. I'm not sure we would have known even if we'd gotten closer. His hair was a different color, almost black. His brows appeared to be very heavy. If it was him, he changed his appearance."

"Something that we know he can do," Della murmured.

"Well, tonight will be a good learning curve," Mason said. "From now on, when anyone sees anyone acting even remotely strangely, we divide and conquer. If that was Jesse Miller—and while he may not be our killer, he's the only suspect we have at this time—we'll never know now. We'll spend the day tomorrow studying every detail possible about the past and the present—and do better when we head out tomorrow night."

"We have an amazing artist, Maisie, back at our headquarters," Della said. "I'm going to ask her to whip up some pictures of different ways Jesse Miller might look based on his bone structure."

"We'll get a solid estimate from our forensic people on

the height of the bloke seen leaving the alley," Edmund said. "For now, we should get to our lodgings."

Della laughed softly. "Do we know where they are yet?"

"Let's call François Bisset!" Mason said. He did so.

And he discovered that they were going to be quartered in the townhouse where they'd already been—the London police had held on to it through the week and they needed only to extend the rental so long as it might be required.

"That's great. We only need to walk a block or two!" Mason said. Thanking Bisset, he ended the call and told the others. Sean was going to head to his own home, but he'd be with them in the morning, ready to answer anything about his area, history, the streets—anything he could possibly offer.

Edmund and Jeanne were also going to stay at the townhouse. It held six bedrooms so they'd be fine. Also, the kitchen was already stocked with tea, coffee and essentials.

Before they walked away, Mason felt he had to acknowledge the presence of Abigail Scott, the ghost who hoped that she might help them in some way.

He nodded to her, giving her a thank-you with his eyes.

She smiled, amused, nodding in return. "I will see you again," she promised.

She'd heard him speak to the others, of course. She knew where they were staying.

It had been a long—really long—day. But Mason called Jackson again, thinking it was about time he should be leaving the office, but then Jackson and Angela never really considered themselves to be off.

Jackson answered the phone, telling him that he had just been about to call. He was sending the duo of Philip Law and Jordan Wallace. They would look after their witness, standing in for each other when necessary, seeing that no harm came to the woman—whether her danger was perceived or real.

They reached the townhouse near Grace Church and quickly determined rooms. Della wanted a shower and so did he—as of yet, there was no shower on their very nice private plane.

Maybe one day, Adam Harrison had teased.

Soap, water, heat, mist...

Life. They were alive. And no matter how tired either of them might have been, the sheen of water on flesh, the spray of heat, the touch of their bodies...

It was good to make love. Good to feel the ecstasy of love and life.

Soon enough, they dared to sleep.

Because the morning would come quickly.

Morning was coming. Even in London—even in Whitechapel—the sun could begin its ascent in the sky with an array of beautiful colors. At that hour, no rain touched the sky, and the mist that could cover the ground in the shadows of dusk was nonexistent.

Beautiful, beautiful morning.

Ripper smiled, watching the house. They were in there.

They were stumbling around in the dark, even as morning came.

He had a few days to wander. Of course, his second event needed to occur next week. He couldn't maintain the exact locations—the original Jack would have had to change, had there been cameras and surveillance back in his day.

But sticking close to the time pattern? Yes, he could do that.

He smiled, thinking about what was to come. Ripper's second victim. He'd already picked her out. She'd been loud, laughing with her friends in the bar, flirting and then cutting men short with humiliating ease when they responded. Whore. Yes, she was perfect. Of course, he knew where she was staying and what she was doing. He was following her social media as his current identity. She was a tourist, and she had looked at him with interest. Of course, for now, he was keeping his distance, carefully making sure that they made eye contact, that she knew that he was interested…

When the time came, she'd know just how interested.

He relished the concept of his next murder! Yes. He would mimic the murder of Annie Chapman to a T. Two slashes to the throat, deep enough to cause striations to bone. Bits of her uterus and bladder taken away. Intestines set above her shoulders… Her pills, bits of items from her life left around her as well. He'd seen the pictures. He'd read all that the medical reports on her death had contained. Now, Annie had been killed sometime, they believed, between 5:00 and 6:00 a.m. He hadn't quite figured out yet how to pull off his murder at that hour…

But he would. And if not… Well, he was prepared to make sure that the victim, as discovered, would appear just the same. And then…

What they called "the double event!" Liz Stride and Catherine Eddowes.

Last…the Mary Kelly murder. And that victim was planned as well. He stared at the house where she slept right now. He knew where she was while she and her comrades went crazy, not knowing how to find him. Stop him.

And she…

Young and beautiful. She would be his finale. She had been Dante's obsession. And when he competed this initial quest, becoming king of the Rippers with his very special Mary Kelly victim, he would not just be a king, he would be emperor of the world...

He'd have finished what Dante had coveted. Indeed, he would steal every title from Dante, and he would be the true ruler of all.

CHAPTER SIX

"This is so frustrating!" Della murmured.

"What?" Mason asked, pouring cereal into a bowl in the kitchen of their Whitechapel rental. "You mean having a name for a man who might be the most viable suspect out there? Oh! Or having had him—and lost him?"

Della looked up at him. "Frustrating—no known address. No paper trail. How does anyone go through life with no paper trail? No credit cards. Whatever phone he is using—if he is using a phone—is a burner phone."

Mason brought his food to the table where she had been staring at her computer screen. "He learned from a *master*, remember? Stephan Dante knew how to become friends with criminals, visiting them in prisons, learning where they had stashed money, learning how to find the best creators of false IDs—and while he wouldn't have given away all his connections, he probably set his followers up with connections to money and false IDs. But remember this— we did get Dante. And we will find his followers, too."

"All right, so going back. There's a lot to determine. Dante didn't kill the girls who had been killed in London. Someone did. Those murders were committed with instructions from Dante, but now our latest murder has been committed by this person determined to be the best Jack the Ripper ever. But he's like Dante. He's arrogant and confident. So, here's the question. Is the person who committed this latest murder the same person who committed the vampire murders? And, is he the person we stopped as he flirted with an American tourist, or someone else entirely? Are there two murderers or is just one person responsible?"

"Isabelle Ainsley, a local girl, was found on the banks of the Thames like a Sleeping Beauty, and Leslie Bracken, an American tourist, was found in the same condition. And there was also Colleen Denton. But Stephan Dante denied committing those murders while gleefully confessing to the others that were committed in his blood-draining vampire mode. But we know that he trained others and..."

He paused, shaking his head.

"What?" Della asked softly.

"It's terrifying, really. That Dante could find followers. That there are that many sick people out there, eager to be apprentices to a serial killer."

"Terrifying and worse. This killer intends to outdo Dante. But like Dante, he knows how to change his appearance, like a chameleon. Like Dante, he seems to know how to get friendly with imprisoned thieves—and find access to stashes of stolen cash and IDs and...everything it seems that he needs. Or they need. I was thinking that—"

"We need to go back to the beginning?" Mason asked.

She nodded. "We need Sean and Edmund to help us. If we go back to the beginning, we'll go over every little bit of information available on the two *sleeping beauty* victims. We'll look into every possible witness and we'll speak to the people who discovered them and check to see if Forensics discovered anything at all at the sites."

Della nodded and shook her head. "And while we're doing that—"

"Della, we can't stop every bad thing that might happen. Because, I believe, in law enforcement we discover that the greatest possible monster living on earth might well be the human being. Most creatures hunt and kill to survive while some men—and women, most thankfully, a small percentage of both—are wired neurologically different than most in that they delight in deviously planning bloodshed and murder. We can't stop it all—we can only strive to do our best to swim through the mire to discover the monsters as quickly as possible."

Della nodded. "I know. But—"

"If this fellow follows Ripperology, we have several days before another murder."

"Right," Della murmured. "So! Let's get on it."

"May I finish my cornflakes?"

"If you must."

Mason laughed softly. "Thanks! None of the others are even down yet," he reminded her.

"Right. But I'm going to go and get through to Jackson or Angela and find out how Maisie is doing on her sketches of the many appearances our suspect may have, from dark to light and old to young, hairy and bald, and so on!" she told him.

"I'm right with you," he assured her, rinsing his cereal bowl and beating her out of the kitchen.

Della booted up her computer and checked for messages

from Maisie. She had a quick note explaining that the first of many were through and she downloaded and quickly studied the images with Mason standing behind her and looking over her shoulder. He came around and joined her on the sofa in the parlor and they studied the images together.

"Maisie is so incredibly talented," he murmured.

"There are three exceptional artists working at headquarters," she told him. "But I admit, Maisie is my favorite."

They sat in silence. A minute later, Edmund came down from his bedroom upstairs, with Sean, François and Jeanne close behind him. They headed first for coffee, and then joined Della and Mason in the parlor.

"We've all received these images, and Jackson is going to arrange for them to be sent to law enforcement all over the British Isles," Mason told them. "Because if this killer is taking all his cues from Stephan Dante, he will change his appearance."

"Especially if he's the man the two of you and I already met," Edmund said, nodding. By then, rather than drawing them up on their own devices, the three men were standing behind Della and Mason, all studying the sketches.

"He was light and all-American or Northern European the last time we saw him. Do you really think that he could appear to be Middle Eastern or—" François began.

"Yes," Mason said flatly. "He can look like anything."

"How the hell do we begin to find him?" Edmund asked.

"If he's following Dante, he'll work on his face and hair. Dante got his moves from the movies. He won't change his weight or his height. We need to be ready for anything. But we also had an idea to go back, to look at everyone and anyone who was interviewed when the so-called vampire victims were discovered."

Edmund nodded. "Most of the information can be sent securely to our stations here, but Sean and I can go to headquarters and find anything in the evidence room that might be of some assistance." He paused, shaking his head. "I was lead on the cases. And I was entirely frustrated. Then, of course, we learned that Stephan Dante had moved on to Norway, and by the signature, of course, we assumed that our killer had moved on, and that the international task force was going to be the way to find justice for the victims."

"We will find justice—for all of them," Mason promised.

"Trust me, we've all worked incredibly frustrating cases, and sometimes, fresh eyes on a situation may help with something you've been worrying in your mind and just straighten out the thread."

"I'm fresh eyes on this," Sean said. "Except for—"

"The recent victim. We're all fresh on the recent victim," Jeanne said.

"I hope they won't call you back," Sean said quietly. "And, sorry, mates—there was an extra room so I decided that while my flat is near, I should be here with you."

"Perfect!" Della assured him.

"This is our assignment," Della assured him. "And you don't know our bosses. We will be here, and on this case until we find the killer—or, should I say, all the killers that Dante trained." She looked at Mason, an idea having come to mind as they'd spoken. "Edmund, perhaps you and Sean could sign out the evidence boxes. I'd like to take a walk around Whitechapel and the area with Mason and—"

"I'm going to go back and see the medical examiner," Jeanne told them. "They were checking stomach contents on our victim, and if we discover exactly where she'd been before…before her death, we can follow up."

"I'll work with Jeanne today," François said. "Nothing like a trip to the morgue."

"Then we're decided. Let's move," Mason said.

It wasn't until they were outside that he looked curiously at Della and asked her, "Okay, what are we doing? I'm assuming we're looking for our lovely Victorian ghost to show her Maisie's sketches of possible disguises our killer might assume."

She nodded and smiled. "If he's trying to play Jack the Ripper to a T, at the beginning, of course, he might be testing his disguises, walking the streets, finding out where there might be cameras, looking at the original sites and trying to keep his murders as close as possible. Then again—"

"Because a hundred-plus years does make changes on the landscape, he may be determining new areas in which he might strike," Mason said. "Sean told me they've heightened police presence, but no country or city could provide an officer per city block—which is the only way there would be a guarantee that this killer wouldn't strike somewhere unseen." He hesitated and shrugged. "This isn't the same area, and this killer isn't going after the same women, though…sometimes, I don't think that we look at the original Jack's victims in the right way. Times were terrible back then. The area was poor—dirt poor. Some of the victims had been married, they were mothers. Bad things happen in life, and when they became addicted to alcohol, there was no Alcoholics Anonymous or addiction centers to help them—not that they could have afforded an addiction center if such places had existed. Many—of course, not all—but many women at the time resorted to prostitution because they were desperate. And because they had become alcoholics, they had to keep finding more money. Before the Ripper got to them, many were leading tragic existences. Not that it matters any less, the horror that was done to them."

"I know," Della murmured. "British historian Hallie Rubenhold believed the only real *prostitute* among the victims was Mary Kelly and that, as you said, the others resorted to the sex trade out of desperation. I'm just glad that I didn't live in the East End of London back in the day!"

He smiled, nodded and took her hand. "Not an easy existence. Where do you think that we might find our ghostly lady?"

"I was thinking that we might walk around St. Botolph's Church because in the Ripper's day that was the prostitute's church. She might be looking for us there. Our kindly Victorian lady knows where we're staying and might be hanging around somewhere near, not that all this isn't within walking distance. So—"

They hadn't gone a block before Mason pointed down the street. "There she is. Mrs. Abigail Scott." He waved.

Della smiled. Normally—having learned as a child that people might well think him crazy if he were seen waving to or speaking with a ghost no one else around them could see—he would have been careful *not* to do so. But the streets were busy and he might have been waving to anyone.

Abigail Scott waved in return and made her way to them as they made their way to her.

"Anything?" she asked anxiously.

"Not yet, I'm afraid," Mason told her. "But we have some images we'd like you to see. We work with a woman who is an amazing sketch artist and she has drawn pictures of ways that the killer might disguise himself. Would you take a look at them and see if you've seen anyone resembling any of these pictures wandering around the streets, heading to any particular pubs?"

"Of course! I will do anything to help!" she assured them. She sighed, looking around. "The world changes. Some things are the same—and some are so different. Now, well, many decent and hardworking people who have good jobs and stable families live here. Young people come to rent their first flats on their own and businesses may thrive. There is health care for all. You can't imagine what it was in the past. Such crowding and such poverty. My heart was broken when I read about the poor women so viciously taken from this world. And now, again, so, yes, please, let me help in any way!"

Della inclined her head to the woman. "Mrs. Scott, it's thanks to people like you, those who pointed out the plight of others, those who cared, that the world changed. And we're so grateful that you're here and ready to help us."

"Of course, of course. I've often wondered..." Abigail Scott's voice trailed.

"Why you're still here?" Della suggested softly.

Abigail nodded. "Somewhere in my heart, I know that my husband waits for me, and my children, and I can tell them about their children and their children's children. I've seen others leave, and yet..."

"Maybe you are still here to help us," Della said.

"To make a real difference. It's what I always longed to do," the ghost said. "So. I shall see these images."

They were on the street, of course, with others walking by them. The good thing was that it appeared Mason and Della were just speaking to one another. When Mason brought his phone out to show Abigail the images, he appeared to be sharing something with Della.

Maisie was truly talented. She'd made use of a computer program, of course, but all the little touches were hers and she'd created what Della considered to be an amazingly reasonable display of a man's facial structure being changed in many simple ways.

As Mason flipped through the pictures, Abigail Scott began to point to a few.

"This fellow, dark hair, dark beard…or, our killer in this disguise… I believe that I saw him right in this area, perhaps a block down, just last night!"

Della glanced at Mason. They were both wondering if the killer had knowledge that a group of international law enforcement was on his trail—and that they were housed in the area, determined to be right on his stalking grounds.

"Oh, and this! How amazing! How wonderfully talented your artist must be! Yes! I've seen him look this way, too!"

The image she pointed was that of their killer, assuming that their killer was Jesse Miller, with light red hair, a clean-shaven face and an enlarged nose.

"He was following the crowd at a Jack the Ripper tour the other night!" Abigail said. "Can—can it really be the same person—and is he the killer?"

Mason shook his head. "He behaved suspiciously," he told Abigail. "We don't know. But if he is changing his appearance to avoid being questioned by the police, he is definitely a person of interest. And thank you. Thank you so much."

"Wait," Abigail murmured. "I've seen him one more way, too!" she said.

She didn't quite understand the way Mason had been showing her the images on his phone, but she touched the phone and looked at Mason.

He quickly began to run through Maisie's renderings again.

"There!"

She pointed to the image of Jesse Miller as a bald man with a neatly clipped brown mustache and beard.

"Where?" Della asked.

"City of London Cemetery," Abigail said.

Mason frowned. "That's almost eight miles from here, I think."

"Yes," she said, hesitating a second. "I visit the graves. Mary Ann Nichols—Polly—and Catherine Eddowes are buried at the City of London Cemetery," she added quietly. "I go sometimes to see them, and others, where they are buried."

"Have they—remained?" Della asked.

Abigail shook her head. "No. And I'm thankful because I truly believe that there is a heaven and that their poor souls are at rest. I just go to pray. And to make myself feel better, I believe. And I do believe, as I said, that they are in a far better place, and still..."

"I understand," Della assured her. "And you saw someone resembling this image there? Interesting." She glanced at Mason. Was there would-be Ripper King trying to learn everything he possibly could about the past—including visits to gravesites on the canonical victims?

Abigail nodded. "I saw him. But he didn't seem to be... Well, he didn't seem to show any empathy. It wasn't as if he went to pray. He stared at the graves and he... I think he smiled. I didn't pay that much attention to him. Many people come, just as they come to go on the Ripper tours. But now that I've seen this image..."

"Yes?" Della prodded gently.

Her voice trailed. "I tried—others tried. You must understand the world back then." She winced. "You see, murder in the Whitechapel and Spitalfields areas was not rare. Three other women might have been early victims, though detectives through the years believe that his victims were limited to the five. But there was a file on the Whitechapel murders that included others like Frances Smith, Emma Coles and Martha Tabram. For many in the establishment, violence in Whitechapel was something shrugged off—the crime rate was horrible and our so-called more refined society considered that violence to be part of life for the hard people here living explosive and dangerous lives. When it came to the victims at first, it was lamentable, of course, to good Christians, but it was also almost as if they were..."

"Throwaway people, disposable," Della said. "And please, don't worry. We do understand how hard living conditions were for these people. We don't think poorly of them, or that they were disposable in any way."

Abigail nodded, her eyes closing briefly, the hint of a smile on her lips.

"This present-day killer—this monster—he thinks nothing of any woman. All are prey for him. But he's a fool, because it's not the same world the original Jack knew!" Abigail said fiercely. "And you won't let him get away with more murders. Will you?"

"We're taught never to make promises because none of us can give guarantees," Mason said. "But I swear to you that we will do everything in our power to apprehend him."

"We won't stop," Della added. "Know this, we will not stop."

Abigail nodded again. "Well, you will have me, too. I never was a detective, but I hope that I will be..." She paused and then smiled brightly again. "I will be a secret weapon against this monster!"

"A highly valued secret weapon!" Della said. "Thank you!"

Abigail nodded somberly. She appeared to straighten her spectral shoulders.

"We'll keep walking the area. We know that he's out here somewhere," Mason said. But then, he excused himself; his phone was ringing.

He took a step away to answer the call. As he did so, Della smiled at their determined Victorian ghost.

"Was it hard for you, being a journalist, an advocate, in the 1880s?"

Abigail smiled. "Almost impossible. But my uncle was a man ahead of his time. And he owned the paper. He didn't even insist that I use a man's pseudonym. He was... Well, I miss him almost as much as I miss my husband. Of course, my husband... Strange, isn't it? I saw many marriages in my day that were forced. I knew many *respectable* couples who were miserable. And, of course, it was far more accepted for a man to seek solace elsewhere than it was for a woman, but..." She paused, shrugging. "To exist so long, I see that laws change, that morality may change, but the human being remains the same. Love is beautiful. Sometimes it twists, and couples turn on one another. I had a good marriage. My husband was a truly good man. His mind was filled with the brightest health, but his body was ravaged by disease."

Della hesitated. "Abigail, may I ask you something?"

"Of course, dear."

"You were young yourself," Della said softly.

Abigail smiled and nodded. "Yes. And I had children. A boy and a girl. Maybe I care so much about these women being maligned because...when Allen died, I drank too much. Oh, I could function—I wrote well. And I was a good mother. And I would have died, just not so soon. My body did not do well with what I was doing to it, but, you see, I know what it is like to long to feel numb, and...well. The good! My uncle had a daughter about my age and she hadn't been able to have children and Jane was happy to care for my babes and I always loved her, so... Well!"

She stopped speaking and Della knew that Mason was returning to them. He nodded to Abigail and told Della, "Edmund and Sean have a list of those who might have witnessed something during the vampire murders. They're headed to see someone named Reginald Alder and we're off to see a Gary Hudson. Mrs. Scott—"

"Abigail, please," their ghost reminded him, glancing at Della with a smile.

"Abigail," Mason said, nodding. "You know where we're staying and, of course—"

"I will find you if I hear or see anything," she promised. She hesitated. "I keep walking but I don't believe that our killer stalks his victims until night falls."

"I think that you're right. But I also believe that while his first Ripper murder might have been a killing of convenience, I think he's already chosen his second victim and is watching her routine. He'll take a week, possibly, which is good for us. It would be wonderful if you could keep your eyes open for us."

"Of course!"

"Della?" Mason said.

"I'm ready. Are we driving?"

"No," he told her. "Mr. Gary Hudson is a bartender. Right on Whitechapel Road."

"Isn't it too early for the pubs to be open?" Della asked.

"They'll be setting up—a perfect time for a little chat. And apparently, Mr. Hudson was interested in the case, very happy to help the police. With luck, he'll want to talk to us."

"Ah!" Abigail said. "Those who try to put themselves into a case are often involved?"

"Sometimes," Della said, glancing at Mason. "Profilers, officers and agents who study human behavior, believe that it's often possible that certain criminals do like to ingratiate themselves, become involved with investigations, perhaps to determine just what police know, and also to prove their own prowess over law enforcement. And you knew that because—"

"I often haunt the home of one of my great-great-great grandchildren," she said, smiling. "And I do love to watch their television set. I've even managed to push that little box thing—"

"Remote control," Mason said.

"Yes. I can change the channels."

"And no one suspects?" Della asked. "They don't think that they live in a *haunted* house?"

Abigail laughed. "Oh, they just roll their eyes and say that the cable company is crazy," she explained. "There are some wonderful programs. Many silly ones that are a waste of one's time, but some very good ones, too."

"Of course. We shall see you later," Della said.

She turned to Mason.

"We're off!" he said.

Mason looked up at the sign that read simply Ye Olde Pub.

The place was certainly in an area that would allow for easy access to almost any of the dark alleys that remained in the original Ripper's old haunts. He'd always believed and still believed that if modern forensic techniques had existed during the original Ripper's time, the man would have certainly been caught.

And here they were today. With all manner of forensic techniques.

Then again, the original Ripper hadn't known not to leave fingerprints or a single hair or fiber that might be traced back to him. He didn't know that he needed to avoid security cameras that were placed at banks and so many other establishments.

Stephan Dante had been aware. And while the knowledge to take care because of the ever-evolving field of forensics might suggest that someone in forensics or law enforcement might be involved, the internet allowed for knowledge to spread across the world—for those who sought to study and delve further and further and from site to site.

Dante had never been in law enforcement. He might have learned all he needed to know from his time in prison, from those who had fallen to whatever detection or forensics had been out there. More than anything, Dante had known how to use people.

And he had surely taught his disciples to do the same.

"Mason?" Della said, nudging him lightly. "We can't talk to him if we don't reach him."

"Right."

Mason put his hand on the door and quickly discovered that it was locked. But within, he could see that waitresses were setting the last of little battery-operated "candles" on the tables and that one of the three young women moving about was setting up a small poster board with the pub's daily specials.

One of them noticed him at the entrance and hurried over to the door, opening it. She was a pretty young woman, dark-haired, in her early twenties, Mason surmised.

"I'm so sorry," she told him. "We do need a sign on the door. I'm afraid that we don't open until eleven."

"And I'm sorry to disturb you," Mason said. "But we're here to see Gary Hudson. I realized that he might be with the night crew and that you stay open—"

"We all switch up now and then," the young woman said. "As it happens, we had a meeting this morning and Gary is here. Are you friends of his?"

"We've never met," Della explained politely. "We're hoping to meet him now."

And they were about to meet him. Mason saw that a man had come out a door behind the bar that must have led to offices or stockrooms or both.

He was about six feet tall with sandy-blond hair that was cut short but still framed his face. He presented a handsome figure, with a good face and light eyes and a quick smile.

"Cindy, what's going on here?" he asked, a semi-smile on his face to take the edge off words he apparently figured he might have spoken a little too harshly.

"Cindy was politely letting us know that we're too early to come in."

"Not by much!" Cindy said. "We could let you sit. I'll be unlocking the doors in just a few minutes. Gary, they came to see you?"

Gary Hudson arched a brow, studying Mason and Della.

He grinned. "You," he informed Della, "I'd let in anytime. Now, about you, sir…?"

Mason grinned in return. The words had been said

in good humor. Hudson was intrigued, wondering why Americans had come specifically to see him.

"We need your help," Mason said flatly.

"Of course. But how can I help you? I mean, you're obviously American, and I'm not the best tour guide around, though I do create one hell of a dirty martini—any bloke out there will testify to that on my behalf."

"We are American—obviously," Della said, smiling. She was especially beautiful when she smiled, Mason thought, and, well, of course, she'd won him over heart and soul, but her ability to judge people and use whatever mental or physical assets she had in any given situation also made her an incredible partner.

"Right," Hudson said slowly.

"We're part of an international task force," Mason said quietly.

They were still standing in the doorway.

And Cindy was still watching them, listening.

"Oh, dear Lord!" Cindy exclaimed suddenly. "You're here because of that horrible business with a madman thinking he can recreate the killings perpetuated by Jack the Ripper. Oh, I mean, not that horrible excuses for human beings haven't done such things before—"

"The Yorkshire Ripper for one," Gary Hudson said dryly.

"But…how can Gary help you?" Cindy asked. "How can any of us help you? And international? I'm so confused. He killed here…"

"We believe that he's a man who was specifically trained by an American killer. We also believe that he committed murders before he decided to emulate the Ripper—and I believe that Gary will know what we're talking about."

He looked at Gary Hudson. The man was staring back at him. The bartender nodded gravely. "I gave the police everything that I had at the time," he said, sounding pained. "But come in. I'm not on duty until seven this evening, so it's easy enough for you to have a seat and... Well, I just don't have that much to tell you. You should stay for lunch, though. Cindy is a great waitress and the food here really is good."

"Thank you. Maybe we'll do just that," Mason said.

"I..." Cindy shook her head, looking ill. "I don't leave here alone anymore. I make my boyfriend come and meet me right after work. And... I have things to do!"

She quickly disappeared. Gary Hudson held the door for them and Mason and Della went on in. Hudson indicated a two-seater high-top table and drew a third bar stool over for himself.

Mason and Della sat and Hudson did the same. "How can I help you?" he asked.

"Well, we've read the files, of course," Mason said. "Mr. Hudson, you were the one who found the first victim on the banks of the Thames. Colleen Denton. An American tourist. I read your statement. You were just walking down to see the river and you were stunned to see someone lying there and you thought at first that she was sleeping."

He nodded. "It was morning. I was surprised that someone else hadn't noticed her." He shrugged. "I'm a water lover—I even love the Thames, since... Well, it's what we've got in the area! And there was a time, of course, before modern sewage, that the river itself was a cesspool. But these days, there's something about standing on the embankment that... Well, it's beautiful. Especially when the sun is rising or falling." He paused, looking at Della, frowning. "You're really an FBI agent?"

Della nodded. "Really."

"Oh, are you usually in an office? Are you a profiler?"

"I've attended a number of profiling seminars," Della said pleasantly, "But, no, it's not my expertise, and no, I'm not an office tech."

"Artist!"

She shook her head again. "Please, Mr. Hudson, can you think of anyone around you? Was there someone watching you?"

He frowned. "Well, hmm. I was alone. I was watching the water when I looked down the embankment and saw her. As I said or wrote or both, I thought that she was sleeping. I went over to wake her up and I thought right away that she had to be a tourist, probably an American—you know, being a bit showy, maybe, wanting to tell friends at home what she'd done. In fact, I looked around, thinking she'd want a photo, that it was something she was doing for social media. There were people up on the street...and maybe..."

"Maybe?" Mason asked.

"Maybe there was a guy watching."

"But he was wearing a dark hoodie?" Della asked dryly.

"No, he was in a T-shirt and..."

"And?" Mason prompted.

"Well, I guess I didn't think much about it before. But he was wearing a T-shirt and jeans and carrying a briefcase. You know, like a man might use for work as a banker or such, like an accountant or a barrister. Except, what bloke goes to a job like that wearing a T-shirt. In fact, I remember the T-shirt. It was one of those you buy at a concert. There's a new group out now, The Slackers, and I think they had a concert recently and you know how they sell T-shirts at concerts. I... I mean I noticed him but didn't think anything of it until now. Until..." He paused again, making a face, shaking his head. "Well, of course, the Ripper murder is all over the media. Oh! I also thought that someone had been arrested in those killings. That the bloke was an American—not to be offensive, but not surprising."

"We're not offended," Mason said. "But you should also know that sick killers come from every country and they might be of any ethnicity."

"Yeah, right. There was that Russian that they didn't want to admit to because the Russians wanted to believe that all such sick people were only American. What was his name? Chink-o-something."

"Chikatilo," Della said. "Among others," she added sweetly.

"I'm sorry. I just wish that I could help."

"Can you give us more of a description?" Mason asked.

"Dark hair," Hudson said thoughtfully. "I don't know—he was at a distance. Maybe six feet tall, with an average build, I think. I was paying attention to the woman. I went to her and I nudged her, speaking softly—didn't want to scare her. Odd, I never thought that she was drunk. Drunks fall and pass out in awkward positions. I thought she was sleeping because she looked so sweet and beautiful and she was lying there in such a restful position. Then, of course, I realized that she was dead and I panicked and I pulled out my cell and ran back to the street, calling for the police. Naturally, I went to the station and told them what I'd seen. I didn't mention the bloke in the T-shirt because my concentration was on the woman and... Well, I had worked late the night before and I was so shaken and... "

His voice trailed and he lifted his hands.

"I'm so sorry. I wish I could tell you more. Maybe…well, maybe whoever discovered the other women on the embankment can tell you more," Hudson finished.

"Maybe. But, of course, we thank you—"

"Did you want to have some lunch? I can call Cindy over."

"I think we'll skip it for now. As you said, we have others we need to speak with," Mason told him, rising, waiting for Della and Hudson to do the same.

"Right, yes," Della said. "And thank you so much. Of course, if you think of anything, please reach us through Detective Inspector Edmund Taylor—any police station will get you in touch."

"Of course," Hudson said, shrugging. He seemed an easy man, capable of being charming, listening. Bartender at a pub might be the perfect profession for him since he seemed entirely affable and ready to converse or not as a patron might want.

"But again, I thought you got the killer," Hudson said. "How could the same guy be at it again? Oh, and I thought that killers killed in a certain way. Isn't this—different?"

"We think this killer might have had some practice, copying another killer," Mason said honestly. "Again, thank you for your time."

"Right. Thank you," Della said, turning to head for the door.

Mason followed her.

Outside, she turned to him. "I don't know if he's the man who is killing again now, but he killed that first girl!" she announced.

"Della, he's probably more than a bit of a chauvinistic ass, but that—"

She shook her head strenuously. "No, Mason, I'm sure

of it. He was making up that story about a man in a T-shirt with a briefcase. And he reported that he touched her, nudged her, trying to wake her. That would explain if anyone found his print, a hair, anything that might forensically attach him to the killing. Mason, I don't know about the rest of the murders, but I'd bet a year's pay that he was guilty of the first. So, what do we do about it?"

CHAPTER SEVEN

Della wasn't sure about the way that Mason was looking at her and she felt that she had to explain herself. "Mason, I'm serious. And not because he acts like women should be kept in the kitchen. It's the way he was describing the person watching and the way he found the body."

She was glad that Mason nodded. "I don't believe that we can be certain, that's all. The police questioned him—"

"Of course, they did! He found the body. But he was working under Dante's tutelage then. He would have seen to it that she was left just as Dante would have left her. He would have learned all about making sure that he didn't leave any evidence to suggest that he was the killer."

"But," Mason reminded her, "if he was using Dante's methods, he would have needed to get rid of his tools of the trade—his way of removing all the blood from her body."

"She wasn't killed there—she was dumped there," Della reminded him. "Or, I should say, displayed there."

Mason nodded again. "All right, so...gut-wise, I think

that you're right. What we need to do is find a way to prove it. Curious…" he murmured.

"What's that?"

"We both believed that he killed the young woman he claimed to have found. Did he kill the others? And is this the Ripper King we're looking for now?"

"He's certainly in a good position. He's a bartender right in the area—"

"Yes, except, remember. A pub closes. The patrons begin to filter out after last call. The staff has to stay until they've picked up for the night. And, I still can't help but think that Jesse Miller is the man trying to perfectly—as perfectly as possible well over a hundred years later—replicate the Jack the Ripper killings."

Della closed her eyes for a moment. "Mason, this is terrifying. There really might be more than one killer."

"We've already thought of that possibility."

"But…"

"I know what you're thinking. There might even be more than two killers out there—two killers who were followers of Stephan Dante. And now, one of them isn't just being careful not to get caught when he believes the world thinks that the vampire killer has been caught, but who has determined that he's going to outshine his mentor, prove that he's the most complicated killer out there—the one to become the most infamous."

Mason nodded. "Or," he said, crossing his arms over his chest, "there could be just two—one who committed one or more of the previous London killings, and one who is now working on becoming a twenty-first century king of Rippers."

"There's got to be some kind of evidence somewhere!" Della said.

"Yes. Those cases are still open, and they are the reason Edmund came after the vampire killer and joined our little international group. We need to research all the findings on the vampire killings here again. Every one of us. Something may click with someone."

"And in the meantime, Jesse Miller is still somewhere." Della frowned and pulled out her phone, quickly keying something into a search engine. "Mason, Abigail said that she saw a man who may have been Jesse Miller at the City of London Cemetery. And look!" She lifted her phone so that Mason could see the site she'd drawn up. "Isabelle Ainsley, the vampire victim who was local, was buried at the City of London Cemetery as were both Mary Anne—aka Polly—Nichols and Catherine Eddowes. I think we should pay the cemetery a visit."

"It can't hurt. In whatever guise, the killer is probably doing his stalking once darkness falls. We'll head to the cemetery. I'll call Edmund and we'll go over records together early this evening, and then we'll hit the streets."

He lifted a hand for a cab and she frowned.

"We're not walking!" he told her.

"Oh, right. I guess we'll do enough walking tonight. And..."

"And the cemetery may be a lot of walking, too."

They were picked up and dropped off at the gates. Della had drawn up information on the cemetery but he didn't need her to tell him that it was large—a two-hundred-acre site—or that it was well thought out and crafted with a stunning entry that offered handsome stonework and spoke of the Victorian age.

"Opened in 1856," Della murmured. "Not that old as things in Europe may be, but…"

He shrugged. "Human beings have always needed to remember loved ones gone before them. Often, in centuries gone by, people were buried in churches—interred in catacombs or in the walls—or in churchyards. Come the Victorian age and designing beautiful places for people to come and sit and pray or reflect on their loved ones—or life and death perhaps—became a popular concept. Also, they were afraid that the number of decaying corpses would cause diseases to spread. But this place is known for its well-kept roads and pathway, nature and beauty. Not that other cemeteries aren't…but, anyway, anyone of any religion or ethnicity can still be buried here."

"Hey, I'm the guide here, remember?" she teased.

"Where first?"

"Let's find our victims."

They walked through the cemetery like any other tourists, commenting on beautiful funerary art pieces and the landscaping.

Watching people as they did so.

They passed a family bringing flowers, a young couple, a small group of young adults who appeared to be tourists and a lone older man kneeling at a gravesite, his head bowed in prayer. No one they saw resembled any of Maisie's sketches, or Jesse Miller as they had seen him at the pub in Brixton.

They reached the grave of Jack the Ripper's first canonical victim. A stone was set with a circular brass plaque with the words *City of London Cemetery* and then *Heritage Trail* set around the center, and in the center, just the name, *Mary Ann Nichols*, and the date of her death, *August 30, 1888.*

"May you rest well now!" Della murmured.

Mason set his arm around her shoulder. "I hope she knows, too, that her death—with those other deaths—brought attention to those in the East End. And she is remembered."

"Just as a prostitute and alcoholic, most of the time," Della said.

"No. There's a good documentary out about the lives of the victims. You would like it—they become very human in the documentary."

"Hmm. You haven't mentioned that before!"

He shrugged. "I watch lots of documentaries. Let's... let's keep moving. I don't see anyone suspicious hanging around here today."

"Onward to Catherine Eddowes."

They followed the directions to the grave that Della had brought up online.

There, too, was a circular memorial set into place by the City of London Cemetery. And there was the name, Catherine Eddowes, and her date of death.

As they stood there, Mason knew that like him, Della was watching the people who were near them and the grave in the cemetery.

"There," Della said softly. "By the family vault over that way."

"I see him."

"Head back up the path and split up?"

He nodded.

He took her hand and they turned, heading along the roadway. Della pretended to admire an angel statue and he let her hand go.

He took off to the left.

She took off to the right.

They circled around the vault. He was surprised to discover that the man they had been watching was still there.

He was even more surprised to discover that they knew the man who was behind the vault, leaning against the stone of the back side.

He straightened, seeing the two of them come at him, and his frown of concern quickly turned to a smile of relief.

"You two!" he said.

"Trey Harper, Metropolitan Police," Della said.

"Visiting a loved one?" Mason asked him dryly, curious that the one-time undercover policeman who had approached Della the night before was there at the cemetery.

Watching?

"Watching for a freak," Harper said, as if he'd read his mind. Or, as if he was telling a simple truth. On the one hand, these killers were so good eluding capture by leaving no evidence behind, it just might suggest that the killer was a cop.

"You think that the killer is coming here?" Mason asked him. "What makes you think that he might?"

"I'm off duty, but you know, in this line of work, when a case is a haunting one... Well, you're never off duty. I figured that this killer is so determined to mimic the Ripper that he might feel obliged to visit the graves of Jack the Ripper's victims."

"Have you seen anyone?"

"I thought I did the other day. I mean, obviously, tourists come and because it's an active cemetery and crematorium, people bring flowers and—" he shrugged "—coming to honor their loved ones. But there was a fellow behaving oddly the other day. He didn't go to any of the graves, but he walked around and around and I thought that he was talking to himself."

"Did you talk to him?" Della asked.

"I was going to, but I heard a scream, and being a cop by nature, I ran to the scream... It was a kid who had never seen his father's headstone and I guess seeing the name on the headstone was too much for him. But by the time I knew that nothing was wrong, the man I had been watching was gone."

Mason pulled out his phone and keyed up Maisie's images, asking him first if it was the man that Abigail Scott had identified.

"Was this him?"

Trey Harper frowned. "Yes, and no. I mean, it looks something like him, but..."

"What about any of these?"

"There!"

Trey pointed to an image of their suspect with long tawny hair and thick shaggy brows.

"That's him!"

"These images have been sent to the city and Metropolitan Police," Della told him. "Study them when you have a chance. I don't know why this man would keep coming to the cemetery—"

"He was in an area with a new grave. That of the English girl who was killed as one of the vampire victims," Harper said, his tone hard. "That in itself had made me wonder—she's over there," he added softly. "Family plot. Her great-great-great grandfather was one of the first internments here."

"We haven't been there yet," Della said.

"Will you show us?" Mason asked.

"Of course." He winced. "Her death is fresh and deeply

painful for many and I'd like to think that she isn't on any historic or other tour maps yet. This way."

They followed him around one of the paths, passing majestic angels and other memorials. Trees lined the main road and the cemetery was meticulously maintained.

They reached an area that was secluded by a small stone wall. In the center was a tall monument that bore the family name. The first grave dated back to the year that the cemetery was opened.

But Trey Harper led them to a grave where the grass was just growing back. A simple wooden cross marked the newer burial.

"Her headstone hasn't arrived yet," Trey said, his voice sounding bitter. "The family has ordered it, of course, but it can sometimes take a few months for markers to arrive and be installed."

"But you saw this man here, and wandering near the Ripper's victims?" Mason asked.

Trey nodded. "I haven't seen him today."

"Thanks for showing us this area," Mason said. He looked at Della and wondered if they were thinking the same thing.

Their "Ripper King" had visited this cemetery—before his first Ripper murder—his "Polly" Nichols murder.

Where was the Ripper's second victim buried? Had he visited that grave already, or would he show up there. And seriously, why was he bothering, or was it just a part of his organized madness?

"Thank you," Della said quietly. "I guess we'd best get back. Trey, I'm sure we'll meet again."

"And it will be great to meet again," he said. "We can hope for better circumstances."

"Absolutely," Della said.

Mason lifted a hand in goodbye and he and Della headed

out of the family plot and through the cemetery, back to the street where he looked at her, shrugged and said, "Car service?"

"Let's try. I don't think that many cabs will be out here."

"Rideshare is everywhere," he said, looking at the apps he had on his phone. "But where are we going? All right, we believe that our killer came here—then, he struck for the first time. The first victim is buried here, but the next—"

"Manor Park Cemetery and Crematorium, East London, near Epping Forest."

"Maybe?" he murmured.

"All right. Off to Manor Park Cemetery. And then—"

"Then back to the house. We'll meet up and everyone can report on their day, any new findings—"

"And there may be...nothing," Della said.

"There may be nothing to share as yet."

"And we may be going to Manor Park Cemetery for nothing, but..."

"We have to see what we can see," Mason agreed quietly. He was silent a minute.

"You don't think that we have a chance of finding him until night, do you?"

He dialed and a car came for them within a few minutes. The driver was chatty; they chatted back, talking about the landscaping of the cemetery and the odd way tourists liked to visit cemeteries.

Della told him that he'd just have to visit New Orleans, and the atmospheric "cities of the dead" to be found there.

He asked them if they had an English relative or friend buried in the cemetery.

Mason answered that one. "We just heard that it was beautiful. Victorian art and all."

"And the grave of a Ripper victim, right?" he asked, amused.

"That's right. Annie Chapman," Mason said simply.

They were dropped off.

It was true that the cemetery was beautiful. And atmospheric. Grand angels and crosses and other monuments adorned many sections, along with headstones at different angles, twisted in the earth by time and nature.

"Opened in 1874," Mason said as they wove through pathways and monuments to find the grave of Annie Chapman.

A standing plaque had been erected for the woman.

"'This plaque is dedicated to the memory of Annie Chapman, died eighth of September 1888, a victim of the infamous Jack the Ripper, her remains are buried within this area,'" Della read. She shook her head, pulling out her phone to read about Annie. "Mason, it's all just so incredibly sad. She liked alcohol too much from a young age, but apparently managed to clean up with help from her siblings. She was married to a man who had respectable jobs, she had three children, two daughters and a son, and the son was born crippled and had to be put in an institution and one of her daughters died at the age of twelve from meningitis and Annie wound up drinking again. She and her husband separated, but she received a payment from him while he was alive. No life insurance, no help from anywhere after he died. She didn't grow up thinking, wow, I am going to be a prostitute when I grow up! She crocheted and knitted and tried to sell her wares, but she couldn't always make enough and she was an alcoholic and as we noted earlier, there was no help back then. There weren't a lot of job openings for her, but she did try at workhouses and the like. Such a different world. Five feet tall, dark-haired and blue-eyed, she was known as Dark Annie, bright and courteous—when she was sober. Don't get me wrong, I am a believer in personal responsibility, but... Oh, Mason, what a sad life!"

He nodded and said quietly. "Despite all her problems, she was a fighter, so I've read. She intended to be a survivor, but..." His voice dropped low. "Careful, but glance to your left. There is a large winged angel and someone is watching us while hovering behind it."

Della pretended to study the graves by Annie's plaque. She saw what Mason had seen—a small portion of the left side of the body of someone standing behind the angel.

"We are being watched," she murmured.

"All right, we'll stay together down the path, split right and left."

She nodded.

They turned to leave the grave. The person behind the angel tried to move slightly, to shield himself—or herself—entirely behind the stone body.

Della spoke as they headed in the direction of the angel, weaving around tombs and artful crosses and other monuments in the area. "Oh, Mason. There—it's a mass grave for fifty-seven people who died during a bombing in World War II. And there, Sarah Dearman, known as Sarah Chapman, no known relationship—initiated a strike that helped change the world. She was known as the match girl, and started the match girls' strike because she was able to gather others and start a union that went international and changed dire working situations for women—she was a true pioneer for women's rights!"

"Impressive," Mason said. "There is such incredible history to be found in a cemetery. We can learn so much from those who went before us." He glanced at his own phone as they walked, coming closer to the angel. "That strike was in 1888—the year of the Ripper. But thankfully, Sarah lived a good long life—she died in 1945."

He gave her a nod. She split off to the left, and he moved to the right. They moved fast.

The person behind the angel took flight. They did the same.

But the cemetery was full of twists and turns between memorials and headstones and tombs. He disappeared. Della continued to the left, slowing when she reached an area where there were multiple angels and crosses and large stone mausoleums. She flattened herself against an angel, easing along to see beyond it.

Someone slid behind her.

Someone who warned, "There's a knife in your ribs, my lovely!"

Her first thought wasn't fear; she was furious with herself. Furious that she hadn't heard or felt the man behind her.

But she could feel the knife.

"Really?" she asked. "How clever of you. Stab me in a cemetery. No one will notice? I'm an FBI agent on special international assignment. Do you think this is smart?"

"You were after me!"

"To question you. And my team knows that I'm here—"

"Yeah, yeah. And that fellow is with you, but you think you're so tough. He's not here now, is he? He's looking for me in the wrong place. You two gambled and lost."

"We don't gamble. But I can promise you this—stab me here and Special Agent Mason Carter will find you within minutes."

"I'm not leaving you here. You're going to walk with me to my car."

"You think?" she asked.

"You can't feel the knife?"

"Yes, I know the feel of a knife."

He started to laugh. "You've had a lot of knives in you, have you? Well, I can see that. You are a beautiful woman, but...what a bitch. Of course, most of you are bitches. Or worse. I could tell you what you really are, but that would rather ruin things."

"Why? What do you intend?"

"You're just going to have to wait and see. And do what I say, of course. Because everyone is the same. Everyone wants to survive. So, you'll do what I order you to do, thinking that if you do, you'll get the chance to escape me." He leaned his face close against her neck and ear and whispered softly, "To live! To survive! You may just keep thinking that, my lovely! But you'll obey me, and I am so, so sorry, but hope all that you might. You will die!"

Mason reached an area where the monuments and stones were low enough to allow him to see far ahead.

He'd lost the man, but then, of course, that's why they'd split. Della would be on him. He needed to run hard to the right now, into an area that was a veritable maze of graves and funerary art. As he neared one angel, he could hear a man talking.

"We need to move. Now. Actually, it's a shame that I can't take the time to play with you more here and then kill you—right here! Just a murder in a cemetery. How fitting. A dead woman—among the dead. There's little I can do to make it proper, but then you FBI people are so predictable. You think *signature* all the time, and, well…sometimes, there are people who just need to go! Then again, maybe we'll have some time."

"Time with you? Wow," Della said dryly.

Mason moved carefully and drew his gun, grateful that François Bisset had made the arrangements for their task force to be among the specialized law enforcement allowed to be armed in the United Kingdom. He came around to see who was holding Della.

But even as he did, Della was taking matters into her own hands. Mason saw first that the man had slipped silently behind her, sliding one arm around her while holding a knife against her ribs with his free hand. But even as he appeared before them, Della slammed back an elbow with strength and determination—catching the man in the ribs, possibly cracking one of them. Her would-be killer was taken entirely by surprise and was sent back a few feet, staggering in pain. Della swung around instantly—knowing that she couldn't depend on him being down—and approached him with a leap and a sound kick that might have felled a far bigger man. He was slammed up hard against another angel.

Ironic.

Mason moved forward with his Glock aimed at the man's chest.

"Don't kill him—we need him!" Della cried.

"Only if I have to, you know that," Mason said.

"I'm wounded! That bitch attacked me!" Hudson cried.

Mason stared at the man against the angel.

"Of course," he said, shrugging to Della, "it won't bother me in the least to blow out his kneecap and maybe his wrist—if he doesn't drop that knife right now."

The man stared back at him. Mason wasn't sure if he was

surprised or not that the attacker was the barman, the man that they'd just met that morning.

Now, Hudson stared back at him, hate burning in his eyes.

For a minute, he held onto the knife.

Mason cocked his gun, aiming straight at a kneecap, as he'd promised.

"I'm already injured! She attacked me!"

Mason looked at Della. "He'll be able to talk just fine if I just blow out his kneecap."

"Be my guest," Della said.

Hudson dropped the knife.

"Hey, what are you going to get me on? Visiting a cemetery? They'll bloody well need to arrest you, too, if that's a crime. And wait, you're American, you can't arrest me. You have no authority here! I didn't do anything—"

"Except for attacking a woman with a knife," Mason said.

"I didn't attack her! She's a paranoid FBI agent—a woman! She's desperate to pin anything on anyone lest she be sacked for being useless. Her word against mine, poor female trying to compete in a man's world and attacking a man in a cemetery. It will never stand up in a court of law and—"

"She's a woman who kicked your butt, you ass!" Mason said. "Hands above your head, turn around—"

"No!"

Mason took aim at his kneecap again. The man's hands went up and he cried, "You are idiots. I'm not the bloke you're looking for. I'm not—"

"I don't care what or who you think you are," Della said. "You're coming in and we'll find out more about you. Turn around, hands up behind your head."

Mason smiled. They could all be vulnerable at any time.

But Della was good at her job. Without firing a shot, she had saved herself. He hadn't needed to be any kind of knight in shining armor, though he was glad that he'd had her back in case something had gone wrong.

Gary Hudson listened at last.

He was smart enough to fear a gun. But maybe it wasn't the gun.

Maybe he was more afraid of Della than he'd ever admit.

And he was the right type to be their killer. He obviously held women in low esteem. Possibly because, despite his ability to charm and socialize, he had probably been rejected, perhaps even been under the thumb of a powerful mother or maternal figure as well.

But was he their current "Ripper"?

He wasn't sure. And if not, what was he guilty of?

Della had Hudson cuffed and when she had completed the task, Mason lowered his weapon at last and pulled out his phone again, putting a call through to Edmund.

Della had stepped away from Hudson and stood watching him. Her expression was hard.

"They're on their way," he assured her. "Edmund will meet us at Scotland Yard. He has a car coming for him now."

Even as he spoke, he heard sirens.

He was glad that the London police were on the way. He didn't want to be responsible for the man. Not after the way he'd seen the knife the man had brandished against Della.

She was good. She had proven her ability in the field many times.

And he still didn't trust himself.

He'd been going through a determination that there was always going to be another way, that he was sick of killing.

But now…

He was grateful that he didn't have to be alone with the man.

He'd want to strangle him with his bare hands.

And they didn't even know how much blood might be on the man's hands, just how many victims the man might have claimed.

But that would come.

He'd be questioned. And questioned. In a room where others could observe, and someone would stop Mason if he went after the man's throat.

CHAPTER EIGHT

Gary Hudson did not accept being in custody easily.

Edmund had been at the station as Della and Mason arrived—in a separate police car from that which had escorted Gary Hudson. Held in an interrogation room, Hudson spent his first minutes pacing the room and banging on the one-way mirror.

Sean arrived while they watched Hudson, listening as he raged about being abused by the police—and how he had been viciously attacked by a sick and perverted woman who was now falsely accusing him. She wasn't even a Brit!

He went on and on and on.

"You attacked him?" Edmund asked Della, curiously amused.

"I elbowed him," she admitted. "Pretty hard. Okay, and when he backed up a bit, I did give him a pretty good kick. I really didn't want him coming back at me again."

"Had something to do with the knife at her back," Mason explained.

"We saw him watching us at Manor Park Cemetery where the Ripper's second victim, Annie Chapman, is buried. When we went to find him—" Mason began.

"He found me first," Della said, "to my great embarrassment. Slipped up behind me and set his knife against my ribs and told me that, desperate to save my life, I would do what he commanded me to do. Thankfully, Mason came around right when I did *attack* him, elbowing him so hard it sent him back a foot so that I could give him a kick. Then, he finally dropped the knife. Oh, he didn't want to kill me in the cemetery because he knew that Mason was walking around somewhere. He did say something true—victims obey a kidnapper because they cling to every moment of life, hoping that someone will come to their rescue or that they'll find a way to escape."

"Except he had no idea just who he was attempting to kidnap," Mason said. "And while I thought the man might just be a misogynistic jerk, Della knew from the beginning that his hatred of women might lie a lot deeper."

"You had questioned him?" Sean asked.

"He was at the pub, but not on duty yet. We suspected that since a figure resembling one of Jesse Miller's possible disguises had been seen at City Cemetery, the murderer might be looking at Manor Cemetery, too, visiting the grave of the Ripper's second victim," Della explained.

They glanced through the window. Greg Hudson was still ranting about being attacked and railroaded by an American woman. She couldn't get her job done, so she attacked him, trying to do anything to look like she was halfway competent. Because, of course, a woman can't possibly be a reliable agent.

"Do you think that he's our Ripper killer?" Edmund

asked. He winced. "Of course, he discovered the body during the vampire killings and we interviewed him immediately after. But…well, he pulled the wool over my eyes. He appeared to be so sincerely distraught. I can show you the tape of that interview. He managed something close to tears—he'd been so horrified to realize that she wasn't sleeping, she was dead."

"We've all interviewed a suspect and not seen what was lying beneath," Mason assured him. "The question is, who do we send in now?"

"You are a team player, huh?" Edmund said.

Della lowered her head, smiling. Edmund had expected Mason to take the lead as apparent "head" of their specialized international unit. But Mason had no desire for the spotlight, which made him a great leader. He listened to others and gained from their insight and experience.

"Edmund, you met him first, if you want to go in. I'll join you in a few minutes, maybe get him aggravated, and then we'll hopefully get him to say something that gives us a clue as to his involvement in the first murder and perhaps others," Mason said. He hesitated. "I don't know why—gut reaction, or logic, not sure which—I don't think that he's the Ripper killer. The vampire killings were all abetted by Stephan Dante, whether at the scene or through his instructions and descriptions. These new killings are organized, well thought out, even studied. I do think Gary Hudson is guilty of something and that he might well have been one of Stephan Dante's disciples. He might well have killed one or all three of the vampire victims in London, and he might well know about any other followers Dante trained."

He paused, frowning, excused himself and looked at his phone.

"Carter," he said.

He listened, and then looked at the others again. "That was Jeanne. He knows that we have Hudson here, but he suggested we let him stew a little—we might want to meet him at the medical examiner's office. I think I have a working grasp of English law, but—"

"I have suggested legal counsel, I've gone through all the formal steps. And, yes, we can hold him for twenty-four hours before charging him," Edmund said. "Sean and I already went through the evidence on the previous cases and we're ready to try to put it all together at some point, but here's my suggestion—Sean and I will observe Gary Hudson as he *stews*, while you and Della meet up with Jeanne and François. In fact, I think it's a good idea."

"We need to let him think that we consider other things more important than him," Della said. "Ego is everything to this man. Dante would be the Vampire King—he wants to be a king, too."

"Very true," Sean murmured, shaking his head. "I'll watch him while he waits. Bring him coffee or water or whatever he wants, and I'll make sure he knows that you will all be with him just as soon as you can—but that there are other pressing matters."

"There's a plan," Mason said lightly.

"If we leave him to sit a while, he may be ready to say all kinds of things," Della said. "But he didn't bring up a right not to speak with us—"

"Nope," Edmund said. "He assured me he was completely innocent—and that I should be arresting you. He's innocent—he doesn't need legal counsel. But when you do talk to him, you'll hear more about that. Poor man!

You were so terrible to him, Della. He's really out for your blood."

"I noticed," she said dryly. "All right then—"

"ME's office isn't far," Edmund said. "I'll have an inspector drop you off and bring you back when you're ready. Follow me."

A morgue was a morgue.

And there was no way out of the fact that the empty shell of a body that had once housed a human being was a sad sight.

But today...

In the military and in law enforcement, Mason had seen his share of death. But there was something exceptionally sad about seeing a beautiful young woman with her life ahead of her stripped of that future on an autopsy table.

Worse when Dr. Cyrus Monroe described her injuries—and why he had suggested that they really understand what they were up against.

"I don't claim to understand the workings of the human brain and mind," Monroe told them as Mason and Della joined Jeanne, François and the doctor's assistant around the table, "but your killer is a truly deranged individual who is also something of a historian. I drew up the autopsy reports from 1888 and this poor lass was butchered in nearly exactly the same way as Mary Ann Nichols was killed—down to the bruising at the throat that suggests a sound knock to subdue the victim. Both women were strangled. Mary Ann Nichols was missing teeth, unlike this lass, but the loss of teeth had nothing to do with the murder. One other difference, this young woman was drugged, but I believe you know that. Date-rape style, dropped into her drink. But once the killing began—" he paused to demonstrate two gashes that nearly severed the head from the body "—on the left side of the neck, you have an incision that is about four inches in length. It has completely severed the tissues down to the vertebrae. Then, an inch below, you have a similar incision, running just below the ear. Both are caused by a strong blade, the same blade. Then…"

He paused and his assistant moved the sheet that had given the body a semblance of dignity.

"You see the slashes just below the abdomen. Downward and jagged here. They were done with exceptional strength and brutality. They cut through the tissue deeply." He looked at them. "I believe that your killer has seriously studied the autopsy reports from 1888 and that he is doing everything in his power to recreate the original killings in every way possible. The difference, of course, is that Polly Ann Nichols was older, destitute and living a hard life, resorting to prostitution. And this young lady… But, of course, I understand that this killer believes all women to be of one ilk. And I'm hoping that my work might in some small way help you to stop this man."

He looked around at them all.

"If this murder is in any way indicative of what is coming, it's indeed terrible. I'm no historian myself, but certainly aware of the past. But the original killer advanced with his savagery and while I, more than anyone, am aware that death itself is the great equalizer, and the victims are dead before the mutilation of the body and organs begin, thinking of more young women departing in this fashion is a concept far too horrible to entertain."

"Dr. Monroe, thank you," Mason told him. "We, and every member of every kind of law enforcement in Britain, are seeking to stop this killer, rest assured. We have a suspect—we need to find him. He's a chameleon."

"Ah. Monsieur Bisset said that you have a suspect in custody?" Monroe asked.

"We believe that we have a man in custody who killed the vampire victims—I don't believe that he killed this young woman," Mason told him. "We are hoping that he may shed some light on what is happening."

"The vampire was arrested in the United States," Monroe said, frowning.

"No. He had followers. He was an instructor in murder and killed many, but not all, of the victims in the States and in Europe," Della said. "But, Doctor—"

"You mean there may be more killers this savage and brutal out there than the one committing these crimes?" He paused again, shaking his head, wincing. "We've all heard this, of course—I speak for the dead. Many wonder how anyone does this for a living, a vocation. But it is very true—I speak for the dead. And while I constantly seek justice, in this instance…"

"We understand," Mason said quietly. "And it does help to know the extent of this man's obsession with a past killer. It will help weed out the truth when we interrogate those we seek as witnesses or persons of interest. We appreciate your dedication to detail."

Dr. Monroe nodded, studying Mason and then Della.

"Take care," he said. "And rude though it may sound, I hope we do not meet again."

"Understood," Mason said.

Monroe's assistant covered the body once more. There were thanks all around and they left the morgue. He studied Della's face as they left. She was stoic.

"You know," he murmured softly for her ears alone, "you can talk to Jackson. You are an exceptional agent, Della, I know that more than anyone. But—"

She turned to him. "Mason, I have seldom been more determined to see a killer brought to justice. And you know that I can take care of myself—more so, because I have your backing and that of the others. And now we have Gary Hudson. And while I'm convinced that he's guilty of a murder, he's not guilty of the Ripper murder—he's not that organized. But he may know who is—these men who followed Dante had to have seen each other at some point, or... Mason! How? How does a man turn others into killers? Maybe Philip can get a grasp on such a thing, but..."

"There are people out there who feel wronged. In this case, Gary Hudson is lying through his teeth. But somehow and somewhere along the line, he was wronged horribly by a woman or believes that he was wronged by a woman. We can look into his history, but... Dante was an incredible Pied Piper for finding those who were disillusioned and on the verge." He hesitated and winced, his focus on the past as he said, "We saw it often in small ways during the pandemic. People home and in their own company for hours and hours. They'd get on social media and because they were frustrated, they'd find a cause and embrace it, real or imagined, and they'd let their hate and anger at life boil over into horrible passions on the internet. In this case, a person lives focusing on how they've been wronged, perceived or otherwise, and they let it simmer and grow...and in real life, meet up with a Stephan Dante. They've wanted to lash out. To kill. And he convinces them that it's their right, that they should spew vengeance on others, that they can be the best ever, excel at killing and becoming not just noticed—but infinitely famous."

Della nodded. "I always remember the academy. The statistics. There are twenty-five to fifty serial killers active in just the United States at any given time. That remains terrifying—and doesn't include domestic killing or events fueled by robberies or revenge or… Mason, this is still so sick. We must end this. We must find this man. We saw this poor girl on the table. Dr. Monroe is right. The violence and brutality escalate. Annie Chapman was horribly mutilated. Again, reading past medical reports, they suspect that he strangled his victims to keep them from crying out before he slashed their throats, deep slashes, almost to sever the head from the body. But with Annie Chapman, Mason, he removed her intestines and laid them on her shoulder and he took parts of the bladder and the vagina that were never found. Elizabeth Stride had her throat slit, but she wasn't mutilated. Ripperologists through the years believe that he might have feared he was about to be interrupted. She was killed on the night of the double event. He went on to murder Catherine Eddowes, again with the throat slashed, and the stomach ripped open, and this time a kidney gone and… If it had been now, of course, we'd know whether the kidney sent to Mr. Lusk of the Whitechapel Vigilante Committee was, indeed, her kidney, or… Well, the killer claimed to have eaten some of it when he sent what they call the From Hell letter, which they suspect might have been written by the real killer. Mason, how far will this man go to play out the past?"

"Not far because we're not going to let him."

She smiled. Their escorting inspector was waiting for them. Jeanne and François were coming from behind.

"I wish I could take a shower," Della murmured.

He grinned. "You're not too stinky," he told her.

She made a face at him. "Trust me—I am going to take a shower. Just as soon as we finish with Mr. Gary Hudson!"

"François will accompany me back to the house," Jeanne said. "We have records from the English vampire killings and we'll organize. We didn't mean to take you from such an important interrogation, but Doctor Monroe is deeply disturbed and…"

"Right. We understand," Mason said. "And we decided on letting our suspect mull on his own for a while."

"He says he's a victim, that he needs no legal counsel, and… Well, of course, he's all into being helpful. But letting him sit long enough…"

"*Mais, oui.* Get him agitated," Jeanne agreed. "We will be at the house and expect you when we see you. And then…"

"Tonight, again, all of us out on the street," Mason said.

He turned to the inspector waiting to drive them back, thanked him, ushered Della into the car and joined her.

She had her phone out and was busy texting.

"What's up?" he asked her.

She smiled at him. "I'm writing our great research master at headquarters—Angela Crow. There must be something in Gary Hudson's past—something that caused him to be so hateful. Strange, fathers tend to be the abusers when there has been child abuse, but—oh, and I'm not Gary! I'm not man-bashing—"

Mason grinned. "Statistics are statistics!" he told her.

"Statistically—should have started with that!" she said. "But there are cases, of course, when the mother has done something. Or, perhaps his parents are dead. Or maybe he was just married at one point to someone that they might refer to as a ballbuster. Or—"

"Angela will get something back to us. I know her. It will be fast."

"Faster than ever!" Della said, looking at her phone. "Wow. She's amazing. Okay, worse than I thought. His mother killed his father and claimed domestic abuse, but— Cliff notes on this—she didn't make it through court because a forensic detail gave away her elaborate, premeditated murder plot. Her sentence was reduced because there were many character witnesses to attest to the abuse she had suffered through the years, but apparently, Gary's father loved the kid, and he hated his mother for what she did to his father. He went into the foster system and bounced around—"

"Wait. Where is the mother now? Did she die under mysterious circumstances?"

"No. She died of cancer when Gary was twelve. He went from foster family to foster family." She looked at Mason. "Do you think that he feels he never avenged his father's death? That he wanted to kill women because his mother killed his father and that made him an easy mark for Dante?"

"Could be. We'll have to ask him," Mason said.

It was time to have a chat with Gary Hudson.

Mason and Della met up with Edmund and Sean in the observation room.

"I went in," Sean said. "Hudson has never met me, so we figured that I should be the one to explain that we were sorry, it was going to be a bit. Could I get him tea, coffee, water—anything to make the wait better. He was fine at first. Then he paced the room. Then he started talking to himself. Of course, I politely offered him legal aid again

and he said that he'd be working on his own representa-
tion—once he got someone to arrest Della, too. I said,
of course, that Della was a highly respected guest in our
country, and... How the hell has that bloke been a barman,
chatting up women every night?"

"How else do you make a fool of anyone?" Della asked
quietly. "He's been wearing a mask a long, long time." She
quickly caught Sean and Edmund up on what they had
learned about the man's past.

"Well, I guess he didn't have much of a childhood,"
Sean said.

"Many people go through terrible childhoods—though
that was bad. But many people rise above, too—some of
the best law enforcement people I know grew up in rough
circumstances," Edmund said. "Those with strength rise
above it."

"All right, then. Time to not be so pleasant. Sean has
kept our detainee politely entertained until now, so, where
should we start?" Della mused.

"Twist a little bit harder and harder. I'll go at him," Edmund said, nodding gravely. "We can add on and then
add on."

Mason nodded to him.

They watched as he stepped from the observation room
and in to sit across from Gary Hudson in the interrogation room.

"You!" Hudson said. "You know that I'm innocent! And
that bi—that witch of a woman is just trying desperately
to prove that she's up to par with a man! That's a serious
problem these days. She has something in her head. I am
being persecuted because she's inept and feels that she must
prove something. My God! She attacked me! They're claim-

ing that they just wanted to talk to me because I was in the cemetery, then—"

"Why were you in the cemetery?" Edmund asked.

"What?" Hudson was startled by the question and looked confused.

"What were you doing in the cemetery?" Edmund repeated.

"I was just… Well, the cemetery is beautiful! I like to go there." Hudson quickly regained his indignant behavior. "I like the peace of the cemetery, the landscaping. I walk and I just enjoy the peace before heading to the pub and being the barman. Believe it or not, my work at the pub is much harder than you can imagine. Everyone wants to tell you about their problems. I need to get some time that's just sweet and clear. Sometimes it's good just to feel the air, see the sweep of the landscaping, why even smell the earth."

"Hmm. You know," Edmund said, "I'm from London myself. And I love to feel the air and enjoy nature. We have forests and parks for that."

"Well, you know, Manor Park—"

"Is a cemetery," Edmund said.

Mason nodded to Della and the others, and headed in to join Edmund, sitting across the table from Gary Hudson.

"Ah, look!" Hudson said. "Here he is, the lapdog for the witch!"

"Ah, well, pretty hot witch, huh?" Mason said.

"I keep explaining to them that they're American. They cannot arrest a Brit. That wicked witch of the west has no power here," Hudson said to Edmund.

"Technically, you were arrested and taken into custody by a Detective Inspector Watson, the good fellow who brought you in from the cemetery," Edmund told him.

"You can't hold me! You have no evidence. You have nothing to charge me with. It isn't illegal to walk around a cemetery!"

"Wait, even I, an American, know the answer to this. Oh, by the way, much of our law is based on British law, going way back. But that's neither here nor there at the moment—I know that you can be held for twenty-four hours before being charged."

"So, I bloody well sit here for twenty-four hours!" Hudson said, leaning back and crossing his arms over his chest. "Then I do something very American! I sue for police harassment!"

"Good luck with that," Edmund said, shrugging.

"And here's the thing," Mason said. "If you were in the cemetery so innocently, I'm just curious as to the reason you like to hide behind funerary angels," Mason said.

"I wasn't hiding behind any angel!" Hudson protested.

"But, um, hmm, yes, you were," Mason said thoughtfully, his eyes unwavering as he stared at the man and assumed his position, leaning back and crossing his arms over his chest. "You were watching us when we were at the grave. And you pulled a knife and set it against Della's ribs."

"No! She attacked me. I was just coming up to say hello!" he protested.

"And got your butt kicked by a woman," Mason said pleasantly.

"No, I didn't want to hurt her!" Hudson cried, trying again to appear to be sincere and innocent, a man who could explain everything.

"Well, I secured the knife you were holding on her. And your fingerprints are all over it," Mason said, shrugging.

"Yeah. 'Cause it's my knife," Hudson said.

Della decided it was time to make her entry to the interrogation room.

She opened the door and walked in, smiling. "Yes, but you see, your fingerprints will be on the handle and my blood will be on the tip."

"You attacked me! I defended myself," Hudson said. He didn't sound quite so wounded. She had stirred something in his temper.

Della sat in the free chair next to Edmund and leaned across the table, close to Hudson. "No, Mr. Hudson, you attacked me. And I fought back. And you're such a sorry excuse for a man that one elbow and one swift kick sent you flying. Then again... Well, you've never had any kind of normal understanding of reality, have you? And all women are enemies. After all, your father had to be the biggest dickhead known to man, your mother killed him, and neither of them was a shining example of how to live, but, apparently, you've just decided you hate women and Dante gave you everything that you need to vent all that awful frustration you've had through life!"

For several seconds, Hudson stared at Della, his eyes burning, his hatred creating an almost palpable tension in the air.

The he rose to his feet in his rage, lunging toward Della.

CHAPTER NINE

Gary Hudson did little but hurt himself since a table sat between him and Della, and while she remained still, Mason and Edmund were up in a flash, walking around and catching the man by either arm. Heedless of being held back, he went into a frothing rage at her, screaming.

Mason and Edmund caught him by the shoulders, forcing him to remain still even as he continued spewing his venom, so angry he was garbling his words until he ran out of steam.

So angry that there was froth at his mouth.

Once he was seated, Edmund handed him a handkerchief—assuring him that it needn't be returned as he did so.

Despite his show of fury, a glance from Mason assured Della that she needed to keep pressing while they had him in such an angry state.

"Seriously, pathetic!" Della said. "I do mean a sorry excuse for a man."

She was dismissive and casual.

And she managed to truly ignite something dark within him.

He was calmer, no longer foaming—but still furious.

"Oh, you go ahead and talk, you bitch! You need to have two men protecting you now as you sit there, thinking you know me. Protected and acting like you're all tough. I would have had you! I could have had you a dozen times. Sorry excuse for a man? You tell it to that pretty girl I left on the bank of the Thames! You tell her because she loved me and wanted me right up to the minute she looked into my eyes and knew that she was going to die!"

"We've got him," Edmund said, shoving the man back in his chair. It took another moment for Mason to release him.

When he did, he spoke dryly, "He's all hot air, Edmund. He didn't kill anyone. He gets beat up by a woman, and now he thinks he needs to prove his manhood or something."

"Stupid, stupid Yank!" Hudson was all but frothing again. "I didn't kill just one. I got two of them. I like to be international, too, just like you. The first girl. Her name was Colleen something. She was an American tourist, so silly and ridiculously in love with a man with a British accent, a bloke who was going to show her all around London. She was a pathetic slut, so eager! So easy to drug. And the media, of course, went crazy! It was so wonderful. Then, of course, I didn't want anyone to assume it was someone with a thing for American tourists, so I had to go for a British lass. Poor, poor baby! She had been having a rough time getting over a romance and she eagerly accepted a drink from an understanding man, a good-looking bloke—"

"Good-looking?" Della interrupted. "Passable, maybe."

"Cunt!" Hudson raged.

She shrugged and he went on, determined that she realize his prowess.

"She was the pathetic one, I'm telling you! I might have done her a mercy. But women are…universally stupid and wretched! I practically spiked her gin and tonic right before her eyes. Their names aren't even important, not to me, but I do remember her name, given and surname— she was Isabelle Ainsley. The headlines on that kill were exceptionally wonderful! Oh, I was so damned good and it was so easy, you would have laughed! Easy to get her away, easy to get her back. There was no one about and I was able to *lead* her from the street, dead as the proverbial doornail! I had time and I wrote on the embankment *Dracula lives*! I think Dante was jealous, I did such amazing work." He paused for a minute and stared hatefully at Della. "Pathetic! You don't begin to know, but you will. Because you will find yourself the pathetic one in the end! I will not be held. I will be free. And I will prove to you what a man you see before you!"

Della looked at Edmund and shrugged. "I might have a drink with a man like you, but I'd never have one with a fellow like him. And it seems that he must drug a girl to get her to do anything with him. I'm guessing that he drugged Leslie Bracken, too, and even if she was an American, that would be the only way that he could get her to look at him twice."

Hudson was tense and silent.

"He didn't kill Leslie Bracken," Mason said, speaking to her and Edmund. Then he turned on Hudson. "She was killed by the man who now wants to be the Ripper. The one who is stealing all your thunder."

"He's not as good as me! He had to find a new thing and he's a horrible copycat—couldn't even think something up on his own!" Hudson spat out angrily.

"Who is *he*?" Edmund asked.

"Wouldn't tell you his name if I knew it!" Hudson said.

"I would tell us anything that you could. It might help with your sentence," Mason said.

Hudson started to laugh. "What, you stupid American? We don't have the death penalty in England. We're civilized!"

"Well, you could shave off a few years of incarceration," Edmund told him.

Hudson smiled, gleeful that it seemed he had them on something at last.

"You don't know his name, do you?" Della asked him. "Because your great leader, your Vampire King, taught you all not to use your real names. I believe that he might have taught you, too, that the reason was so that if one was arrested, he couldn't give away the others. And, of course, he was able to bring you all into the fold because you just couldn't get a real relationship going. Maybe your mom beat you, too, when you were a child—before she killed your father, of course, and wound up in prison." She leaned forward, smiling. "She made you feel like a speck of dirt, and maybe you dated someone who did the same. And you couldn't even fight like a man so you had to resort to drugs and that—"

"Don't be ridiculous!" Hudson told her. "I never had to drug anyone for sex, and, baby, you really blew it, because you… Well, you'll just die. Slowly and painfully. Vampires! We needed our women drugged so that we could draw the blood, drink the blood, savor the life and strength it sent into our systems!"

"You said *we*. I'm guessing that Dante helped you, either through instruction or by being there," Della said. "And

without Dante, you were powerless! You killed two innocent young women who did want to give you a chance as
a man, as a human being, but now that Dante has been arrested in the United States, you're powerless and pathetic.
Of course, if you'd tell us the name—"

"You are an idiot-bitch!" Hudson told her, angry and
then laughing. "Did you hear? Oh, man," he said, looking at Mason. "You really saddled yourself with an idiot-
bitch. She just said that Dante would have taught us not
to use real names so that we didn't give each other away
and we cleared the world of scum, and now she's asking
me for a name!"

He laughed as if he had managed a one-upmanship that
was truly amusing.

"Sorry, idiot-bitch here just testing you," Della said
sweetly.

"I'm going to be with you again!" he said, eyes narrow-
ing. "And next time—"

"I'll kick you again if you attack me," Della assured him
with a shrug.

"Hmm. I don't think so," Edmund said, saving Mason
the trouble. "I don't think you'll be anywhere with a chance
to hurt anyone for a long, long time."

He glanced at Mason and Della, and she shrugged and
said, "He doesn't have a name. Once he's been charged
with premeditated murder—"

"You have nothing on me!" Hudson roared suddenly.
"Nothing—"

"Other than your confession," Edmund informed him.

"No. No. You tortured and coerced me and—" Hudson
began.

But Edmund quickly corrected him. "I offered you legal

counsel when I first came in to question you. Mr. Hudson, you refused that offer. And that was all recorded, too."

"No, I don't remember you offering me anything!"

Edmund smiled. "Again, I don't know how I can make it any clearer. It's on video, sir, along with your confession. So, if you'll excuse us now..."

"What?" Hudson said, annoyed. Then he laughed. "There is no excuse for you—any of you. All of you are just so sadly inexcusable!"

"Yeah, well, late night," Edmund said. "I believe that, well, it's just time to move on, sir. You have nothing else to give us."

"No, seriously! That's it. You think that you're done with me?" Hudson demanded

"You have said that you have no names of anyone who was with you when you were studying—or whatever it was that you were doing—beneath Dante. You killed two women. You didn't kill three, and you aren't the new Ripper. And you have said that you can't help us."

"I want legal counsel!" Hudson raged.

"I am sure that can be arranged," Mason said, glancing at Edmund.

"Of course," Edmund said.

"It will all be thrown out!" Hudson roared. "All. What you've done to me will be plastered all over the papers. London police with the help of American FBI idiots try to railroad the innocent so that they don't get their bloody arses fired! You don't have half of what you need from me."

"Okay," Della said. "What can you give us?"

"What can you give me?" he asked. He started to laugh, then. "Oh, you idiots! You always think you have the upper hand. And you are just going to have to dig, dig, dig to get anything else." He burst into laughter as if his words were hilarious. "Dig, dig, dig, dig, dig!"

Della shrugged. "Okay. We'll dig, dig, dig, and we'll see that you get that legal counsel. In a civilized society, you are entitled. I don't understand English law—I don't always understand every little nuance of American law—but I know that you have rights, too. But, of course, you did waive those rights when you came in, and for us… Wow. It has been a long day."

"And we are going home," Mason said quietly.

"She needs to get you alone to beat you up, too?" Hudson taunted.

"She doesn't beat me up and guess what, I don't beat her up, either. This may be surprising to you, and in a way, I almost understand. Most of us don't need to beat each other up. And, gee, none of us are threatened by Della—or other women, for that matter. We think it's fantastic that she's strong and capable, as are so many others. I think you have a problem with any woman who does anything at all better. Except wash dishes maybe. And guess what? I wash dishes, no problem. And I think it's cool that we get to be with such a bright, quick agent. But seriously, we wasted enough time on you today. I need something to eat."

"Now I get it. The little woman is going to cook for you?"

"I may cook for her," Mason said. "But—"

"Yeah, let's do this," Edmund said. "Seriously, running way too late. We've got to get out of here! And Hudson isn't going anywhere, so…"

"No!" Hudson protested. "You dragged me in here. You made me wait. You—"

"Good night, Mr. Hudson," Mason returned. "Edmund,

this is like dealing with a five-year-old. We do need to move on."

"Right! Let's go!" Edmund said

He rose and Della and Mason followed him as he headed toward the door to exit the room. Hudson tried to run after them and push his way out.

Edmund politely but firmly pressed him back in. Hudson immediately went berserk, pounding on the one-way mirror to the observation room. But uniformed officers were in the hallway, waiting to take him to a cell.

They happened to be big men, both well over six feet tall, strongly built, and despite his protests and the fact that he let his body drag, they quickly had the man under their control.

Della watched and, frowning, glanced at Mason and turned to Edmund. "Think he needs to be under suicide watch?" she asked.

"This has been like watching Dr. Jekyll become Mr. Hyde," Mason said. "The mild-mannered, friendly bartender has become a combustible pile of anger and nerves."

Edmund looked at them, arching a brow. "He could save British taxpayers some pounds were he to end it all himself. Not very Christian of me, but the man is surely a devil—a demon, at least."

"As much as I may agree—" Della began.

Edmund put a hand on her shoulder. "Della, I've given an oath to uphold the law as well, remember? Different countries, very similar values, as in so many nations, the point being, I hope you are coming to know me. I won't risk—"

"Edmund, right, yes, I know. But it seems that he's been going about his regular work, a barman at a pub, doing it all right, charming and lucid by all appearances. But I think that he's beginning to unravel now. It seems that since we caught up with him at the cemetery—or he caught up with me," she corrected dryly, "he's lost all semblance of trying to play the innocent and intelligent man watching a crazy world go by around him."

"I've already seen to it," Edmund said quietly. "With an ego like his, I think it unlikely. Then again, with an ego like his, anything is possible. And, yes, indeed, I'm aware. He might still be useful and I don't intend to become an animal like those we arrest because we're sworn to uphold the law, not become part of the problem."

She smiled and nodded.

"Meeting, back at the house," Mason said. "We'll need our full crew to decide how we proceed next. We do have new information. We need to focus on how we'll use all that we know."

Della nodded.

It had been an eventful day. It was, she realized, evening.

Darkness was coming.

And a new night when a Ripper just might strike.

Mason knew that he had to let go of the interview with Hudson and the rest of the day, just a bit, just enough to look back at it all with a clear mind.

But there was something teasing at the back of his mind. Something that Hudson had said, and he wasn't sure what it was. It was most probably true that Gary Hudson didn't know the names of anyone else who had become a follower of Stephan Dante. Dante would have been protecting himself first, of course, but he had laid the groundwork for his groupies. And while Dante was incarcerated, awaiting trial, he surely heard news.

And he was just as surely delighting in the Ripper murders. He would proudly consider himself responsible since he had trained the killer.

He was quiet as they returned to the house, thoughtful and aware, of course, that Della was watching him, wondering what was wrong and perhaps understanding. They had a remarkable way of communicating even in silence. Maybe, for the first time in either of their lives, they had found the one who not just loved them but truly understood them.

He realized that they had all been quiet when Edmund finally broke the silence by saying, "We need to organize our thoughts from today, but first! Dinner, please, for the love of God!"

"That will work," Sean agreed, "Seeing as how we missed anything resembling lunch or even a lovely tea break."

"Can we order in?" Della asked. "It will be easier to converse when we're here, all in the house without having to worry about being heard by others."

"That's perfect," Jeanne Bisset said. "And, as your liaison, I've taken on the task of knowing what's around us and who will deliver! I suppose for Americans the standard is pizza—"

"Pizza goes around the world!" Della protested teasingly.

"If you all are up for it, there's a pub not far from here that creates one of the finest shepherd's pies known to man and since the pandemic, they're excellent at providing a family style that will work beautifully for us all," Bisset said.

"Shepherd's pie it is!" Della said. "Of course, if all agree."

"I was thinking of coq au vin with excellently seasoned rice and perhaps a fine salad and an aged red wine to be followed by cigars and cognac," Jeanne LaPierre teased. "Oh, but, of course, this is England. No fine French cuisine!"

Edmund groaned loudly and they all laughed.

"That's why it's good to be American," Mason said. "We have cuisine from all over the world since our people are from all over the world."

"Wait, now, the world is moving all over, you know!" Sean protested.

"Children, keep fighting about food and I'll call in our order," François said, sighing.

They all laughed and Della headed into the kitchen, calling over her shoulder, "I'll put the tea on. And coffee! Love tea but coffee helps keep Americans up and ticking."

"And we have another long night ahead of us," Mason said.

"Do you think that he'll strike again so quickly?" Edmund asked. "If he's really trying to follow in the Ripper's footsteps, we have several days to go. The Ripper killed Mary Ann Nichols on August 31, 1888. Annie Chapman wasn't killed until September 8."

"I believe," Mason said, "that this killer wants to follow the Ripper's pattern. But he's already segued in his victimology. If he finds that he might have difficulty keeping to the time pattern, he'll change it up. But right or wrong, we all believe it's possible that the real killer is the man we saw in Brixton—Jesse Miller. We also believe that he was seen in the City of London Cemetery—Della and I learned that because we showed the various sketches of what he might look like to a few visitors when we were there." He looked at Della as he spoke. He couldn't explain that they knew he'd been at the cemetery because of a very reliable witness—Abigail Scott.

They needed to find Abigail again, of course. And find out what else she may have witnessed.

Jesse Miller was out there somewhere.

"This is really ridiculous," Edmund murmured, heading into the kitchen. The teakettle was whistling and he went about measuring tea into the teapot as he spoke before adding the water. "That man is out there. One man, brutally murdering women, and there are six of us plus all the law enforcement in the country and we haven't been able to find him!"

"We will," Mason said determinedly. He headed into the kitchen himself. The coffee had brewed as well and he helped himself to a cup.

"Now, what's that?" Sean teased. "I just brewed the finest cup to be had!"

"Hey, nothing wrong with tea," Mason assured him. "More caffeine here."

"Per pound, tea has more caffeine," Sean told him.

"Maybe. But you're not drinking a pound of tea!"

François glanced at his phone.

"Food has arrived. I'll get it—"

"Wait. I'll go with you," Mason said, setting his cup down.

François frowned. "You're worried? If the killer comes to the door, we'll drag him in!"

"The killer won't come to the door. But if it's gotten out in any way that the six of us are here, we still have to take care."

François smiled and showed Mason his phone. "We're riddled with security cameras. In fact, tonight I need you all to download the same app I have. While we sleep in shifts with extreme caution, this allows us all visual aids to anyone arriving here—or slipping around the sides and back of the place."

There was a single man with a large delivery bag at the front.

"François, you are worth your weight in coq au vin!" Mason assured him.

Jeanne LaPierre groaned and laughed and headed with Mason to the door.

Soon, the table was set, the food was passed around, and while they'd been teasing and joking with one another— so necessary when their hours were filled with continual tension—it was time to assess the day.

"All right, we have the files from the vampire killings and we can begin to go through them again. We all watched and listened to Gary Hudson today—I believe that he did kill two of the victims in the so-called vampire killings. That leaves a third victim, and a second killer. And in listening to him today, I believe that *he* believes— or even knows—that our Ripper today is the second killer in the vampire murders. We believe that man to be Jesse Miller. But Miller has managed to live off-the-grid for years. I believe that he is English, but the best tech people on two continents haven't been able to find an address or anything else on him. We know how Stephan Dante managed to hop from country to country—he ingratiated himself with all kinds of criminals. He got his funds by finding the stashes of robbers who were incarcerated—he found the right people to create false IDs. In Jesse Miller, I think he found a kindred spirit and not just an able follower. Jesse Miller has been existing with no known source of income, so, Jesse Miller might well have been playing the same game over here, somehow managing to befriend those who are locked away, enough, at any rate, to gain access to stolen funds. Or, he may be working—under an assumed name."

"Something else that we can get on tomorrow," Della said. "He's changing his appearance like a true chameleon. I believe that he may have worked in the movies. Even as an extra. That would allow him to be this familiar with cosmetics and prosthetics, changing even the shape of his face."

"I can get on that," François said. "First thing in the morning; I'll find out about everything that is being filmed and has been filmed recently."

"There are also theaters, wonderful theaters in London," Sean reminded them.

"Theaters, yes," François said.

"I can work with you on that," Sean said, explaining, "if I weren't an inspector, I'd have loved spending my days in *Hamilton*—even if he was an American, oh, wait, it was a whole British/American thing, or *Wicked* or... Well, you know. Wait! Wow, *Hamilton*! Sorry, Della—any relationship to the man?"

"I have no idea," she said, laughing. "My mom's family is Norse. My dad's family are a totally mixed-up bag of different nationalities. If I have famous ancestors, no one ever knew it. But, hey, I love the play myself!"

"I recently saw *Evan Hansen*. And before that *Six*!" Sean said.

"I haven't seen *Six*, but I have the cast album downloaded. Love it!" Della said.

"Um, I think we'd all like a night out at the theater," Edmund said, "but..."

"Sorry. The point is that I still have friends working in

the theater and the movies, and that could help," Sean said, grinning at Della. "We will get to a play!" he whispered as an aside to her. "And if they're nice, we'll let the others come!"

"It's a plan!" she whispered back.

The others were all staring at them.

But then Mason laughed softly and they all agreed—it would be really cool if they were going to a play instead of being involved in someone's play at life and death.

"We definitely want to make use of any helpful connections. You and François are on searching for our fellow through the makeup angle," Mason agreed.

"I don't think that the medical examiner can help us anymore," Jeanne said. "And, of course, we are working with contradictions. The killer was careful to create the wounds on his victim just as the Ripper did on Mary Ann Nichols. He was precise. But he made it clear that he's choosing different victims. While to this day no one knows who Jack the Ripper was, it is believed by many that he may have suffered at the hands of a prostitute—perhaps having acquired syphilis from one of them—but he chose his victims because he could whisper to them for sex and lure them into alleys or away from sight. This killer thinks that all women are, in his words, whores."

"The world has changed. Dating has changed. Both sexes like to have fun when they're young—and not so young. You can find a date online. Men and women both pick each other up at pubs. Maybe our killer has decided that while his victims may appear to be different, they're really all the same," Edmund said.

Mason frowned and looked around the table. "Did anyone gain anything else from Gary Hudson's rants? He said

something that I keep feeling I should have gained something from—and I admit, I'm going a bit crazy trying to
fathom what it might have been."

They all stared back at him.

Then Della suddenly frowned and spoke. "Dig, dig, dig.
Dig, dig, dig. He said that we're going to have to dig. I don't
think that he meant that we needed to dig into information."

"Dig. An architectural dig?" Edmund asked.

"There was a dig going on in Norway when we were
there. We inquired there, but all digs need more than just
archeologists and anthropologists. They need grunt workers, too, getting through tons of upper layers once something has been discovered. Maybe—"

"Maybe Jesse Miller—under an assumed name—went
on to Norway, ready to do Stephan Dante's bidding there,"
Sean said.

"But we know that Dante did the killing in Norway,"
Jeanne pointed out.

"That might have been the catalyst," Mason said, "for
the killing here. For this man's need to be the king of the
Ripper killers. He might even be pleased that Dante was
apprehended—that allows him the opportunity to become
even more famous. Jack the Ripper was never caught. To
this day, scholars still argue over who it might or might
not have been—they go by the five canonical victims, but
there were eleven murders in the area at the time—one
probably a robbery, but one possibly a practice for what
was to come. The lack of definitive knowledge on many
fronts regarding Jack the Ripper is allowing our copycat a
lot of leeway, which means we need to be careful in making any assumptions about what he will and will not do."

"How does he know so much about forensics?" Della wondered.

"You're suggesting that an inspector or someone else in British law enforcement might be involved?" Edmund asked her.

She shook her head. "There are dozens of people in forensics, working for law enforcement, or even for universities or other establishments. I'm not suggesting—"

"But there is that possibility," Sean said. "Except that we think it is Jesse Miller, a man who disappears just like a wisp of fog. Someone we might look straight at—without a clue that we've got our man."

"We will get him," Mason said with determination. "And we're set. Tomorrow, Sean, you and François will be talking to the theaters and any movie productions going on. And, of course, stores that sell professional grade makeup."

"That is going to include getting around—"

"I can work with them," Jeanne LaPierre offered. "That will leave three of you to research whatever archeological digs are going on in the area now. Trust me, there's always something. Bits and pieces of old Roman waterworks, walls and more are sometimes discovered along with bits and pieces from medieval times."

"Edmund, Della," Mason said. "As Jeanne has suggested, we divide and conquer. In touch all the time, and for now—"

"We hit the pubs again. Two by two. Sean, this is your area. You tell us where we're most likely to spot our suspect."

"There's always the Ten Bells—supposedly frequented by both Annie Chapman and Mary Kelly," Sean said. "And there's the Red Rose—it's new, but the building was there during the Jack the Ripper spree of 1888, and it's near the apartment where Mary Kelly was killed. I was thinking that might be an interesting place to enjoy a nightcap. And there's a place right across from us that's also gaining popularity because it, like us, is close to the prostitute's church or St. Botolph's."

"All right, we'll split up and get out there. Everyone on speed dial, ready to move at the drop of a hat," Mason said.

"Or a pint," Sean reminded him good-naturedly.

"Or pint!" Mason agreed. "Let's do it." He glanced at his watch. "Almost ten. Close to closing time for many of them once we get out there, and..."

"Wait, midnight tonight, for most, as we're moving toward the weekend."

"We have patrol personnel out on the streets, all aware of the chameleon we're seeking—and all on the lookout for trouble of any kind," Sean assured him.

"So!" Edmund said. "Let's do this!"

Cups were set in the sink, trash was collected and dinner was done. They left the house, with both Mason and François Bisset checking the security of the lock as they left.

They should have been exhausted. Maybe they were.

But adrenaline had set in. And they knew that they were on a time limit. Their Ripper wanted to be perfect.

But he didn't mind segueing in the least if it fit the picture of perfection in his own mind.

And they all knew that he might strike just about anyone. At just about any time.

They were leaving.

Heading out for a night on the town, thinking that they

would find him. They were clever but, of course, he was smarter than they imagined.

Smarter than they were, and eventually, they would know that. They would know it—right before they died. He had something extremely special intended for *Special Agent Della Hamilton*, but he had decided now that all of them had to die.

Not an easy task, but he was up to it.

Seeing the door open and the team heading out, he melded in with a group of about ten college boys—all too far gone into their gin and tonics to notice a newcomer.

The oh-so-special international team had gotten the man Ripper had met as Grey. But in Ripper's mind, Grey had been an idiot. Yes, Grey had managed two kills, but only because Ripper had been with him and because Ripper had kept his phone on, receiving minute directions from the Vampire King all the while.

The third kill had been Ripper's.

All Ripper's.

And he had done it right without help from anyone.

Aye, they were all out and about now, searching for him in the pubs of the city. And, of course, Ripper did frequent the pubs, he watched. He needed to know who was alone and who was not, who was friendly and who was smart enough to be wary of strangers. A pub setting was a good setting. People tended to be friendly. Americans loved pubs—they loved to be in a "pub" rather than a "bar." And because everyone spoke at least a semblance of the English language, American women were easy to spot and find.

And because they tended to be friendly...

They were easy prey.

But for the team of special *whatevers* staying in the house by the church…

He hadn't really conceived of the thought of taking them all out at first. He wanted the woman. Of all the victims in 1888, Mary Kelly had been young and beautiful—and a whore, of course, but young and beautiful. When the Ripper had finished with her…

Mary Kelly had been—according to most so-called scholars and Ripperologists—the last of the Ripper's victims. And he had been able to spend time with her—she'd been the only one killed in an apartment. He'd flayed most of her skin from her body, including her face. She had been unrecognizable as a human being. The apartment had been covered in her blood, in flesh, in body matter…

Ripper could just imagine the house where they were staying.

What he would do to Special Agent Della Hamilton. He would have time, lots of time, and he would use it all to good advantage.

How he would leave the house, bathed in blood, her blood… Maybe he'd drink just a little bit of it, too, in memory of the Vampire King, locked away across the pond.

Of course, as Ripper was always smart and careful, he'd watched. They thought that they watched. No, he watched, with far greater superiority.

She was never alone. That was a problem. Problems, of course, were simply items that had to be put in order and figured out.

Ripper had seen what had been happening in the city.

He'd seen the way that the man he'd known as "Grey" had been taken, and he was sure that Grey, being an idiot, had said too much. But no matter what he'd said, he couldn't pin anything on Ripper. There was no evidence. None—at all.

He felt incredibly good. They had nothing. And watching now…he had everything. He had the answers to pesky little problems. He was that good.

He laughed aloud, walking down the street, feeling the cool night air. Grey was an idiot! He wouldn't know Ripper if Ripper walked right up to him and slammed him in the shoulder.

And that was thanks to the Vampire King.

Now, however, Ripper was managing a feat as difficult as—or perhaps far more difficult than the Vampire King might have ever imagined.

And while he might be just a bit cliché himself…

Many people had wanted to be vampires through the years. Many played at it, drinking one another's blood in cult groups or the like. Vampires were, in fact, as the Americans said, a dime a dozen! And, yes, he was no fool. There had been other "Rippers."

But not like him. He was a true king, studying, reading, walking the streets, knowing the sites, understanding all there was to understand.

And planning a finale like no other!

It hadn't been until tonight that he'd figured that out. Watching. Watching, watching and watching…

And now, knowing.

Knowing just how he would get his eager hands around Della Hamilton's throat when the time came. Knowing just how he would get through it all…

And the very thought of it was delicious, something to be savored and he continued to watch, watch…

And choose his other prey, of course.

Oh, yes, so good.

So very delicious!

"Boys, eh! Out for a lark, are you now?" Ripper said, addressing the group who had barely seemed to notice him. "Come on with me, my good lads! Time for a pint or two, on me!"

CHAPTER TEN

Della and Mason chose seats at the bar, conveniently at the rear of the pub where, looking across the bar, they could see the whole of the establishment, looking over the heads of a few of those sitting on the other side of the oblong mahogany structure.

They ordered pints and nursed them.

There were two bartenders on that night, both in their late twenties or early thirties, one with an unruly thatch of red hair, one with darker hair.

They'd been there a few minutes, nursing their pints, when Della noticed that the redheaded bartender was leaning back against a shelf filled with bottles, taking a bit of a breather.

It had been busy when they'd arrived. Now, the crowd was beginning to thin out.

"Taking five, Reginald," the man called to the other, who nodded and tended to the two women who had just walked in.

He was close to them and Della decided she'd find out what she could from the man.

"You're American!" she said with surprise.

He turned to them and grinned. "Damn. That accent gives it away every time!" he said.

"I'm going to say it's probably the same for us," Mason said.

"It's just curious—an American here in a pub," Della told him.

He shrugged. "I'm attending an institute of higher education—City Lit. Went to Yale, I'm proud to say, and here I am—a bartender. No, not complaining. I like my job. Nice people here. I was a working journalist but wanted to improve what I'm hoping will be my skills in fiction. And I love getting to see more of the world."

"Wow, nice, and good for you!" Della told him.

"Well, we'll see. I do love London. And I'm able to broaden my knowledge of world literature. Oh, and hey, my mom and dad use it as a great excuse to travel—they stay at my place and save on hotels. My sister comes—now that's fun, she's pretty and attracts more pretty girls, so... Anyway, how are you finding it here? Enjoying the sights?"

"It's a fascinating city, certainly," Della said.

He grinned. "Cool stuff—and a lot of grisly stuff. One of the Ripper tours makes us their last stop. And there's so much more. Visiting the Tower of London. That's always fun, seeing where some of the great nobility lost their heads! People go to see the Crown Jewels, and some go to see the way man practiced cruelty on his fellow man. Oh, we haven't stopped that, have we?"

"There's always a war somewhere," Mason said dryly.

"Seriously, what you're doing sounds great. When you are home, where's home?"

"Hartford, Connecticut," the man said. "I'm Joshua, by the way. In case you come to hang around again."

"Thanks. I'm Della, this is Mason," Della said.

"Great. And, um, I'm not sure how long you've been here, but I'm thinking you've seen the news—it's going around the world, so I've been told. There's a killer out there. Around this time of night, I'm always warning single women in here not to go walking back to a hotel alone—the locals around here are so steeped in history that they don't have to be warned twice. I even…" He paused, shaking his head. "They don't know. No one knows who it might be. I'm not sure how up you are on Ripper lore—I wasn't into it at all until I got the job here, but… Okay, I'm rambling. The point is that there are about seven serious suspects from the 1888 killings. One was a butcher and one, of course—ridiculous, in my opinion—was that the Crown might have been in on it, either Prince Albert Edward himself or his physician, Sir William Gull. There was Montague Druitt, respectable fellow in a bit of trouble, but it could be anyone. Someone who is charming and looks like they have the best job and best upbringing in the world. So—"

"We're very careful," Della promised him.

"Well, cool, enjoy, Oh, hey, that's Jessica over there, alone," Joshua said. "I guess the tours must be down these days. Oh, she does other tours, too, and what a historian she is! Westminster, the Tower, Buckingham Palace, the British Museum… Anyway, enjoy!"

Joshua moved on over to help the newcomer he had called Jessica.

He pointed to the two of them, probably as prospective customers.

She smiled and waved, a pretty brunette in her mid-to late-twenties.

"Maybe she's seen something," Mason said quietly.

"We might as well be honest with her. We're not under-cover," Della reminded him.

"Okay. And they're about to give last call. I say we meet Jessica," Mason said.

They walked over to the other side of the bar, Della smiling and offering Jessica a hand as they approached her. "I'm Della Hamilton and this is Mason Carter. Joshua has said that you're the best guide in the city."

She smiled at that and shook Mason's hand, too. "I'm not sure if I'm the best, but..."

"You just came off a Ripper tour? I thought you brought your groups in here when it was over," Mason said.

She sighed. "Well, it's strange. Some people would think that a Ripper tour was in the worst taste known to man with what has happened here. But there are others who... We're so full, it's ridiculous. Maybe people are trying to see where not to be, I'm not sure. But we've also decided that we're going to be done early and get our people out of the area, home for the few locals we get now and then, back to their hotels."

"Maybe it's a good policy for the time," Della said. She shrugged. "Finish the tour and get them on their way, or... Well, if they insist on staying, you've made the reason they shouldn't clear."

"Right." Jessica smiled. "I come here because Joshua and I are mates and he sees to it that I get home safely. We live in the same building just across the bridge."

"That's great. I'm glad that you're watching out for each other," Della said.

"Jessica, we're going to tell you the truth. We're with the American FBI, but assigned here on a special task force," Mason said.

Jessica narrowed her eyes suspiciously.

"For real," Della said.

"But this is England. You have no authority here."

"We're working with local detective inspectors," Mason said, "through Interpol. And we have an interest in this case because we believe it's associated with the vampire murders—"

"You have a fellow locked up in the US! That's what the news says," Jessica said.

"No. The man we have locked up is the main killer— or the killer who taught others. But we believe that this new Jack the Ripper is an acolyte of his. And like Stephan Dante, this man knows how to change his appearance. Would you mind looking at a few pictures for me?"

"Why?"

"We're curious as to whether he's gone on any of the Jack the Ripper tours," Della said.

"There are many, you know," Jessica reminded him.

"Yes, and many guides," Mason said. "But maybe you can help us."

Joshua and the other bartender were announcing last call. Jessica looked at them and shrugged. "Fine. Just… I go when Joshua goes!"

Della smiled. "Right. We will all be gone when the pub closes!"

Mason brought out his phone and flicked to the gallery of sketches Maisie had done for their group. He went through them once, and then again.

On the second go-around she frowned and stopped him.

"There—wait! Are these all the same person?" she asked.

Mason nodded. "The many ways he may look. He is a master of disguise."

"I think he may have been on the tour about a week and a half ago. But…he looked something like this—this one, where the hair is dark and the face is furry. He…had a look like this, but his hair was a reddish-blond color. I can't be sure. It may have been him."

"It was before the Ripper murder?" Mason asked her.

She nodded. "A few days before. Oh, God!" she exclaimed. "I might have had this monster on my tour?"

"We can't be sure. Do you remember anything about where he went after the tour?" Della asked her.

"Here. He came here, with several others. He chatted up a lot of the others, a very friendly man. He was…likeable!" Jessica said, horrified as she stared at them.

"Thank you, and we didn't mean to upset you," Della told her. "You're doing the right thing, meeting Joshua and making sure you're not alone." She hesitated a minute. "Jessica, don't drink anything that anyone buys you. Don't have a pint or anything else unless you get it straight from Joshua."

"He's drugging women?" she asked.

"Yes. He's adept at slipping drugs into drinks and making his targets pliable. We believe that he killed before he became a Ripper killer, and he's practiced at it. I think you're going to be fine because you're smart and careful. Just keep that in mind because I'm sure that people on a tour want to buy you a drink."

She nodded. "Thank you!" They all realized that Joshua and the other bartender were standing near them, waiting.

"We've got to lock up," Joshua said. "This is Reginald, by the way. If I'm not around, he's almost as good as I am," he added, indicating the dark-haired bartender.

"Reginald, great to meet you."

"So, you're FBI!" Reginald said. "Cool. Even if it's not quite as cool as something British."

That allowed them all a smile and seemed to relax Jessica. Mason and Della stepped out with her and waited; Joshua and Reginald came around another door and once Jessica was with Joshua, heading for his car, they waved to Reginald and started back across the street.

"You don't think it's Reginald, do you?" Mason asked.

"I didn't get any...indication," Della said.

"I wonder if we will."

"I didn't see him overly charming with any of the women in there," Della said. "I don't think that... Mason, I think that he prowls the streets at night and works by day. Maybe just sometimes. He might be living on a stolen income and supplementing it...but, I'm willing to bet that he is out here most nights, watching. Watching where people go when they leave the pubs. Watching what women just may be alone. Oh! I think Edmund should hold a press conference tomorrow."

"And warn women to be extremely careful with their drinks?" Mason asked.

"You do read my mind."

"We should have done it already. Between the messages to the media, what happened... I guess they were hoping to avoid a panic, but since the Jack the Ripper case is probably the most famous unsolved murder mystery across the globe, I think a press conference could contain panic rather than cause it."

"We'll get our charming François Bisset on it. As our Interpol liaison, he's probably best suited to be diplomatic and political in every way necessary."

"That's a plan," Della agreed. "Mason!" she said, setting a hand on his arm and stopping him. "There, across the street. Abigail is there, waving at us."

"She must know something," Mason said. "Come on."

They hurried across the street to greet Abigail.

"I was hoping to see you," she said. "He was here—he was walking around St. Botolph's tonight! Oh, he was in one of his disguises. I don't know much about theatrical things, but…his nose was quite different. He had a well-trimmed beard and a mustache. He appeared to be young and he was blending right in with a group. I tried to follow them, but in the end, they all hopped into cars and I didn't see if he got into one of them, or…or if he disappeared into the crowd again. It wasn't quite closing time— I don't know if he's on the streets now, hunting!"

"Thank you, Abigail! Where were you—"

"When they got into the cars? By Whitechapel Road."

"Della! Mason!"

They heard their names shouted and turned around. Edmund Taylor was hurrying their way, Sean keeping pace with him.

"Anything?" Mason asked, swinging around to meet them.

Abigail stood silent, not wanting to cause Della or Mason any difficulty.

"No, we didn't see anything. We heard people talking about what was going on, heard women telling men that they were together and would be staying together... Nice to see that people seem to take this seriously and want to be cautious. What about you?"

"We were introduced to a tour guide. We believe that Jesse Miller—in disguise, of course—was on her tour about a week and a half ago," Della told him.

"So he was checking out all the sites, determining just where he could and couldn't leave a body himself," Sean said bitterly. "Well, we have men and women patrolling the streets, watching for anything, but..."

"We were going to see what was going on around Whitechapel Road," Mason said.

"Any reason?"

"We were casually asking a few people if they had seen anything strange on the street," Mason lied. "A slightly older man was hanging with college kids, and a lady thought it might be suspicious."

"Aye, then, why not try Whitechapel Road?" Sean asked. "Though we should divide and conquer."

"We'll do a bit of patrolling and head back here," Mason said. "I don't believe that he is going to strike tonight. I believe he's doing some stalking, finding out who might be alone when they head out of the pubs at night."

"We'll take the church. Meet you back at the house."

"Sounds good. Della, you ready for a walk?"

"Through dark alleys after midnight. Sure!" she said.

They started out. Della was glad to see that those who had been out late were walking in groups or as couples, heading into apartments or to their cars.

She and Mason walked the distance to Whitechapel Road.

They skirted into dark alleys—prepared for whatever they might find.

But the night was quiet and eventually they headed back.

Edmund was waiting for them in the parlor. He was alone.

"The others?" Mason asked.

"Gone up to try to get some sleep," Edmund said.

"You didn't need to wait for us," Della said. "We're extremely careful with the locks and the alarm. And it's our turn on first watch."

"I did need to wait up for you," Edmund said.

"Why? Did something happen?" Della asked.

"You tell me," Edmund replied.

"Oh?"

"When were you going to introduce me to your ghost?" Edmund asked.

"Pardon?" Della murmured.

Edmund grinned. "I've wondered. But I've been careful, as you've been careful. I'm assuming that in the United States as well as England and around the world, those of us who see them and talk with them are taught not to let others see you—you might just wind up locked away in an asylum. But since I saw the woman and the two of you clear as day, I'm assuming that you're both ghosties."

"Ghosties?" Mason said.

Edmund shrugged. "Seers, whatever one chooses to call those with this very strange gift or curse."

Della glanced at Mason and then shrugged, sitting in the chair across from Edmund's perch on the sofa.

"Okay. We're ghosties."

"You need to introduce me to the woman you've met."

"Abigail Scott," Della said. "She was here during the day. And she's hoping she may be able to help with this go-around with the Ripper."

Edmund nodded. "And she's the one who told you that she saw him tonight, on Whitechapel?"

Mason nodded, taking a seat as well. "She was also the one who said that she saw a man resembling our sketches of Jesse Miller at the cemetery. After tonight, we believe that he's studied everything possible about Jack the Ripper, drawn a few of his own conclusions, and that he did take a tour and that he has gone to the cemetery. Cemeteries, I should say."

"But," Edmund said, frowning, "it was at the cemetery that you came across Gary Hudson. Do you think that he and Jesse Miller are still in contact with each other?"

Mason shook his head. "No. Hudson believes that he was far superior to our Ripper, if it is, indeed, Jesse Miller. I'm sure that Jesse Miller also believes that he's far superior to Gary Hudson. There's too much competition between the two for them to be working together or even in contact with each other."

"Have you had any help from anyone?" Della asked.

Edmund smiled. "You mean anyone dead?" he asked.

"Of course. Because I'm assuming if you'd had help from the living, you'd have told everyone."

Edmund grinned. "Yes. There's a Royal Air Force ghost killed during World War II who believes he might have seen the murderer on the night of the murder."

"And you didn't tell us," Mason said.

"Excuse me, if you weren't ghosties and I'd have told you, you would have asked for a new man to be assigned to your unit. And, from his description, our killer is Jesse Miller. Since our task isn't so much trying to discern who it is as it is how to find him, it wasn't something necessary.

Had it been necessary... I'd have done the same thing you did, and I'd have made up a witness out in the crowd."

"Touché," Della murmured.

"This has been with you all your life, Edmund? Or something that came to you later?" Mason asked him.

"Early in life. My mom died when I was just five."

"I'm so sorry," Della murmured.

"It's okay. She's still around, though she prefers to haunt our family home up in Stirling. And you?" he asked Mason.

"A grandparent when I was a kid. I came into it gently," he said, glancing at Della.

"A friend was killed in an accident when I was in high school," Della explained.

"And he saved her life—oh, and helped catch a serial killer while doing so," Mason said.

"He was able to warn me and point out a rock and... I was able to bash the guy in the head and then the police got there and... Well, he's still a good friend and I see him whenever I can." She shrugged. "I go to the cemetery, but he still loves hitching rides to sporting events when he can, and, of course, like Abigail, he haunted places where he can watch TV and stay up on current events."

"That happened to you—and you went into law enforcement anyway, after that kind of trauma?" Edmund asked.

"That incident made it very important that I go into law enforcement," Della said. "Our gifts are something that we can use. And, of course, we're incredibly lucky because—"

"The Krewe of Hunters is also known as the ghostbusting unit," Edmund said. "I've read up on the Krewe and, of course, I wondered. Still, it's not an easy thing just to ask about, but tonight, when I saw you and saw your ghost, it seemed the time to clear the air."

"We're lucky," Della told him. "Our founder—"

"Adam Harrison," Edmund said, interrupting with a smile. "He recruited Special Agent Jackson Crow and a team and because the first case for his new unit happened to be in New Orleans, you became the Krewe of Hunters. In the Bureau, some may tease and call you the ghostbusters because your cases usually revolve around the unusual—like vampire killers and Jack the Ripper copycats. But you also have their respect because you manage to make arrests and stop whatever horror is going on. When the vampire killings began in France, someone in the know called your founder or your field supervisor and here you are."

Della glanced at Mason. "Yes," she said simply.

Edmund smiled. "I'm grateful. When the vampire killings fell to me, I was beyond angry and frustrated and grateful for help. Right now I'm hoping that when this comes to a conclusion, they decide that we are a great unit and that I'm considered to be part of it."

"Edmund, from what we've been told, yes, this is going to be a continuing unit. Killers don't respect country boundaries. Interpol has been with us, and now this team, and now you've been an integral part of it." Mason paused and frowned. "What about the others?" he asked.

"What about them?" Edmund asked.

"Are they *ghosties*?" Mason asked.

"I don't know. I've worked with Sean before, but not closely like this. And, of course, I met François and Jeanne when we started on the vampire killings."

"Interesting," Mason murmured.

"You think that—" Edmund began.

"I'm curious, certainly," Mason told him. He shrugged.

"Our powers that be may have had an idea about people and that may be why we were put together."

"François Bisset was chosen, but Jeanne LaPierre caught the case in France, just as I caught it in England," Edmund said.

"We'll find out in the days to come," Mason said.

"Subtly," Edmund suggested.

"Subtly," Mason agreed. "And you should go up and get some sleep. Della and I are here, on watch for two hours, so…"

"I'm going up. But I do want to meet Abigail Scott. Oh, and if you're nice, I'll introduce you to some royalty along the line!"

Della wasn't sure if he was joking or not; it didn't matter. What mattered was grasping the fact that they didn't need to pretend anymore, not with him.

And that Edmund's abilities would enhance their own, possibly bringing them closer to solving the case.

When his footsteps could no longer be heard on the stairway, Mason looked at Della and said, "That took us long enough!"

She smiled. "You can't blame him for wondering."

"I don't. I blame me for not being more observant!"

She laughed softly. "Want coffee? Tea? It's been a long day and it is really late."

"Tea, maybe. I always had it as a comfort beverage, lots of milk and sugar in it."

"Sounds good to me," Della said.

She headed into the kitchen. Mason leaned back for a minute and then joined her.

"I've checked all the video screens. No one in front of, in back of or on the side of the house. And I've still had the strangest feeling at times that we're being watched."

"Me, too," Della told him. "Of course, that may be the nature of being us."

"Paranoid?"

"Smart," she argued.

He shook his head. "No one out there now. We have until two thirty. Oh, I sent a query to Angela early. She's going to see what's going on with archeological digs and such in the area. She'll be back with us by the time we're ready to go in the morning."

"That's great. So. Hmm. Two thirty. And I'm tired now."

He smiled, leaning on the counter, looking into her eyes. "How tired?"

"Well, first, a shower. I must have a shower."

"Showers are good, definitely. After a day like this one. A shower and then…"

"Hmm. We'll have to see if I have any adrenaline left."

"Hmm…"

He went to get the sugar container and asked her how many cubes she'd like. Della went for the milk and between them they had two cups of sweet tea all set.

Mason checked the screens again.

"He's not coming here tonight," he murmured.

"But he has been out there. We both think so."

"Maybe Abigail would stand watch tomorrow night for us. If she's by the church, she can see if someone is standing across from the house and watching it."

"How could he know that we're here?"

"Obviously, the crew at Scotland Yard knows where we are. And who knows? In one of his many guises, he might have followed one of us here."

Della nodded thoughtfully. "This is maddening! One man! One man, and he's being as elusive as the real Ripper.

And we have six dedicated individuals—not to mention the country's law enforcement system—and he's watching us!"

"At least we know it," Mason said.

"Well, we don't *know* it," Della said.

"Yes," he told her quietly. "I think we do."

"Mason, we will get him."

"But I don't want him to murder anyone else!"

"I know. Well, let's frustrate him. We'll talk about a press conference with François in the morning. We'll make it damned hard for Jesse Miller to find a woman to kill."

Della drank her tea and walked around to the sofa. Mason took a seat beside her. She closed her eyes.

She jumped, aware she had been starting to doze off.

Mason laughed softly. "It's all right. I'm here. I'm awake. We only have another thirty minutes. I'm glad you had a little nap."

"Ah, ulterior motives?" she asked him.

"You're accusing me!" he teased.

"I'm ever hopeful," she said.

Their last thirty minutes went by quickly. Sean came down, assuring them that François was taking second shift with him and would be down any minute.

They headed upstairs.

Della immediately turned on the shower and stripped as quickly as she could, only to discover that, of course, Mason had followed her.

Her clothing lay in a clump on the bathroom floor. His had been strewn across the bedroom.

She turned into his arms for a brief moment and then pushed him away.

"Shower!"

"Shower!"

He lifted her behind the curtain. She'd set the water hot, and it felt wonderful as it rained down upon them, the heat entering her muscles, soothing away tension she hadn't known she'd been feeling. It had been such a long day. But now they were together. The shower was equipped with liquid soap, and they both filled their hands with it, adding the sleek feel of it to the water as they came closer and closer, teasing with every touch, and still...

Washing away the day.

"How's the adrenaline?" Mason whispered.

"Keep working on it!" she teased.

"Hmm..."

She felt his fingers sliding over her, the warmth, greater than that of the water, in his lips as they trailed along her shoulder.

"My adrenaline is doing just fine," she whispered. "Let me show you..."

"Oh, do be my guest!"

They touched, and they laughed, and they affirmed all that they felt for one another, and how they drew strength from just being together, speaking or in silence.

The water rinsed away the last of the soap. They emerged, drying one another as they had washed one another. Then, of course, Mason decided he needed to be romantic and dramatic, sweeping her off her feet, carrying her to the expanse of the bed.

And they made love. Beautiful, life-affirming love. Something that kept sanity in a world where they both knew that they had to continue fighting demons.

And later, when they lay just breathing and touching together, Mason murmured, "I'm afraid I've cut down on our sleeping hours."

"Some things," she assured him, "are better than sleep."

And they were.

But that didn't stop her from closing her eyes. And enjoying a deep and dream-free sleep until the sun had risen and it was time to begin the day again.

Another day...

One in which they needed to find a monster before he could strike again.

CHAPTER ELEVEN

"Professor Arnold Goodridge, Colorado State!"

The man who greeted them was lean, well muscled and bronzed from the sun, though Mason doubted he'd acquired his tan from working the Thames embankment near port—one that had been used since Roman times. He'd known they were coming, and he had made it easy for them to find him when they'd reached the center. It was, François Bisset had told them, a comparatively small dig, but it was already being touted in archeological circles.

Tents had been set up and boxes of supplies stood about in the roped off area while archeologist with small brushes and trowels were working in dug out areas.

Professor Goodridge shook hands with them both, intrigued that the FBI was in England and that they were interested in the multinational dig he was working.

"This has been quite a remarkable find. Not Roman, mind you, but medieval. You've heard of Thomas Becket, of course, St. Thomas à Becket?"

"Yes, of course. But wasn't he killed in Canterbury Cathedral?" Della asked.

"Yes. He was archbishop of Canterbury from 1162 until his murder in 1170. Blamed on the king, of course, and I imagine that his followers were more than just trying to make him happy. No proof, and history has it that his men, acting on words that had been shouted out in anger, came to Canterbury Cathedral, argued with him over his fight for the Church against the king, tried to drag him out but wound up murdering him in cold blood right in the church."

"We aren't near Canterbury Cathedral here," Della noted.

"And there's the wonder of this find!" the professor said. "Of course, all of Christianity was enraged by what happened. Shrines were created, many destroyed during the Reformation when Cromwell took charge. But that's another piece of history. Pilgrims wanted souvenirs from their journeys to pray at a shrine, do homage to a saint. They chipped away at tombs and just about anything, and to stop the loving vandalism, artists were commissioned to create badges—much like the souvenir pins we have today for various places and events. Trying to make a long story short—too late, I know!" he said, possibly afraid that they might not want to hear his academic speech and therefore threw some humor into their conversation. "A little boy playing along the embankment here found a badge. There had recently been dredging in areas of the river—time and weather shift the earth's crust sometimes. Storms can come along and sink ships, earthquakes and volcanos can consume towns, and sometimes there are just more subtle changes due to time and the elements. It's amazing what we've discovered on the banks of the Thames—including many Tudor theaters! Anyway, sorry. The kid's parents brought his discovery to the museum, a crew came out and bones were discovered and… Well, so far, we're seeing a picture of medieval robbery and murder. The relationship between Henry II and Becket has always intrigued me. Becket had been chancellor before he became archbishop—he didn't want to be the archbishop of Canterbury because he knew he would honor the church before his old friend, the king. As the archbishop of Canterbury, Becket changed, living an austere life, truly embracing his position and the Church. The act of his murder even changed the king who finally did penance himself. I'm sure you know that pilgrimages were important to the faithful back in the day. Here, pilgrims who had been to Becket's shrine were set upon by highwaymen. It's been amazing to touch history this way. What we've learned! They fought… We're finding a treasure trove of a microcosm of time, the bones of the dead, their relics, and those indications that the pilgrims fought back fiercely—and took down a few of their attackers in the process. But…"

He paused, wincing. "I'm sorry. I'm sure that you didn't come for a lecture."

"Fascinating, if we had time!" Della assured him.

"Right. Well, I don't think that the American FBI can arrest any Englishmen for a crime that occurred hundreds of years ago, so?"

"We're working with an international task force," Mason told him. It was the way to start—it kept them from having to explain why Americans were investigating an English criminal. "We—"

"Oh, we all read about the vampire killings and the self-titled King of the Vampires," Professor Goodridge said. "But he was caught in the States, right? The killer was an American."

"The man was apprehended, yes, but he didn't do the killing here. And now—"

"Oh! The Jack the Ripper murder!"

"We're trying to find out if a man has worked here for you—is still working for you, perhaps—or if you might have ever seen him."

"The people I work with are respectable professionals, highly regarded in the field!" the professor said, frowning.

"But you do hire people to do some of the heavy lifting—digging before you're close to artifacts, carrying boxes and supplies, right?"

"Well, yes. And that may be just day labor. Or scattered labor—when researchers are coming in or going out with specialized supplies and tools or when an artifact is large, carefully boxed and ready to be sent off to an institution. But—"

"Professor, please, we need your help," Della said pleasantly.

"For the living," Mason said.

"Of course, of course!" Goodridge said.

Mason pulled out his phone, drawing up the images Maisie had created of Jesse Miller in his many guises.

Goodridge frowned almost instantly.

He pointed and had Mason stop at the image of Jesse Miller with dark hair and a clean-shaven face.

"That's Lucas Braden," Goodridge said. "And he worked here a few days when we first arrived. We had heavy lifting, and he was happy to take just a few days' work. He was well liked among the crew—our labor force and our academics. He was willing to help in any way at any time. I was sorry to see him go. Wait! You mean this man—"

"He's a person of interest," Mason said.

Goodridge shook his head. "No, no, it can't be him. I mean, this man was a good fellow. Hardworking, and just...just a nice guy! I'm telling you, everyone liked him."

"Be that as it may," Della said quietly, "he is a person of interest. If he should come back here—"

"I asked him to come back.

"And?" Mason prompted.

"He said that he'd be busy for the next several weeks. That... Well, after that, he'd check back with me and see if there was anything that he might be needed for."

"If you do see him, please, it's imperative." He handed him a card. They'd been especially made for the current situation and had numbers for the entire team listed on them. They didn't want to take a chance on anyone who had any information not being able to get through to a specific person.

Goodridge nodded, looking confused but agreeable—even if unhappily so.

"Did he tell you where he was staying?" Della asked. "Did you have an address for him?"

"He was what we call work-for-hire, hires who are responsible for their own VAT and records. I think that he told Lucretia he was staying in..."

He stopped speaking and blinked.

"He was staying in?" Della pushed gently.

"Whitechapel," Goodridge said

"Who is Lucretia?" Mason asked.

"Lucretia, sorry, Dr. Mayberry. She's a forensic anthropologist, invaluable to this project. But she's not on site right now. She had a meeting with one of her societies at a nearby restaurant. I can call her—perhaps you could speak with her as soon as she's free," Goodridge said.

He had been in such denial that the man he had known as Lucas Braden could be a killer. Now he seemed confused— still in denial, but unable to completely trust his own mind. An uncomfortable feeling for such a man, Mason imagined.

"We'd be grateful," Della assured him.

Goodridge put through the call. As he did, Mason excused himself and put a call through to Angela, having her search for any activity under their newest pseudonym for Jesse Miller. He doubted that there would be anything on record; Miller was too smart for that. But they had to try with any means possible to find the man.

They would find him. Eventually, Jesse Miller would make a mistake. There was a small army of law enforcement looking for him.

But he was also a master of disguise and illusion. Besides taking on any appearance that fit his need, he could take on different personalities. He was exceptionally talented at using a charming persona to achieve his ends.

People liked him.

Young women would easily find him fun and pleasant, unerringly polite.

He finished his call; Goodridge finished his.

"The hotel is just up the street and Lucretia is just wrapping up her meeting. She'll wait for you in the lobby," Goodridge told them.

They thanked him.

And Mason couldn't help but remind the man that no matter how great Lucas Braden had seemed, they needed to know if he made an appearance back at the dig.

Goodridge nodded. Mason believed that the professor understood the importance of what he was being asked.

They left the site, with Della looking back, fascinated as they did so.

"Dig, dig, dig," Mason murmured.

"And dig some more," Della said dryly.

"I think that means that Gary Hudson does know Jesse Miller—or, at least, that he knew that Miller was making money at a dig. I imagine he's sure that we have no idea what he was talking about. I'm tempted to have another conversation with him," Mason said. "He might not know the real name of the man he was committing murder with under the vampire's tutelage, but he may know a lot more than he was telling us. Della?"

She was still looking back at the dig as they walked.

"Sorry. I was waiting for Indiana Jones to make an appearance. Honestly, though, the real thing looks like it's a whole lot harder! But fascinating."

"The real thing can be painstaking and tedious."

"Of course. Still, fascinating."

"I wonder how deeply Jesse Miller *dug* into this site," Mason said.

"What do you mean?"

"He just wanted cash—he doesn't live on credit cards, unless he's stealing them, using them once and disposing of them so that no trail is left. And in most places, he'd have to have ID to acquire credit cards, so bizarre as it may seem in this day and age, the man knows he needs cash. But some things are easy to sell on the black market."

"Ah, you mean the medieval souvenir badges like the one that the kid found that started the whole dig going?"

Mason nodded.

"I'll call in this time. Angela can see what's going on. She knows how to find her way into almost anything on a computer. She can probably find a black market," Della said.

"If anyone can find anything, it's Angela," Mason agreed. "Hotel ahead—maybe Dr. Lucretia knows something!"

There was a woman standing by the reception desk when they arrived. She appeared to be about forty, hair braided down her back, wearing a denim suit that was attractive enough for a meeting—and utilitarian enough to crawl through the dirt. She had a handsome face and a quick smile and walked over to meet them.

"I'm Dr. Lucretia Mayberry," she told him, her smile fading and her eyes taking on a worried look. "Professor Goodridge said that you had come to see him about Lucas. That Lucas is a person of interest in a murder case?" Her accent was beautiful, British and precise.

"I'm afraid so," Mason said. "Lucas also goes by several names, but I understand that as day labor at the dig, he was exceptionally helpful."

She nodded. "Very pleasant, always. Ready to dig in at any time."

Mason glanced at Della.

"Dig in," she murmured softly. "Dr. Mayberry, Professor Goodridge said that Lucas told you that he was staying in the Whitechapel area. Did he tell you anything more than that? Places he liked to go, perhaps, or things he liked to do."

"No, not really. I didn't get an exact address from him. Oh, he told me once that he'd been born in Liverpool. And he was exceptional with accents! We laughed one day, sharing a cup of tea during a break, because he could slip on a French accent, Irish, Scottish, Welsh—and, of course, a variety of English accents. I asked him if he'd ever gone into the theater. He smiled and said that he'd dabbled in it, but that he wanted to see the world, and—while I didn't quite get this—odd jobs kept him moving. Of course, London isn't far from Liverpool, but maybe he was seeing this as a launch."

"Interesting," Mason said.

"He seemed extremely intelligent. I suggested he continue his education and find work that paid well and allowed him to travel. He just told me that he did dream of eternal fame, but... I don't press, you know. It's quite rude to insist on answers from others," Lucretia Mayberry told them.

"I understand. Of course. But, Dr. Mayberry, it's very important that we find this man—" Mason began.

"You think that he's the Ripper. That he will strike again?" she asked.

"Yes," Mason said flatly. "Please—"

"Oh! One thing. Yes, he did say one thing! He enjoyed a pub in Whitechapel. He laughed and said that Ten Bells was a great pub, but he preferred something called... Daphne's, I think. Do you know it?" she asked worriedly.

"We can find it, I'm sure," Della said. She produced their card that time, explaining that they were a mixed team and that if she thought of anything, she could call any one of them.

She swallowed hard as she took the card. "I sat there with that man! Oh, my dear Lord, I sat there with him. And he..."

"We need to find him. Then we'll know for sure. Thank you. Thank you for meeting with us," Mason told her.

"Of course! And yes, yes! If I can think of anything else...

I… I am an anthropologist and I've dealt with…long gone bodies. But this…"

"Stay in the company of friends. People you know well," Della advised her.

She nodded. "Until today, I would have thought of Lucas as such a man!"

"That's our fear. But a press conference is happening as we speak. Hopefully, women will know to be careful of anyone they haven't known well for some time, and that they won't be easily lured from a bar or a club. So, thank you. Thank you, again."

She nodded, looking shell-shocked as they said their goodbyes.

"That was something," Mason said.

Della shook her head.

"What's the matter?"

"I'm sorry. It's good that we're finding out we are most probably right about this man, that Jesse Miller is switching identities as easily as he switches his appearance. We know where's he been. We saw him in Brixton…but we can't find him now. One man!"

"He's laying low, or he's being extremely careful. But he will make a mistake, Della."

"I just don't want another woman killed!" she said.

"I know. But if he's following Jack, we do have time."

"Some time. And a narcissist psycho like Miller might snap and make a move early!"

"He might. But we'll be there. We have City Police and Metropolitan Police… He'll do the wrong thing in the wrong place, and we will get him."

She nodded. "Let's stop for lunch on our own—see if we can find a pub showing the press conference."

François Bisset, along with Edmund and Sean, had headed to Scotland Yard for the press conference at the same time Mason and Della had been heading for the dig.

It was right that the English inspectors and the French liaison be the faces on camera; they were in England, and while they were announcing that an international task force was working on finding the man, it was still best that an Englishman be in the spotlight.

"There!" Mason pointed at a place called Ye Olde Scotsman. "I can see the TV at the bar, and it looks as if the BBC is rerunning the press conference right now."

"I'll guarantee that they have fish and chips!" Della said.

"And you're in a fish-and-chips mood?" Mason asked.

"Why not? Best place in the world for fish and chips, I think!"

They hurried in, taking seats at the bar in front of the television and quickly ordered.

Fish and chips. The bartender smiled. Americans ordering a typical British meal. He was friendly, offered them a local pint, and was only a little disappointed when they said they would stick with tea.

When they were able to give their attention to the television, they saw that the mayor was introducing Edmund, and while the sound was low, the bartenders had the TV on with closed captioning so they could also read every word being said.

Edmund said he was relieved to tell the public that one of the murderers responsible for the "vampire" killings in England had been detained.

But another was at large and it was believed he had moved on to being a copycat version of Jack the Ripper.

They were actively seeking Jesse Miller, who was most probably going by many other names as well.

He was charming and cordial, a polite and courteous, good Englishman by all appearances. He was also capable of assuming many different accents and many different appearances. While they did not want to create an aura of panic, it was crucial that women be aware and exceptionally careful when meeting men in pubs and restaurants and other social venues. It was imperative that they watch any drinks they intended to imbibe as police believed that the man made his victims pliable by drugging them. Then came a spate of questions from the press gathered before them, but Edmund lifted a hand and explained that they had images to show of what the man's appearance might be; they would be displayed online as well for anyone to study with greater intensity.

"Damned good!" Mason murmured.

Their food arrived and the bartender noted the TV.

"Wretched bad business! I hope they catch that monster quickly."

"Indeed," Della murmured.

"They will get him," Mason said with determination.

'Never got the first one," the bartender murmured, moving on.

Della spoke quietly after taking a bite of her fish. "He covered it well, and he's fielding the questions well. He announced a hotline for police just now and I'm afraid that they're going to be inundated."

"The press helped create Jack the Ripper," Mason commented. "In good ways, I believe, and, of course, there's always the negative, neighbor turning on neighbor, but, as I'm sure Abigail would agree, the press also highlighted the condition of Whitechapel and Spitalfields at the time, so that was important. And, of course, there was what Jack did himself—and the letters with which the police were inundated."

"There were two letters that they thought might be real. What they call the Dear Boss letter and the From Hell letter. Although I think journalists later took credit for them, it's still likely that they might have been from the killer. The Dear Boss letter changed the Whitechapel murders into the Jack the Ripper murders—because it was signed Jack the Ripper. And in that letter, he said that he'd clip a lady's ears—it was written before Catherine Eddowes was murdered and when she was discovered, her ear had been clipped. And... Well, with forensics, we'd have known for sure. The From Hell that was sent to Mr. Lusk contained a piece of kidney with Jack claiming that he had eaten part and that it had been very nice."

"Mason, look!"

Della was pointing at the television. The anchor was interrupting the rerun of the news conference with breaking news.

"We have recently received an email from someone claiming to be the killer, calling himself the Ripper King," she announced. "The police have been informed, and since it has apparently gone many places, we wanted to share it with the public as quickly as possible. The email reads, I laugh when they think that they have me, that they know me. They will soon realize that they know nothing at all. They may post all the pictures that they like, but if you meet saucy Jack—for I am him, reincarnated with greater power—you will never know that you have had the honor. Unless, of course, you are one of the lucky ones I hold in my embrace. I am eternally yours, Jack the Ripper, risen to be king, King of the Rippers, for all who came before me just played at the part. And she must know, she must feel, that she will be the one, for this Jack will find her, and find the time, and she will then be known as Mary Kelly.'"

The anchor turned her attention from the scroll to the audience.

"Again, we cannot emphasize how careful and vigilant we must be!"

"Of course, he sent a letter," Della said. "He would have to—after the news conference."

"But he's angry," Mason said.

"And that's dangerous!"

"Maybe. And maybe it will cause him to make a mistake. I believe that they've moved on to speak with producers and directors on any movies being filmed, directors, stage managers, cast and crew at the theaters, and owners of makeup shops. He'll need to become more inventive if he really wants to change his appearance now."

Mason set his credit card on the bar and they quickly paid, anxious then to meet up with the others and find out where they were—and where they should be—to try to trace Jesse Miller through his disguises.

"Edmund is quite a find," Della said as they headed out.

"Should I be jealous?" he teased.

She smiled. "He's one of us."

He nodded. "And we didn't know."

"We should have known," Della agreed. "I wonder about the others."

"We can just ask, you know."

"Think we should?"

He shrugged. "Maybe. As for now...let's get back in the game. And, no, we can't stop to see a play!"

"I wasn't going to ask and you know it. Except that I do love the theater in London. Maybe, once we catch this fellow, we can see a play. I've really wanted to see the show *Six*! It features the—"

"Six wives of Henry VIII?" Mason interrupted, amused.

"They compete to have the best story in song. I have the CD—"

"I know. I've listened," he said, grinning.

"Right!"

"Once we catch him, we'll see the show. It's a deal," Mason promised. His phone was ringing and he glanced at the caller ID and answered it quickly.

"Edmund, great job on the press conference. Hopefully, women will take heed and be extremely careful."

"Thank you," Edmund said over the phone. "Did you get anything?"

"We know he worked at the dig. He needs to take jobs now and then, apparently, to keep himself flush. What about you?"

"We found another job he worked. He was an extra on a movie—one of the makeup crew who worked with the extras remembered him. Different from any of the sketches we have, but your artist couldn't possibly come up with all the changes he might make. I think you might want to join us and have a chat with the young woman yourself."

"What's the movie and where are they filming?" Mason asked. He glanced at Della.

"You'll love this. It's called *Darkness and the Vampire*. Today, they're working on background material. Right in Whitechapel. We're on Whitechapel Road where they have a section blocked off for filming. Security is onsite so I'll meet you at the tape."

"Get me a side street," Mason said. "And we're on our way."

"Our chameleon likes being an actor, too," he said, ending the call and telling Della what Edmund had discovered.

"What is the quote?" Della queried. "'All the world's a stage, All the men and women merely players.'"

"William Shakespeare," Mason said. "Let's get this guy before he turns this show into an even greater tragedy!"

Edmund helped them dodge around the cameras and crew working on the street, bringing them back to a trailer where a young woman was waiting for them.

Stacey Kerry was an attractive young woman in her mid-twenties, green-eyed and sandy-haired, immediately polite and sincere as she spoke with them. She was seated in the trailer's makeup chair, surrounded by the tools of her craft, as she spoke with them.

Della sat facing her on the small seat across from the chair while Mason and Edmund leaned against two of the side counters that held everything from color palettes to face putty and wigs and extensions.

Her accent was American, one that contained a hint of the Southern states. She explained that she was American as was one of the two producers on the film, a man she and the director and others had worked with before on such classics as *Ghosts Gone Ghoulish* and *Zing of the Zombies*.

Della apologized for having missed the movies, which had caused Stacey to laugh. "Not for everyone, but you'd be amazed at the cult following!"

"We will have to catch one of them!" Mason said.

Edmund winced.

"I'm certain that this man worked with us just three days ago," she said. "He didn't appear as he does in any of your artist's sketches, but—"

"No one else claimed to have seen him," Edmund interjected lightly.

"And, I could be wrong," she said, looking at Della. "But because of what I do—and I knew this was what I wanted to do since I was a kid—I know face shapes. Yes, he can change his face shape, but when you're close, the real bone structure is there."

"Stacey, if you think that you saw him, I'm certain that you did. I have a friend who works for a major makeup line at a department store, and even she can point out aspects of a face because, of course, she's always trying to make a woman look her best and accent her best features while playing down those that are so…great. So. When were you filming and what part was he playing?" Della asked. "What name did he use?"

"He told me his name was Ken, Kenneth Rippon. And he wasn't playing a part at all—he was an extra."

Della glanced at Mason. *Rippon.* Miller must have enjoyed that alias.

"You do makeup for all extras?" Mason asked Stacey.

"No, not when they're just background," Stacey said. "But we do walk through the crowd to just make sure that everyone looks all right, as if they're someone who would naturally be in the scene. This film takes place in the 1970s. Beards and long hair on men were common then and we were just looking to see if everyone fit in to the background—we were filming in the studio and the scene was designed to be a '70s nightclub. This man was perfect for it. Long shaggy brown hair and a full shaggy beard. I noticed that he was wearing contacts—"

"You saw contacts?" Edmund asked. "You were that close."

"I talked to him. He was nice, charming—fun," Stacey said.

"You must have information on him," Mason told her. "If he was hired—"

"That would be payroll." She winced. "We had at least forty extras on set that day, and more than half of those were men. And, of course, we can find out about his check, but… I'm not in your line of work, but I imagine he gave a false name and address." She shrugged. "I sincerely doubt they do background checks on extras—the extras just don't want their checks to bounce!"

"No online payments straight into a bank account?" Edmund said.

Stacey shook her head. "Not with extras—checks just written out for a day's work."

"You said that you talked to him. Did he tell you anything about where he was staying, what he was doing?"

"He said that he was a tourist and working on the movie in any way was just cool. I asked him where he was from and he told me that he'd grown up outside of Chicago."

"That was a lie. He's English," Edmund said quietly.

"Really?" Stacey asked. "He sounded so—so Chicago!"

"He can change his accents as easily as his appearance," Mason assured her.

"Did he say what he was doing as a tourist? Did he mention anything that he likes to do?" Della asked.

"Yes, he said that he loved just walking the streets and

seeing where things had taken place throughout history. Come to think of it, he was familiar with British history."

Della glanced at Mason.

Of course. Jack the Ripper history!

"Jack the Ripper history?" she asked aloud.

"Yes, of course—most young Americans like to take the Ripper tours," Stacey told her. "But he knew a lot more British history. Okay, now I know he is a Brit. But he talked about kings and queens from the past, World Wars I and II—he was a fan of Queen Victoria and... Oh, wait! When he talked about Queen Victoria, he went back into the Ripper thing. He said that the theory that the Crown might have had something to do with the killings made sense. Victoria was so very proper and her grandson, Albert Edward, wasn't. He supposedly had an illegitimate child, and maybe Mary Kelly was the mom's friend and maybe she intended to blackmail the Queen! I personally think that a woman like Victoria ordering heinous murders is ridiculous. I said that to him. We talked about other suspects...and he suggested that if I didn't believe that one, maybe it was Montague Druitt. From a good family, educated and then—oh! Then he suggested that it was probably a bobby—a cop who could walk through the streets and not be noted. Cops always act so good and they're usually messed up people who want to be cops because they need to find power somewhere. Or, he told me, maybe it was just an average guy—a butcher or such—who wasn't cool and so news media didn't pay any attention to that idea."

"Did you go out with him?" Mason asked her.

"Oh, no, and thank God!" Stacey said. "But I did sit with him at lunch when we had a break and, as I said, he was nice."

"Besides being a tourist and seeing the sights, did he say anything about where he was staying or what he did at night?"

She frowned, thinking.

"I'd assumed that he'd be back when another call went out for extras. This isn't Hollywood big budget as you may have ascertained—"

"But you must be very good," Edmund told her.

Stacey smiled. "I am and thank you. Experience. And while this may be low-budget, I'm well paid, and when it came up, I was looking forward to spending time in London. I've only been here once before, and I do love seeing iconic treasures like the Tower of London, Big Ben—and we got to see Stonehenge on a day off!"

"Have you put a call out for extras again?" Mason asked.

"I don't do that, I get notes each night about what's going on the next day. There's a schedule, but it changes. Weather can cause changes, and sometimes, a lead player gets sick... Every night we get a sheet that schedules the next day. There are things about filming a move that stay the same—and things that change at the whim of the producers or directors."

"I'll check and see if I can find out about the next call," Edmund said, leaving them.

"Can you think of anything else?" Della asked her.

She frowned and shook her head. "Not really. He said that he just likes to walk...people watch, see what's different here from other places. Oh, and guess nationalities of people on the streets. I'm sorry, I can't think of anything else."

"What about pubs?" Mason said. "Did he mention any pubs specifically?"

"No. He just said that he loved pubs and pub meals.

Pubs tended to be warm and friendly places that he really enjoyed."

"Thank you so much," Della said, noting that Mason had nodded to her; they had gotten what they could from the young woman.

But Della was compelled to speak again as she rose. "Stacey, please, this man is a killer and he is going to kill again. Be careful. We think that he's working alone, but... You know faces, but you know, too, that he is good at changing himself."

Stacey smiled. "Not to worry. I am a complete coward. I go out at night when my call isn't ridiculously early or we don't film too late, but never ever alone. Mike Gantry—our vampire—is a total sweetheart in real life and he and Jon Lund—the human hero—are always with me and few of the other support crew. We're never alone."

"Good," Della told her. "Keep it that way. And thank you again. It's been a pleasure to meet you."

Sean was waiting for them when they left the trailer.

"Edmund is with the director," he explained, "getting access to all the right people to find out if there's a paper trail."

"There won't be," Mason said. "But we have to go through all the motions."

"Exactly. We don't dare miss anything," Sean said. "He suggested we head back, look at all that we do have, and..."

"And wonder how the hell we're going to find him, no matter what we think we know," Mason said. "But he's right. Time to regroup at the house."

CHAPTER TWELVE

Not even Ripper could be everywhere at once.

He had to take pleasure in the fact that there were so many places he could be and not be found or discovered as he watched.

Watching them, he perfected his plan.

He was there when they returned. And, of course, he'd be there when they headed out for the night, looking for him. He'd follow them, their stupid little group of six would split up and, naturally, he would follow *her*.

He'd watched her laugh. And he'd seen the way that she looked at the other American, Special Agent Mason Carter. He thought he was so clever. And, of course, she thought she was so tough. But she could have all of them around her...

And still, he knew what to do now. He smiled, because the idea had come to him, and it was really so evident. All her great FBI training would mean nothing, all the muscle and brawn around her would mean nothing...

And there they were.

She was perfect. So very beautiful with her long flowing hair and bright green eyes. She kept it up often, but when she was with him, it would be down, and he would love touching it, feeling it, until the time came...

Maybe he'd keep a bit of it. Stroke it occasionally, savor and remember.

The Frenchmen walked into the house first, followed by the local copper, Inspector Detective Sean Johnstone who was laughing at something that Special Agent Della Hamilton was saying. Last in the door were Inspector Detective Edmund Taylor and Mr. Tall, Dark and Brooding, Special Agent Mason Carter. Carter was fit... Jerk probably spent half his life in a gym looking at his abs. But neither height nor muscle were going to help him, because people like him never saw just how vulnerable they were. He'd be bringing his strength and his gun against brilliance... just like bringing a knife to a gunfight, as the Americans liked to say. Like the old American West. Gunfight at the OK Corral. But there would be no gunfight; it would be all over so quickly and they'd never know what hit them. Yes, there would be time for them to see him with their dying eyes...

See him. And know what he was going to do to her. Maybe he'd even time it so that they might watch for a while.

He felt good. In fact, he felt incredible. Lesser men would wonder how one man might get to a woman surrounded by five trained and armed members of law enforcement.

Thankfully, he wasn't a lesser man.

His own genius made him gleeful. He'd be ready for a fine pint tonight! And he would be so far superior to the Ripper of yore. In his mind, the fool had carried out iconic murders—and then betrayed himself when there had been no need, when life should have been the fullest.

Ripper would follow the brilliance that had come before, but then rise above where the former had been so sadly lacking.

As he stood there, he slid deeper against the doorway where he'd appeared to lounge, distractedly playing with his phone.

The door was about to open. Food delivery was arriving.

He smiled and walked away. It would be a while before they left again.

And he would be ready tonight, and in the delicious nights to come, planned so perfectly in every detail.

Sean had his nose in his computer from the moment they entered the house. He had barely acknowledged the question Edmund had voiced to him about food. He'd waved a hand and said that he'd be happy with whatever.

Mason pulled up the chair next to him at the dining room table.

"Just what are you studying so intensely?"

Sean looked up at him. "Maybe nothing. But I had some time with Stacey at the movie set and she was telling me the same things she told you. I don't know why, but I'm curious as to our killer's thoughts on the identity of Jack the Ripper, so I was looking them up myself. I have to say that I agree with him on one thing—I really do not see a royal connection. Yes, Prince Albert Edward was a bit of a disgrace to his family. Victorian mores were strict." He looked at Mason. "I'm not sure how this can help, but since Stacey mentioned it was something Jesse Miller—as whoever he was at the movies—was talking about the suspects."

"Can't hurt. It's too early to head out to the pubs and dinner is on its way. What have you got?"

"All right, let's go with ridiculous first—according to my humble opinion. Though they made a few cool movies on the theory, there's Prince Albert Edward, or Eddy. He was heir to the throne when he was born, being the first boy born to his father, heir to Queen Victoria. He was suspected of a scandal when the murders occurred. Supposedly, he loved art and the well-known artist Sickert introduced him to a girl who something modeled for him, Annie Elizabeth Crook. She was definitely a no-no for him, being a Scottish Catholic. But he was madly in love and she bore him a daughter, Alice Margaret. The story has it that Queen Victoria was incensed and the Sickert house was raided. Poor Annie was taken to Guy's Hospital where another suspect, Sir William Gull, proclaimed her insane. She died there twenty-eight years later, totally insane by then, probably true after all that was done to her. The plot thickens! Supposedly, Mary Kelly had also worked for Sickert and was friends with Annie and saved the baby until Sickert was able to get her to safety. Fast-forward to the Ripper. Theory one—Eddy and Sir William Gull created the murder spree to hide the murder of Mary Kelly. Theory two—Sir William Gull did it all by himself to protect the Crown, making use of hints about Mason ritual, as in the *Juwes* mentioned on the wall, wanting to throw off suspicion. Elaborate, brutal, unhinged murders—to hide what might be a disastrous scandal for the Crown. Some even suspected the artist, Sickert—he was known to paint some pretty gruesome pictures. But, in my opinion, you don't help someone and then head out on a killing spree. Okay, so, in my mind, Eddy didn't do it—and evidence is on my side. He wasn't even in London on the nights of several murders. Then, as profilers today would tell you—"

"The killer evolved. By the time he murdered Mary Kelly, he had slit throats and slashed abdomens and genitals and removed organs, but Mary Kelly was just about stripped of all flesh and her face was left as a disaster of blood and bone," Della said, joining the conversation. "I don't believe—even though I agree it made for good movies—that the killer was Eddy or Gull. Not with what we've learned from profiling, except, of course, profiling is a tool, not an exact science."

"Right. But a useful tool more often than not." Sean grinned at her. "On to Montague Druitt. A possible, I say. Numerous members of his family were in the medical field. He'd been dismissed from his post and it was suspected that the dismissal might have had to do with sexual misconduct. He knew the area. He kept an office there when he might have kept it elsewhere with his family's influence. The real kicker—his own family thought that he might be the Ripper, and…drum roll, he committed suicide and his body was found in the Thames after the Mary Kelly murder—and the murders stopped there, right before his death. In a private memorandum, Sir Melville Macnaghten of the Metropolitan Police suggested that Druitt was the suspect he considered to be the killer."

"A possible," Della agreed. "Then, of course, there was the whole *leather apron* concept that it was a man named Kosminski in the police reports, a hairdresser and barber, but as time went by, no one was even sure if Aaron Kosminski was the man referred to, though he was a Polish Jew, as identified. There is tremendous confusion with some of the names because police referred to a suspect deranged and rambling at the end of the murder spree as David Cohen, possible real name Nathan Kominski, who was going to be taken to the parish workhouse but became so violent when they tried to take him under restraint that he had to be sent to Colney Hatch Lunatic Asylum, and died there in 1889."

"Far less movie worthy than a tainted heir to the throne!" Sean said.

"Back to the name confusion. Kosminski wound up in an asylum in 1891 after threatening his sister with a knife," Della said. "But I can't imagine a man to have evolved into the killer who murdered Mary Kelly just stopping— and then winding up institutionalized that much later for threatening someone with a knife. What would he have been doing until that time?"

"I'm looking at notes by Scotland Yard and Ripperologists, but you're… You just know all this?" Sean asked Della.

"I had several classes with members of the Behavior Analysis Unit at Quantico," Della explained. "This was a favorite topic for one of my instructors. Another suspect he didn't think belonged in the pool was George Chapman, born Seweryn Klosowski in Poland, who was finally executed after poisoning three wives and caught because the last wife's mother demanded he be investigated. My instructor disagreed with him as a suspect because of the monetary gain he achieved through his liaisons and because poisoning as a method of murder is far different from brutally hacking them to ribbons. He did, however, have medical training in his youth when he apprenticed to a surgeon and while some think that the Ripper had such training, others believe anyone who had ever butchered a large animal would have the same fundamental knowledge."

"And what about James Maybrick?" Sean asked.

"The diary claiming him to be Jack the Ripper didn't show up until the 1990s and the materials and all else about it are too questionable," Mason put in. Sean and Della both looked at him and he shrugged. "I had similar—though not the same—classes," he reminded them.

"All right, so, who was Jack the Ripper?" Sean asked.

"More important," Mason said, "who does this new Ripper think he was?"

"Robert Mann was a morgue attendant—plenty of scalpels and knives available, but he wasn't really a suspect at the time," Della said. "Then there was Dr. Francis Tumblety—"

"American!" Sean said.

Della made a face at him. "Irish-born American—though we don't claim that America produces no monsters, you know! But he spoke often enough about his hatred for women, he was a huge self-promoter, pulled the wool over many eyes, and most importantly, he was in Whitechapel during the time of the killings. The Metropolitan Police arrested him for *gross indecency* in November of 1888 but knowing that he was a subject of interest in the Ripper case, too, he managed to escape to France with a false ID and moved on with his life from there. Detective Chief Inspector John Littlefield wrote to a journalist in the early 1900s that Tumblety was one of his main suspects, largely because of his blatant hatred toward women and because of his arrest record. But Tumblety died of heart disease in 1903, and whatever he might have shared with the world died with him."

"William Bury," Sean murmured, "The last person hanged in Dundee! He strangled his wife with a rope in January of 1889—also stabbing her many times and living in Whitechapel at the time of the murders. Just another person of interest," he added dryly, "in the mystery with no definitive answer."

"He wasn't taken seriously as a suspect at the time, but some modern researchers and behavioralists believe it might have been him," Mason said.

Edward groaned. "Listening to you... Well, I wish that I might have had a few more classes with some of your BAU professors."

"Or you can open a computer, too," Sean said.

Edward shrugged. "I don't think I need to—seems we have a much lovelier version of such a fountain of knowledge right here!" He nodded toward Della.

Sean grinned at that. "Yes, Della is stunning and a computer is not. But, hey, computers can hold more information than even the most amazing of human brains. I'm not seeing many other serious suspects. Joseph Barnett was a one-time lover of Mary Kelly and certainly knew the area well enough, so, of course, he receives mention. Then there's Albert Bachert—or Backert. He changed the spelling of the name in 1889."

"He is someone studied by profilers these days," Della said. "They've learned through many cases that serial killers sometimes like to thrust themselves into an investigation, to be especially helpful, talking to police. Bachert was a citizen of Whitechapel and he played with politics and letters—sending many to the newspapers and having them published. He claimed to have spoken to a man at a pub who kept asking him questions about streets where he might proposition the ladies of the night. Then he claimed to receive letters from the killer as time went by, sending them all on to the papers.

"But he was never associated with the women nor was there ever any evidence found regarding him—but he did crave attention and, at a later date, he claimed to have been part of the vigilante committee when the murder spree was going on, but he wasn't listed anywhere. So," Della said. "While that behavior is suspicious, he might have just been a man craving attention."

"The morgue assistant was in the right area—and certainly had the right tools," François commented.

"And that is *certainly* true," Sean agreed.

"I say Montague Druitt might be high on the list," Della said. "He had a shady reputation despite the respect afforded his family, his father was a surgeon so he had tools and knowledge. He knew the area. He was respectable looking enough and cordial enough to have lured a woman into a dark alley. And, maybe the most major point, he committed suicide right after the Mary Kelly killing. And that was so savage that it could have sent someone over the edge," Della said.

"Do we think this killer sees himself as a Montague Druitt?" Edmund asked.

"I think he's far too much of a narcissist to commit suicide. But he believes that he's going to be superior to the original Ripper, so, maybe," Della said.

"We know that Jesse Miller has told people that he lives or is staying in the Whitechapel area of the city," Mason offered. "We know that he does odd jobs—movies and digs, manual labor—to keep his finances going. These aren't full-time jobs and they afford him the ability to work when it doesn't interrupt his planned activities. And, I believe, he's organized and careful, that he's a sociopath or psychopath with a fine line distinction between the two. And I do believe that until he kills again and in fact completes his spree of the canonical murders, he will be prowling the streets every night, stalking possible victims, watching for the patrols, times bartenders leave… He's watching, constantly."

He glanced at Della. He was thinking about Abigail Scott, she knew. They needed to speak with her because she was surely out there every night as well, ready to give them any information possible.

And they needed her.

"Whoa! Interesting late entry into the ever-widening historical pool of suspects!" Sean said, looking from the computer to the faces of those around him. "H.H. Holmes, AKA Herman Webster Mudgett, considered by many to be America's first serial killer, though, of course, in our line of work, I'm going to consider him to be America's first *known* serial killer. There are a couple theories here on his involvement. Okay, seems like he might have been in London at the time of the killing. But!"

He paused for dramatic effect and Della picked up the story.

"H.H. Holmes planned his murders meticulously. He would befriend people—and be their friend for years—before killing them for what he probably saw as necessary financial gain. He designed his Chicago hotel ahead of the World's Fair in 1893 with all manner of conveniences to murder his guests—and get rid of the bodies. He hired and fired workmen—a few who might have disappeared—so that no one besides himself would know what lay in certain areas of the basement, behind walls, and down hallways. That's what many believe to be the major difference—Holmes was an *organized* killer while profilers today consider the original Jack to have been disorganized. There is also the manner of murder—Holmes didn't care if he had to hurt people before their demise, but torture wasn't part of his motivation. He was most frequently motivated by money. Nor did he seem to practice overkill—he just needed to get rid of bodies. There was something truly deranged in the Ripper's mind. His need to rip up bodies and slash through organs—including sex organs—was truly pathological."

"But!" Sean said again, glancing at Della and waiting to see if she wanted to go further.

"You take it away, Sean!" she said.

"Some suspect that H.H. Holmes had an assistant with him, a man who helped with his various schemes, and one he *trained*—à la our vampire killer, Stephan Dante—to kill, encouraging a man with all necessary tendencies for truly brutal murder."

"Ah, dear friends!" François said suddenly, glancing at his phone. "Dinner is at the door!"

The doorbell rang as he spoke. Mason and Edmund nodded at one another and headed to the door together.

They accepted the packages from the deliveryman.

And carefully locked the door and reset the alarm.

That night they'd opted for roast and potatoes, both of which were excellent. Edmund explained that England, like so many other places, had embraced the concept of meal delivery. Contact could be completely limited when a meal was left at the door. They had gotten very good at getting food out that was good and even hot when it arrived.

As they ate, they continued to muse on the possible suspects from the past. When they had finished, everyone dealt with the clean up and soon they were done.

"Della and I will head to Daphne's—where the movie

crowd hangs out," Mason said, looking at Edmund. "And if it's all right with you, Sean, you'll join us?"

"We'll take the Red Rose and the streets," Edmund said. He stared at Mason for a minute and then shook his head. "It's too bad we can't take Stacey with us—she might see something we miss. It's aggravating to realize that he could be walking down the street a half a block away—and we might not recognize him because he's changed so completely."

"Maybe we'll run into Stacey at Daphne's pub," Della said. "And maybe..."

"That crowd does like Daphne's so you might well run into Stacey and a whole group from the movie production crew. But—maybe what else?" Edmund asked her.

"Maybe we'll spend another evening out to no end whatsoever, but I don't see anything else we can do that would even give us a chance."

"And that is the truth, and there is always the chance that we will be successful," Mason said. "So, hey, one good thing—we're trying lots of fine English pints!"

"The best," Edmund assured him.

Stepping out front, Mason noticed that what he considered to a typical London fog was settling gently into the air.

Once past the porch, they split up, walking in different directions. Della and Sean fell into step with Mason.

Della was quiet and Mason glanced her way, asking, "What is it?"

She glanced at him, smiling. "I was thinking that I'm glad that the pubs close comparatively early. We could be in Key West or New Orleans or somewhere where they never close. Hey, we usually get to go to sleep by about one thirty."

"The staid English, you know," Sean said lightly, shrugging.

They reached Daphne's and for a moment, Mason stood still, looking. The building was old and had probably been there a couple hundred of years.

Definitely during the Ripper's day. The facade didn't appear to have been updated in years. It was a warm wooden building with a heavy old entry. There were outside tables, but they couldn't have offered easy access for the waitstaff because they'd need to come in and out of the heavy doors after taking orders and with heavy trays filled with pint glasses.

A waitress excused herself as Mason opened the door; he held it for her before they entered.

Mason quickly decided that heavy doors didn't matter—the bar area and the tables were filled, and at the bar, friends without seats stood to talk with those who did. There was chatter and laughter against the music—rock played at a thoughtful level so that customers could hear one another speak.

It was a popular place.

As they stood in the entry, he heard someone say, "Hey!"

Quickly turning around, he saw that Stacey was, indeed, there, apparently out with friends, and she left her chair at a long table to hurry over and greet them at the bar.

"Stacey!" Sean said, and it was evident that the young detective inspector was impressed by and attracted to the young woman.

Mason and Della greeted her warmly, too.

"I'm not out alone or carelessly," she assured him. "I'll introduce you—Jenny and Morgan are from my department, Brett and Max are production assistants. Come on over, please, join us!"

Mason glanced at Della and shrugged. Joining the group

didn't seem like such a bad idea. Their table allowed for an unobstructed view of the bar and it would appear that they were just out with a group of friends. Here, they couldn't see the tables outside, but Sean murmured to Mason and said, "I'll take a walk out now and then have a smoke."

"I didn't know you smoked," Mason said.

Sean shrugged. "Mostly, I've quit. A few here and there."

Della had heard him. "We don't want to turn this hunt into the return of a habit for you."

Sean tapped his head. "It's up here. If I don't let it get me, it won't."

They followed Stacey to the table and met her friends. Stacey didn't introduce them as law enforcement and they hadn't been seen on set since they'd met her in her trailer when nothing was going on in the makeup department.

The crew had pitchers of beer on the table and they were invited to help themselves. Mason thanked them and helped himself to one of the empty glasses, assuring them that the next ales would be on them.

Della launched in, asking questions about the filming, and for a while, there was a lot of laughter as each spoke about the absolute worst movie they had ever worked on. Still, the conversation inevitably turned to the man who would be the Ripper King—with all of them assuring the newcomers that they'd never be out alone at night under the present circumstances.

"And honestly, we aren't seeing people—women—out there alone," Max, one of the young PAs said. "Thankfully, people are heeding the warnings."

"Which will hopefully save lives," Della murmured.

"I hope they get him and nail his ass to the wall," Max said. "But you know, we were here when they found the body of this Ripper guy's victim. The streets turned into a zoo—everyone wanted to see where it had happened. Rubberneckers! When someone had died. Sick"

"Max," Stacey said, "You worked on the *Worm that Ate Chicago, Monster of the Seven Glades* and a dozen other monster and serial killer movies. And all were popular!"

"But this is real," Max said. He shook his head, looking at Mason. "Do you think that people blur the line between what is and what isn't real? They say that the Ripper tours are going crazy right now. I don't know. I don't get—people. And it's the same everywhere, of course. Here, the US, around the other countries I've been in as well."

"We all want to think it can't be us," Morgan, one of Stacey's friends from the makeup department, said.

"Okay, sorry, my bad. Depressing conversation," Max apologized. "So, you're enjoying London?" he asked Mason. "Talk about…man's inhumanity to man. Check out the London Dungeon."

"Hey, that's not cheerful!" Stacey protested. "Let's talk funny. We had a rising star on the set the other day doing a cameo. One line! Took them three hours to shoot it!"

"My favorite was our ninja guy doing his leap—and having his toupee go flying off!" Morgan said. "Do you like the movies?" she asked Della

"Who doesn't like the movies?" Della replied, smiling.

"Depends on the movie," Sean said, "But I'm sure this one—"

"Is going to be a fan favorite among those who love bad movies! Oh, I didn't say that!" Max told them.

Conversation went around, each of the crew entertaining the newcomers with the best and worst of what they'd seen.

Mason listened.

And watched the room. He noted that Stacey was seated on the far side with him.

As much as she might enjoy a late night, she was watching, too.

"Empty pitcher!" the young woman announced suddenly. "And we have a late call tomorrow morning! That means another pitcher!"

"Our turn," Mason said.

"No," she laughed. "This one is mine. You may get the next two! Oh, and we have baskets of chips coming to the table. They should arrive shortly!"

She hopped up and went to have the pitcher refilled. There were still several people at the bar, still several standing behind those seated in the old wooden bar stools. Mason watched her as she chatted with the bartender and waited for him to pour a new pitcher.

As she waited, Mason felt his phone buzzing. He answered it quickly.

Edmund was on the other line.

"I just heard from the paper—they've received an email from our friend, they don't think it's a hoax, the content and syntax are similar to his other missives.

"And what does this one say?"

"Tonight's the night I don't need the light, she'll be two, but I'm far from through. Saucy Jack is deliciously back and trust me, this Jack truly has the most perfect knack."

"So, he's out here somewhere. Anything on your end?"

"I have police as far as I can possibly spread them. We've tried a few pubs and the streets—I can't find our lovely Mrs. Abigail Scott, either. I'd risk being locked up in an asylum tonight to talk to her in front of others if I had to… We need help. There are too many dark alleys and corners and too many people about and—"

"We can only stay vigilant," Mason told him. "No man can do more than his best."

"Right. I know. But I don't want this bloke ecstatic and gleeful tomorrow because he managed to do what he said he was going to do."

Mason had kept Stacey in his sights as he'd listened.

He saw her frown, looking toward the door. Someone was exiting; the heavy door was closing behind him.

"Hey!"

Stacey was suddenly moving, heading toward the door herself.

Mason leaped to his feet and Della and Sean, watching as he had been, did the same.

He was first out the door, anxiously looking up and down the street. Impossibly, it seemed that Stacey had disappeared.

It was growing late, but the pubs were still open and yet the street were crowded here and there as those who had been out knew that it was reaching closing time and were headed home or back to one of the many hotels in the area.

"I'm going left!" Della called to him.

"Right, Sean, talk to the people out here, see if anyone knows—"

"On it!" Sean promised.

They headed in the three possible directions in which anyone might have gone. Mason weaved quickly through the small groups of people moving along the street, having called it a night.

He looked ahead.

There was no moon that night but streetlights offered il-

lumination, filtering weakly through the London fog that
had settled soon after nightfall.

He looked for doorways, for alleys, for any possible corridor through which Stacey might have disappeared along
with the man she had followed from the pub.

Just a friend?

*Or had she thought that she'd witnessed Jesse Miller in one of
his guises and chased after him, afraid that in calling for help, she
would lose him?*

"Mason!"

He turned. Sean, standing by a couple lingering over
their last pints, was waving to him—showing that they
should be running in the opposite direction.

Mason turned. Because along that street, a gaping dark
hole against the row of buildings showed an entrance to
an alley.

A dark alley.

The kind that the man who be the Ripper King might
well determine to be a fine place to meet with a woman.

Sean was already headed in that direction.

Mason hurried to catch up.

CHAPTER THIRTEEN

Della rushed along, not hesitating as she reached a breach in the building walls, a corridor that led to a back alley.

She knew that patrolmen were working hard to cover the district, to keep their eyes on the dark alleys. But since there were not enough policemen to be posted everywhere all of the time, the patrolman assigned to the area might be making rounds.

And might not be back for minutes…

Minutes in which a killer could slice a woman's throat.

She inched along the wall in the shadows and the mist and then heard Stacey talking, begging with her attacker.

"This is crazy. You're not a killer and I don't know what you're doing with that knife. Don't, don't, don't… Don't put your hands around my throat!"

"Hey!"

Della could just see the shapes in front of her, but she was close enough to take aim with her Glock, to give the would-be killer pause.

She moved closer. A man was holding Stacey—but the man wasn't Jesse Miller. She didn't know who he was, and he'd have to doff the dark green hoodie he was wearing for her to see much of anything about him.

But he had gone still. His knife was against Stacey's throat.

"Let her go this instant."

He stared back at her.

"Buddy, I was the best shot in my class at Quantico," she told him. "Trust me, I can hit you between the eyes before you can shift that blade."

That probably wasn't true, but he didn't know it.

The man moved the knife immediately, throwing it to the ground and lifting his hands in the air.

"This isn't what it looks like!" he cried.

Mason and Sean came running down the corridor, quickly ascertaining that she had the situation under control.

Sean, as local law enforcement, rushed forward, reaching beneath his jacket for a pair of cuffs. He began to speak to the man, as Englishmen had rights, just like Americans.

Stacey cried out and came rushing to Della, ready for the comforting hold of Della's arms around her.

But her attacker was talking, words spewing from him. "I wasn't going to hurt her! I swear it. I was just going to scare her and then explain that some friend of hers had paid me two hundred pounds just to get her to follow me out of the pub and… I wouldn't have hurt her!"

"Well, guess what?" Sean demanded of him. "Kidnapping a woman into a dark alley and threatening her with a knife is illegal!"

"It was a lark—"

"There is no such thing as a *lark* when a killer is roaming the streets," Mason informed him. He nodded to Sean.

"Let's get him into headquarters. We can question him, or he can ask for legal counsel, but one way or the other—"

"No, no, no. I can't be arrested, seriously, she was telling me not to hurt her and I was going to explain and then that lady pulled a gun on me and I was terrified!"

His hood had fallen back. The young man couldn't have been more than twenty or twenty-one. Without the hoodie around his face, Della could see that he had serious brown eyes, soft brown hair and a clean-shaven innocent face with fine narrow features.

And he looked terrified.

He called out to Stacey.

"Tell them! Tell them that you know me and that I wouldn't... I wouldn't hurt anyone! That guy who was on the set that day, too, Ken... Ken Rippon! He said that he was a good friend of yours and that you were too careless and that I just needed to get you to follow me to the alley!"

Della looked at Mason.

The story was stupid but rang true.

Which meant that Jesse Miller was out there somewhere. He'd used another extra from the movie, convincing him that he was truly worried about Stacey and that she needed to have a stern and serious warning.

"Sean—" Mason began.

"I've got it," Sean assured them. "I'll get him to a patrolman and have him brought in. Then I'll get back out on the streets. He is out here—go!"

"What do I do?" Stacey cried.

"We're going to need your statement," Sean told her. "I'll get you in a separate car and the patrolmen will help you. We'll be with you soon, I promise."

Stacey nodded, looking at Della, straightening and finding her courage and composure.

"Right," she said.

Her attacker suddenly started crying and calling out again.

"I swear, I'm telling the truth! I'd never have hurt her. Honestly, look at the knife!" the man cried.

Della frowned, nodded to Stacey, stepped around her and hurried over to where the knife had fallen.

It was a damned good facsimile, but when she moved it, the plastic blade fell back into the hilt.

"It is a prop," she told the others. "So, you stole it off the set?"

"No, no, I didn't steal it! He stole it! Said that we weren't really paid enough but that it would be cool to have a souvenir no one would really miss when the movie came out. I swear, I swear, I'm telling you the truth!"

"And you listened to a man who wanted you to pretend to attack a woman with a knife when a killer is loose in the city?" Della asked.

"I needed the two hundred pounds! And I was just about to let Stacey go when you came around out of the darkness and mist and scared me!"

"I could have shot you!" she snapped.

"I made a mistake, a serious mistake. I know it, I just… I needed the money. Please, believe me. I was playing a joke for money for a good reason. He wanted her to start being careful! He said that Stacey followed people too easily."

"He lied to you!" Stacey said angrily.

There was silence for a minute. Della winced, knowing that she shouldn't yell at Stacey as if she were a child, but wondering why she had followed the man.

"I'm not that dumb!" Stacey cried. "I know this guy from the set—he's Rick Fields, and we talked when he was on set, too! I knew that he wasn't Jesse Miller, so when he beckoned to me, I thought he just wanted to talk outside and I should have realized he had a stupid prop knife and—"

"Stacey, he was luring you out for the killer!" Mason said, trying to contain the anger in his voice.

"For the killer?" the man Stacey had identified as Rick Fields said. He sounded stunned. "No, no, no! The point was to get her to realize that she shouldn't be alone!"

"We have to move," Mason said. "We can sort out the rest at Scotland Yard."

He turned, looking down the alley, shaking his head.

"He's long gone now, but..."

"We have to try!" Della said.

He nodded. They headed off through the darkness of the alley.

By the end of the night, dozens of police, Metropolitan and City, along with every member of their Blackbird team, had searched.

And searched.

They didn't give up until the sun broke through and the dampness of the fog begin to lift. Surprisingly, it was going to be a sunny summer day, devoid of the rain that could so easily plague the city.

They were holding Rick Fields before charging him, though Edmund admitted he wasn't sure himself what the charges would be. When they'd had some sleep, they could talk to him.

Their team had broken into twos to search, as it happened, by nationality, Jeanne and François together, Edmund and Sean, and Mason and Della.

Mason, Della realized, was determined to be at her side—at least for the rest of the night. And it was all right. He knew that she was capable, but they both knew that anyone could be taken by surprise. While it wasn't always true that there was safety in numbers, with this killer on the loose, it well might be.

It was right before they headed back to the hotel for the night that Della saw Abigail Scott standing just next door to their rental home. She elbowed Mason, pointing out their helpful spirit. He instinctively looked around, but light was just breaking and they could see no one else near them.

"Abigail," Della said, hurrying to greet her.

"I was going to try to reach you!" Abigail told them. "I saw him. I saw him lurking near the pub, Daphne's, but then I saw the girl rush after another man. And I saw him produce a knife and I was going to risk making fools of you by rushing into the pub for help, but you came out and came after the two of them and I thought that I should follow the killer, but... I lost him! I searched again, all night, but I haven't seen him again!"

"Abigail, thank you. We knew he had to be near, too, but he does have an amazing ability to disappear. We—and dozens of others—searched and searched. We thank you for your help, always. And we're grateful to know that you are here, helping us when you can," Mason assured her.

She shook her head, not looking at them as she stared ahead and seemed to be seeing the past. "They concluded that one of the first murders that awful summer wasn't the work of the Ripper. The poor woman was Martha Tabram. She was killed on a bank holiday and for many, especially in this area, the holiday meant so much. They attended so many outings. August 6, 1888. A young couple lived at 47 in the George Yard Buildings. They didn't come home until after one. Another resident came home, but it was dark, and people were known to sleep anywhere, so...her body wasn't discovered until a gentleman going to work went out in the very early hours of the morning—he hadn't celebrated— he'd had to work too early. He ran for a patrolman and... she was so viciously killed, but as the day wore on, people gathered to stare. The streets were so crowded there that..." She paused, shaking her head. "Time and distance change things. I know that in your field, studying men and the past is important, but after Martha was murdered, more killing began, and if the Ripper didn't kill poor Martha, they never did find out who did." She seemed to give her ghostly self a shake and gave her full attention to them again. "He was out there tonight. And as with the old nursery rhyme, 'Humpty Dumpty,' 'all the king's horses and all the king's men' couldn't find him. But here's something you must realize to be equally important. You saved the life. And every life is precious. Some of us are born into good homes and grow into a world where we manage well. And some are struck with tragedy and poverty. Every life, no matter the material wealth of a human being, is precious. You saved a life. I wish that I might have saved any of the lives lost to that monster!"

"You're helping us. You are helping to save lives," Mason assured her gently.

"I have friends about the city, too. They let me know." She managed a smile. "How convenient it would be if we could use the newfangled things—cell phones!"

Della and Mason both smiled.

"Scratch the phone. I wish I could hug you," Della told her.

She smiled and moved forward. As the ghostly figure embraced her, Della felt a strange mixture of hot and cold.

"You must get some sleep. You must stay sharp. This man has an agenda, but he will kill anyone in his way."

She looked at Mason. He nodded. "Don't worry—we learn early on that a gun is a good equalizer that can often mean size and strength mean nothing."

Abigail nodded. "Now get to sleep, please. Go on. I will watch until morning."

"Thank you!" Della said softly again.

Abigail hesitated. "I wonder if I see him in everyone now. But, sometimes, I do believe that I've seen him, watching the house."

"Oh?" Mason asked.

"He is monstrously alive," she said, "but with the capability of disappearing into the shadows and the mist."

"One of us is awake at all times," Mason assured her. "We have alarms as well. And in the house, there are six of us, all armed."

She nodded. "And I watch!"

"Truly appreciated," Mason said.

"To be a useful human being, even if in soul only," Abigail said.

"And you have a beautiful soul," Mason assured her.

That brought a smile to her lips and she started to turn away, to begin her nightly walk of the streets, seeking to prevent much of the pain she had witnessed in her lifetime.

But she looked back at them.

"By the way, so you know, I enjoy your charming English detective inspector as well!"

Della laughed. Mason set an arm around her shoulder and they walked on into the house.

When they arrived, Sean was seated on the couch, studying his phone. He rose when they came in.

"I just returned myself. And... Well, I'll take first watch. I don't think that I could sleep."

"It is morning, I think," Mason said.

"Right. But some of us need to be functioning." He let out a long breath. "I think that we need to speak more with Rick Fields. I think that I believe he intended no harm to anyone, but who on God's good earth decided it would be all right to play a prank on someone with a prop knife when this is going on? He must know more about Jesse Miller, where he goes...how he's existing here, right here, beneath our noses, and getting away."

"Maybe. We will speak with him after he's cooled his heels, being held overnight," Della said. "Will he be charged?"

Sean nodded. "He may face a kidnapping charge. He's refused legal counsel and is willing to speak to us. Maybe he is innocent of anything but a prank, but sometimes we might be able to lock someone up for sheer stupidity!"

"We'll see what else he knows," Della said.

"And here's something else that frightens me," Sean said. "He meant Sean to lure Stacey out—then I'm sure he meant to kill her, to up his timeline."

Sean was so intense. Della lowered her head. Of course, yes. Stacey had been the "Ripper's" target that night.

And it horrified all of them. But she thought that Sean had a bit of a more personal stake in it. He liked Stacey.

Whether Stacey liked him and whether they'd acted on a mutual attraction or not, she didn't know. But both were young, industrious professionals, and from all that she'd seen, good people.

Maybe there was something there.

"We reached Stacey in time," Mason said gently.

"Yes, and we have a policewoman watching her," Sean said.

Della glanced at Mason and they both knew that Sean would feel better if he was watching her himself.

"Our Ripper wrote a letter. He claimed he'd take a victim. And we stopped him tonight. He's going to be furious," Sean said.

"I guess he will be. He'll look like a fool—his letter is out there, and no one was killed in Whitechapel tonight," Della said.

"No one that we've discovered," Mason murmured.

"I think we did stop him. But this man is truly an organized psycho. He's going to be more dangerous than ever," Sean said.

And that was true.

"Then we must be more vigilant than ever," Mason said. "Sean, I am awake. I can stay awake—"

"No, I'm fine. François went up quickly—he had just returned when I got here. He'll be back down in less than an hour. We thought that while it won't be much sleep, everyone could get a few hours, but we should get back to interrogate Rick Fields before noon."

"A few hours will be fine," Della told him.

Sean suddenly grinned. "If you sleep!" he teased, looking at the two of them.

"Anyway, I'm here until François comes down. I'm keyed up and need to key back down." He hesitated. "You two are main on this. Della, you...you saved Stacey's life. We'll knock on the door at 10:30. You get all the sleep you can."

"We take turns," Della said.

"Not tonight," Sean said. "Humor me, please."

"We won't argue longer," Mason told him. "Della, my love, let's get some sleep."

They were halfway up the stairs when they both heard him murmur to himself. "Sleep, right! If only my life were so...sleepy."

Della grinned at Mason.

"I wonder if he knows we really do sleep sometimes."

"Tonight?" he queried.

She shrugged. "I don't know. Shower first...as always. There's just something about trailing a brutal and bloody killer..."

"Yep. You can wash and wash—and not always feel clean."

"Okay, we're just taking showers," Della said firmly. "Sleep really is a necessity."

"Right. You go first."

"Well, we can still shower together."

"I don't trust myself with you and a bar of soap. Or... Wow. Liquid soap. Nope. You go first."

Della set her Glock on the bedside table first, stripped quickly and headed into the shower.

She'd grown up in South Florida with heat and humidity. It was a wonderful place when you loved being in a pool—except, maybe, in the heart of winter—but it made the refreshing feel of a shower something really special.

It certainly wasn't hot here. But she'd also discovered when she'd begun her career in law enforcement that while a shower couldn't wash away the evil man was capable of doing, it helped wash away the struggle and intensity of a day.

She didn't want to get out.

"Hey!" Mason said.

She smiled. And he stepped in beside her, reaching for the liquid soap.

She turned into his arms. "I have always been told that exercise, especially good physical and cardio exercise, really helps with a good night's sleep."

"Or morning's sleep," he corrected dryly.

"Whatever!"

She curled her arms around his neck and added, "I'm all into good exercise!"

"I'll do my best to make it a real cardio workout, too," he promised her.

In the end, they did sleep. And the few hours might have been more, but they did, indeed, turn out to be very good hours of sleep.

Mason had taken the last watch, started coffee and gone for the others. They'd gotten at least four hours sleep—not bad when morning had been cracking when they'd headed up to their room.

Edmund was on the phone with Scotland Yard while Sean and François Bisset made plans to continue investigating the movie and theater angle, seeking clues to Jesse Miller's hideout—a hideout that might be in plain sight since few people were as alert to a face shape and possible variances on an appearance as Stacey was.

François was going to continue to head to makeup shops while also combing the streets of Whitechapel and the Spitalfields area.

"There is somewhere that he is going when he's afraid that we're close, and somewhere a person can sleep—even if it's an unknown closet," Della said, smiling her gratitude as Mason handed her a cup of coffee. "Last night, dozens of police and members of other British agencies were out with us, and he eluded everyone. That must mean that he has somewhere to go right in front of us where he virtually disappears. If we can just find out where—game over."

"They were going to bring our canine corps out last night," Edmund said. "Except we need something for the dogs to go on."

"Too bad he wasn't a major player in Stacey's movie," Della mused. "We'd have his costume."

"François and I will be relentless today, I promise," Sean said. "We'll go from theater to theater. Maybe he did have a role that needed a costume in one of the movies or shows being filmed or even at a theater—and hopefully one where everything worn hasn't been dry-cleaned already."

"Edmund, you're heading with Della and Mason to question Rick Fields?" François asked.

Edmund nodded. "I'd like to observe while they question."

"When we finish with him, we'll join you on the streets," Mason promised.

They left the house and split up, Edmund driving to the station where Rick Fields was being held. They were assured that Stacey had police protection and that Fields had been under observation since he'd arrived. He'd refused any kind of legal counsel, saying he hadn't done anything.

He'd accepted coffee twice but slept with his head on the table in the interrogation room most of the time he'd been there.

When Mason opened the door to the room, allowing Della in before him, Rick Fields lifted his head, blinking.

He'd obviously been dozing on the table.

"How long are you going to keep me here?" he demanded.

"I told you it was all a joke. Listen, I needed the money for my rent. And you know I wasn't going to hurt her," he said. "You know that I had a silly prop knife, and no, I didn't steal it—I got it from Kenneth Rippon!"

"Mr. Fields," Della said quietly. "You may be young and foolish or you may be one of his accomplices."

"Accomplice!" the young man said, looking from one of them to the other.

"Kenneth Rippon, AKA Lucas Braden, AKA Jesse Miller is a murderer, Mr. Fields. He killed one of the vampire victims, he's entertaining himself with all his missives about his upcoming murders to the media, and we believe that he did commit the Ripper murder."

"Oh, no, no, no. I couldn't even give my dog an insulin shot for diabetes, I had to give him to my sister. I couldn't really put a knife or—or my teeth, I guess, into anyone! Hey, ask Stacey! Ken—or whatever his name really is— comes off as one of the nicest guys you'll ever meet. Like not a sap, but really great to others, and he could have everyone laughing while we were just doing some of the endless waiting you can do on a movie set. Ask Stacey, please!"

"I'm afraid that at the moment, Stacey is under guard— and terrified," Della said.

"No, no, I'm so sorry!"

"But you're telling us that you were supposed to scare her," Mason said.

"Right, but not... I mean, I would have told her right away—I was supposed to scare her just enough so that she wouldn't be careless. I didn't mean to...mess up her life. Stacey is great, so nice, so good to everyone, I mean... She's just nice, if you're a star or an extra."

"She is a very nice young woman," Della said. "But I am afraid that she'd going to suffer for this."

"It might have been a lot worse," Mason said flatly.

"Worse? What do you mean?" Fields asked.

"Please!" Mason said. "We just told you the man is a murderer."

Fields shook his head. "I just—I just can't believe it!"

"You can't be that naive," Della said softly.

"I don't get you—it wasn't that big a deal. Hey, I didn't make her follow me out—I didn't drag her! And you know that I didn't mean harm—"

Mason shook his head impatiently. "One more time. The man is a murderer. He wants to go down in history as a killer more heinous and brutal than Jack the Ripper. He had you lure her out—so that he could kill her."

"What?"

Rick Fields truly looked stunned. But could he really be so innocent?

"Mr. Fields, whether you want to believe it or not, the man you know as Ken Rippon is really Jesse Miller, and he is a murderer. That is a fact, whether you accept it or not. He had you get her out to that alley so that he could swoop in and take over. He knows that Stacey would recognize him—no matter what disguise he might choose for a night. Now, what we need to know is where is he staying?"

"Where is he staying?" Mason asked.

Rick Fields looked more confused than ever.

"Yes. Where is he staying?" Della repeated softy.

"I—I don't know."

"Then how did he pay you the two hundred pounds to lure her out of the pub?" Mason asked.

"Oh, he called me. And I met him and we had a pint and—"

"He called you?" Della interrupted.

"Yes, he called me."

"We're going to need to use your phone," she said, removing it from her pocket. An officer had happily given it to her after it was initially confiscated from their suspect.

"My phone?" he said, startled. "I need my phone. I get work that way."

"Well, you can't do a lot of work in jail, anyway," Della said gently.

"But I didn't do anything!" he cried. "It was a joke, a prank—"

"That could have gotten a woman killed," Mason reminded him. "Please, unlock your phone."

"I haven't been charged. I haven't even asked for legal counsel because I swear, I'm innocent of trying to harm anyone and I swear that I didn't even steal the prop knife!"

"We need to use the phone."

Reluctantly, Rick Fields reached over and keyed in his passcode, tilting the screen so that they could see what it was.

He seemed to shrink into himself, looking very young, almost like a hungry child who had gotten in trouble for raiding the cookie jar.

Were his emotions real?

Della glanced at Mason. He knew that she wanted to talk to him—out of the room.

"Excuse us for just a minute," he said.

"Wait, please! I've been here for hours and hours—"

"We'll be right back," Mason promised.

They headed out and into the observation room where

Edward was seated behind a desk, watching through the one-way mirror. He turned to them as they came in.

"What do you think?" he asked, swinging around in his swivel chair to look at the two of them.

"Mason, I think he's telling the truth," Della said.

"If he's lying, he's damned good at it," Mason said. "Edmund, you're the lawman here when it comes to charges."

"One way or another, we'll need to hold him until we trace the number on his phone. We have lots of hours left, but then, well, laws are similar. We'll need to charge him or let him go," Edmund said.

"The phone is going to be a burner," Mason said. "But if it's still active—"

"You're going to have him call Jesse Miller?" He shook his head. "Miller won't answer. He knows that we picked him up." He hesitated, shaking his head bitterly. "He knew the minute Della reached Stacey and Fields—and he managed to disappear," he added bitterly.

"Edmund, we will get him."

"Before he kills again. So, obviously, we're all thinking about the possibility of using Rick Fields. Of letting him out of here and seeing if Jesse Miller will answer a call— or come after him," Edmund said.

"Obviously, yes, we're all thinking about the possibilities," Della said. "And on the one hand, I feel desperate, too, as if we need to utilize any means to stop Miller. But, on the other hand, I don't know if we dare put this man in harm's way."

They were all silent.

"If we were just to release him—though I'm assuming at the least he could be held for assault, especially if Stacey is willing to press charges—those charges could be dis-

missed, or he could be out on bail. Our legal systems may
have different titles and syntax, but they're similar, and I'm
assuming that in this situation—"

"Yes, he could walk quickly," Edmund said.

"And be in trouble," Della said.

"She's right. If he walks, he could be in danger from
Jesse Miller without our protection," Mason said. "Maybe
our best way to keep him safe is to use him."

"He failed Jesse Miller—that's how Miller will see it.
Maybe we need to let him know that. If he realizes that
he needs to fear for his own life, he might be a great deal
more willing to help us in any way possible," Della said.

Edmund let out an impatient oath. "I really think the
man might be an idiot. I'm still not certain that he believes
Kenneth Rippon is Jesse Miller. Even the stupid play on the
name! You'd think the idiot would get it! But, of course...
Let me take the phone to tech. If it is still active, they might
be able to find his location, but that might be too much to
hope for. When he saw that we had Rick Fields in custody,
he undoubtedly dumped the phone."

"Most likely," Della agreed.

Mason handed the phone to Edmund.

"So, we promise him protection—and if he lets us know
if he sees the man, if Jesse Miller tries to contact him in
any way?" Della asked.

Edmund nodded and looked at Mason, arching a brow.

"What?" Della asked.

"We're both thinking that you should go in and talk to
him." He grinned at her. "We've silently agreed that he
likes you best."

"All right."

"Maybe we'll show him the headlines," Edmund said.

"Headlines?"

"Oh, that's right! He emailed the papers again—the old King of the Rippers! He's furious—and becoming more and more unhinged, I believe. Sorry—we were late this morning and I was here and you were going in and... Anyway, I have an actual physical copy of the paper."

He turned back to the desk that faced the one-way mirror and picked up the copy of the daily paper that lay there and handed it to Mason.

"They think they're so clever, they think they're so smart, but Jack is forever, it's all just the start. The day wasn't right, it just wasn't the night, but trust me, the blood, it will run deep and bright, she can't see that I'm coming, she shines like a light, but Jack is here, he'll put out the light," he read aloud. "Jack even knows his Mary Kelly, her body will be nothing but jelly. Jack is back, but gone in a flash, they just can't see, what will be, well it will be!"

"Is he unraveling?" Della murmured. "Or simply furious, more dangerous than ever?"

"I believe he is unraveling. Which may make him lose the facade of being the nicest guy in the world. But..."

"When we offer protection to Rick Fields, we'd better give it to him!" Della announced.

Mason nodded. "I'm also afraid that Stacey Kerry may be in greater danger from him."

"Trust me," Edmund said quietly. "She will be protected, I swear it, and every man and woman here will vow the same."

Mason nodded. It was hard enough to fear that the man would kill again before they could apprehend him.

He knew that Edmund was telling the truth and that he was disturbed.

Because it was worse when you knew someone, and that someone might well be targeted by the killer they were hunting.

But they could do it. Jesse Miller was one man. Of course, he was one man who didn't offend others, who came off as the nicest guy in the world. Rick Fields had proven to them that like Stephan Dante, Jesse Miller could lure others into acting for him.

Still, he didn't have the contacts and access to the expertly forged legal documents that Dante had. But he did have his ability to disarm others. He might not have the power to turn them homicidal as Dante had with him, but he could make good use of others to attain his goals.

He frowned. Edmund was disturbed—so was he. There was something about the last message that seemed to tease at his mind.

He couldn't quite reach whatever it was that bothered him so.

It was there...just at the back of his mind.

He needed to find it! But he had to shake it off.

If he could, eventually it would come to him.

He turned to Edmund because forefront in his mind was Jesse Miller's ability to disappear into the shadows. "Plans—Edmund, we need any city and area plans—buildings. Work that has been done. Electrical, water, everything on the underground—the first subway system was here, right? Around 1863."

"Exactly 1863," Edmund said.

He glanced at his phone. "Jackson just let me know that Angela and our technical analysts are doing everything they can to trace the killer's emails but he's using a server that's bouncing all over the globe. They'll keep at it."

"And our analysts have the phone, but—"

"We both think it's a burner."

"I'll see that Rick Fields is let out—and given a protection detail."

"We'll keep the detail but keep him in our line of sight tonight as well," Mason said. "For now—"

"You want plans. I'll see to it."

"We'll leave the others on the theaters, shops and stores— I want to figure out how the hell our man is disappearing."

CHAPTER FOURTEEN

Della poured tea from the pot into a cup for herself and a cup for Mason. François, Sean and Jeanne remained out in the field, searching for any possible leads.

Edmund was still on paperwork and details regarding Rick Fields at Scotland Yard.

She had returned to the house with Mason; his determination to understand every nook and cranny in the area made complete sense to her.

She put the cups on the table, sitting next to him and studying the various maps and plans he had spread out on the table.

"In 1888, alleys were darker. From everything I've read, there was a vast difference—truly, the poorest of the poor eked out a fragile existence. You had women like the Ripper's victims who worked when they could—and resorted to prostitution for money. Yes, many spent what money they made too quickly on alcohol, but there was little if any help for them. But the point is that the world Jack the

Ripper walked around in was a far cry from today. Darkness, alleys, the few people walking around in the wee hours of the morning were drunks, prostitutes, patrolmen on their rounds here and there and those who had to be at work at the crack of dawn. Also, workers were different—you had people working in butcher shops. If someone was seen walking around with blood on them, it wouldn't be the shock that it might be today," Della said.

Mason looked up at her. "It was easy for him to just disappear into the darkness and shadows. But that's not true today. All right, not that violence doesn't exist today or murders don't occur. The material world surrounding us changes constantly due to technological advancement, but sadly, the fact that human nature can become twisted doesn't. Anyway, Jesse Miller knows this area. And he knows something that we don't because with the amount of man—and womanpower—we have working on apprehending him, he must have the ability to disappear in a way that we haven't fathomed yet."

"Maybe he jumps into dumpsters," Della suggested.

Mason shook his head. "Not our guy. He doesn't mind being covered in blood, but he'd be loath to put himself into a pile of trash."

"I agree. Not to mention that the police checked all the dumpsters," Della said dryly. "Unless, of course, he went from dumpster to dumpster. There's a back door to something somewhere."

"Or he's going underground."

"Ah. And thus…"

"It's here. We need to find it."

"We're looking for a door to a building or a grate to the

underground in this area? Mason, we could be here a long, long time."

He shook his head. "Not just any door. He wouldn't be heading into an open business. Yes, I know, except for pubs and restaurants and tourist shops, businesses are closed. But he isn't working at a bank or a real estate firm or anything of the like. So, how would he gain access to a closed business and wouldn't a security camera, a night guard, someone see something?"

"There are businesses that can't afford security systems and guards. But I don't think that he's slipping into a business. He thinks himself too clever, too above the mundane."

"Exactly. That's why I believe that he knows something about the area—close to here—that we don't, that not even Sean or Edmund might know about."

"Tube lines, sewer lines…" Della studied the different maps that lay on the table. "It's somewhere near here," she said. "Does that help narrow things down?"

He started to answer her but his phone was ringing.

"Edmund," he said, glancing at the phone as he answered it. "Della and I are both here," he said. "I've got you on speaker."

"Good. The phone, as we all expected, was a burner. It was tossed, but they traced it to towers that indicate he had it until he was out of the area—he tossed it somewhere near the house," Edmund said.

"That's not a surprise," Della said. "We've had…" She paused, and Mason knew that since she wasn't sure if Edmund was alone or not, she wasn't going to say that a ghost had told them that she'd seen Jesse Miller in their area. "We found a few witnesses who have seen him in this area," she continued. "I think he has a hideout that isn't far from us.

SECRETS IN THE DARK

He probably even knows exactly where we're staying—but breaking into a house with six armed law enforcement officials might be a bit much for even him."

"We both think that he's got a hideout near here," Mason said. "Maybe somewhere underground."

"And thus, the maps. Have you found anything?" Edmund asked.

"A zillion miles of underground, so it seems," Mason said. "But I do think we need to start on the possibilities. And it's not going to be anything that's public knowledge or used frequently."

"A basement or cellar?" Edmund asked.

"He has to be able to blend into a crowd to get in and out," Mason said. "And maybe it's not something we'll find on a map."

"Or ever," Edmund said wearily. "One bloke is doing this! One man."

"Edmund, we will find him. We just keep looking."

"At least his messages are scaring people—except that doesn't sit well with the pubs and shops," Edmund said. "It's going to cut down on revenue. And even when there is a killer loose in a city, people start getting crazy when they can't make money."

"On the one hand, that's understandable," Mason said. "People need to pay rent and they need to eat. But, until we do get him, it's good that people are careful. And we're not telling them not to go out—we're telling them not to go out alone."

"And that women shouldn't fall prey to charming men," Della added dryly. "Have you heard from the others?"

"We've changed things around a bit. Sean is with Stacey. I think he's having a bad time thinking that anyone else will be as capable. He really respects her, and…maybe more. I warned him not to get too involved, but he has a good head on his shoulders. We have patrolmen on Rick Fields, and I'm planning on seeing if he's approached myself. Not to worry—I'll keep a distant tail. Jesse Miller may try to contact him—and, of course, wants to kill him, but he can't do that in a public place. He knows that. But he may have other *friends* willing to get a note to him or something. François is going to call you himself—they found a theater where he was working for the makeup department during their last show. You'll appreciate this—he was Reggie Chapman when he worked there and he was let go. The show was a children's play with trolls and monsters, and they were going through too many supplies and it seemed that they disappeared when he was working. They couldn't charge him with anything because they had no proof, but the director wanted him fired."

"That's how he managed his prosthetics," Della said. "We knew he had to be getting them somewhere. Do they have an address for him? If he was on payroll—"

"Oh, yes. They had an address. I guess no one realized that the address that he gave them was an apartment that would be in the middle of the Thames," Edmund said.

"Of course," Mason said.

"We're still at it, but… We can find out where he's been. We just can't find where he is now."

"It's still good to know we're on the right track and so far, our instincts have been right. He is going to want to get his hands on Stacey—that last letter he sent over the air seems to target who he wants for his Mary Kelly."

"And he has decided that he doesn't have to follow the original schedule he set for himself—he may have determined that he's going to go in whatever order he chooses," Mason said. "I'm going to leave the maps and plans. Maybe you'll see something that we don't. We're going to walk around the blocks closest to us and see what we can see."

"Find Abigail. He can't be on the lookout for her," Edmund said.

Apparently, he was alone as they spoke.

Mason had already planned on looking for Abigail.

"We'll meet up here as usual. We'll let you know of... anything," he told Edmund.

"All right. Stacey isn't going out—she's going to work with Sean dogging her every step and another patrol officer on it as well. I have a good crew following Rick and as I said, I'll be following up on that bloke, too. He's ready to jump at the drop of a hat. I explained just how long he might enjoy our penal system but that he wouldn't do time at all if he helped. But Della, whatever you said to him worked. He's ready to help."

"I just mentioned that he'd fallen prey to the whims of a homicidal maniac and that he needed protection, even if he chose the penal system," Della said.

"Well, it worked. He's ready to trip over himself to help us."

"Something will give, Edmund. If we get a true handle on where he has been, we can better get ahead on where he's going to be," Mason assured him. He glanced at Della. "We'll get back to you. We'll head out now and try to find a hideout."

"Right."

Edmund ended the call. Mason looked at Della.

"Feel like a leisurely stroll through the charming streets of Whitechapel?"

"But of course," she assured him.

They left the house and Mason paused to look at St. Botolph's.

"He's not using the church," Della said.

"Oh?"

"Abigail would know."

"True. She walks around it, as the prostitutes were known to do long ago and she watches the house we're in and the surrounding area from there," Mason agreed. "I don't see her now."

"She's out looking for him. She's determined. It's a pity we can't give her a job."

"She'd need to go through the academy," Mason said lightly.

Della rolled her eyes and grinned, walking ahead of him, turning onto the main street of their block.

The first building housed a candy store.

The second was a clothing shop and the third was a pub.

"Shall we ask about their wine cellar?" Della suggested.

"Might as well. But..."

"You think we're missing something."

"I do. But maybe what we're missing is at the pub."

They went in and Della murmured to him, "Maybe this is a place we should try at night. If he has been watching the house, he might use this as a lookout point—if he sits at the bar, he can see outside. Mason, I think he might have watched the entrance to Daphne's from here—you can see the door! He would have seen Rick Fields go out—followed by Stacey. But he wouldn't have gone after her—because he saw us follow right on her heels."

"And he'd know that Rick was going to be taken—and

that there wouldn't be any way to get Stacey farther back into the darkness of that alley."

"Let's see if they've seen him."

Like many of the establishments in the area, the building was old but much of the inner facade had been updated. The bar itself was rich polished wood, the stools were crafted from the same material, the front windows were sheet glass and shiny chrome accents created an appeal that made the place feel comfortable, historic and modern all in one.

They ordered two pints, with Della smiling and chatting up the bartender, an older man who turned out to be George Harley, the owner of the pub. They had arrived before the early evening time when workers, off for the night, stopped by, so the two carried on a pleasant conversation before the bartender mentioned that they were never sure if they were going to be dead slow—or slammed, what with the news and the warnings going out.

It seemed the right place to get truthful and serious so Mason pulled out his badge and phone, explained that they were on an international team and asked him if he'd seen the man in any of the sketches Maisie had created.

Now, they also had a picture of Jesse Miller—as Jesse Miller—provided via email by Angela and her team.

Harley wasn't put off by their questions; he studied the pictures and handed the phone back. "Maybe, I'm not sure. There's been a chap in here a few nights who might... Well, he's not exactly like any of these, but... Well, something is similar in these renderings and the man I've seen. Not like the actual pictures you have of him. The man I've seen is... I don't even know how to explain. He has dark, dark hair, blue eyes. No beard, but a mustache. His nose is big, though, and he has a funny pointed chin. An Aussie or Kiwi, I think, from his accent."

Mason produced a card from his pocket. "He's not an Aussie or a Kiwi. He's a master of accents, changing his appearance and his story wherever he goes. He's a murderer, and he's being hunted all over the city. Surely, you've seen the news."

Harley swore and then quickly excused himself to Della. She smiled and waved a hand in the air before saying, "Trust me, I share your sentiment. We want to get him before he has a chance to kill again."

"I will call, so help me, if I see anything at all!" Harley swore, looking at the card. "My father owned this pub and his father before him. If he continues preying upon young women, he will send us all back to the days when poverty ruled here. Whitechapel today is a district that is diverse and thriving, rebuilding all the time. I will help in any way."

"Well, you *can* help more, if you don't mind. Do you have a wine cellar?" Mason asked him.

"Wine cellar, storage room, old stone foundation basement, really, here since the late 1700s when this building went up,"

"May we see it?"

"Of course," Harley said. "But—you think that this man is hiding in my cellar?" He shook his head. "I don't know how that could be possible. I close here, and I'm the man who opens, too."

"We don't know, either," Della said, "but we'd love to see the cellar and get an idea of what is underground."

"I've got some good wine down there," Harley said dryly. "And some okay wine, too. I have some kegs, and some spirits and… Well, come along. You'll see."

There wasn't another bartender, or even a cocktail waitress to be seen.

There was an older man at the bar and Harley called out to him. "Jagger, keep an eye on the place if someone stumbles in while I'm gone. Back in a flash."

He nodded to Mason and Della, indicating that they should follow him around the bar. Della glanced at Mason and he knew what she was thinking. The place was popular with a local crowd. Mr. Harley was well liked by his clientele. But apparently, the stairs to the cellar were behind the bar, and she doubted that anyone slipped in and out of the pub without being noticed. Still, they should see the cellar.

They followed him down an old wooden stairway.

Mason didn't think that Harley had a housekeeper, or even swept down in the cellar often.

But there were kegs lined up against a wall with a refrigeration system that was also used for wines that needed to be kept cold. The latter were stacked up in a new chrome-and-glass shelving unit. Shelves lined the floor as well with bottles of vodka, rum, whiskey, cordials and more.

There was a door at the far rear of the cellar.

"Where does that lead?" he asked Harley.

"Cleaning materials, lad, but come, I'll show you."

He led them to the door and opened it.

"I think they put the woodwork in here in the 1800s," he said. "Odd that they paneled a room like this—can't think of anything done down here that would require this room to look a bit nicer—as far as I know—and that's from way back, nothing was ever kept here except for cleaning supplies and the odd bit of necessary machinery now and then. Like I said, it's an old place, an old building, and while I'm old, I'm not that old!"

As Harley had said, the room had shelves that were stacked with all manner of cleaning supplies. And while the cellar might not be swept or dusted often, the bar and restaurant area of the pub were clean and shining.

Della smiled at him. "Mr. Harley, this place is wonderfully historic, and still so comfortable a pub! It's a great place."

"Then you'll come back when it's not on business?" he asked.

She glanced over at Mason.

"I think we should come tonight!"

"First pint is on me, lass!" Harley promised.

"Now, there's a deal," Mason said. "Thank you. Mind if I walk around in here?"

"Of course not. Go ahead, my friend."

Mason walked into the room, curious. The shelves were everywhere but the far wall, but the wood paneling there appeared to be just what it was. He saw no possible place in it that might give way to a secret door.

And, unless the man was lying and he was among the Oscar-winning category of actors, the only way down was from behind the bar.

They headed back up the stairs, thanked him again and went out.

He glanced at Della. "All right, what's bothering you?"

"Why would you put paneling into a storage room? The rest of the place is just…ground, I guess. The flooring looks as if it's been there since the pub was built!"

"Still, there was no sign of a blanket, a bucket for a bathroom or personal objects of any kind," Mason said. He paused. "I think we might want to talk to our archeologists again. Seriously, think of all the digs that have gone on when something is discovered when a new tube station or the like is being built. Maybe there's something here that we don't know about. And something that isn't going to be on the maps or plans for the city."

"We didn't try the candy store or the clothing shop," she reminded him.

"I know. But we might want to go in having some idea of what we're looking for."

Della nodded. "Good point. Okay, so one of us can have a chat with Professor Goodridge and Dr. Mayberry. They may know something about this area that wouldn't have come up in our conversations before," Della suggested.

"Mayberry or Goodridge?" he asked her.

She shrugged. "They both seemed like nice and decent people. Okay, coin toss."

He nodded. "We won't bother with the coin. You can have Lucretia. Let's do this. Despite his missives to the public, I think we infuriated the killer by getting in the way of his murder last night. He'll be speeding up his agenda because he has to prove to us that we can't stop him. I'll call Bisset and he'll set it up."

She nodded and listened as he made the call.

They headed out from Harley's cellar, thanking the man again for all his help.

Mason noted that Della looked back at the man curiously as they were leaving.

"What? You have a feeling there's something wrong with him?" Mason asked.

She smiled and shook her head. "No, I'm hoping that everything is right with him. He seems like a decent guy— keeping a family business going through generations. I like him. And I hope I'm not wrong."

He smiled. "Your people radar tends to be good. I just—"

He broke off and she prodded him quietly, "You just…?"

"We had him. We had him before we knew we were looking for him, and he got away."

"Mason!" Della chided. "You must stop haunting yourself with that thought! Even if we had stopped him, he would have disappeared again. We had absolutely nothing to hold him on. It's not illegal to flirt with a young woman at a pub. Seriously, he would have walked away no matter what, and we'd still be trying to find him."

"Right. I know."

"Then let it go," she said firmly. "Onward!"

"Lucretia is at her rental flat. Bisset says it's right across the river. Edmund is sending a patrol car—the officer will drop you and then take me on to speak with the good professor."

"Meet back at the house after?" she asked him.

"Yeah. Edmund said you can call for a car—"

"I'm not wasting police on a ride across the river," Della said. "This is their city, Mason. They're on it, too."

"True, but—"

"Special dispensation, Mason. I'm armed. Armed and capable."

"I know."

"I worry about you, too!"

"I know. But I'm not the Ripper's type."

"I'll be careful!" she promised.

The car came for them, a good-natured officer driving, assuring them that he didn't know a man or woman in law enforcement who resented anyone's help in catching a killer, and his current assignment was just to move people around to where there might be something they could discover. He gave them his number to ring straight through if they needed him.

They thanked them.

It was after they left Della off at Lucretia Mayberry's flat that he finally realized what had been bothering him about their new Ripper's messages to the media.

The *she* the man wanted might just be Della.

Lucretia seemed honestly glad to see Della.

Maybe she was just happy when someone was interested in the past and the peoples of the past.

"I've been at sites in the Middle East and Africa that are truly amazing as far as discovering the evolution of man," she told Della, "But I admit, I love being right here, in London. There's just such a richness in the many centuries and the population through the centuries. And the discoveries that we make, and for me…sadly, much has to do with the tragedies man has faced. The bubonic plague that seriously struck London in 1348 killed about sixty percent of the population—we unearth bodies from those days more often than you'd care to think. Before the plague, circa 1315, there was a famine—and we find truth of events throughout history through the bones of the dead frequently. Even Professor Goodridge unearths a microcosm of amazing human events. Plague, of course, would continue to arrive every few decades, taking more and more people. And, of course, no one can forget the Great Fire that burned down about eighty-five percent of the city! We discover so much!"

Della smiled and nodded while she listened.

"I'm curious. Is there anything you can tell me about the area where we're staying in Whitechapel. Were there previously digs in the blocks surrounding St. Botolph's?" she asked.

"Whitechapel, of course, has a rich and varied history," Lucretia said. "The center of the area is Whitechapel High Road—the name derives from the little chapel of St. Mary's, and it ran through with the old Roman road. Through hundreds of years, it was where immigrants came. At one time, there were over a hundred and fifty houses to shelter the poor and desperate. Entire families lived in one-room flats. No sanitation... I can't imagine the misery of being there!"

Della thought of Abigail Scott. She had been an impressive woman, determined that others see the way that some had to live.

She nodded again. "What I need to know is... We think that the killer we're seeking is moving underground, but we're trying to figure out how."

Lucretia was thoughtful. "Well, sad to say, in the area, there were murders that occurred before the Ripper. Domestic disagreements, robberies gone bad... In fact, when the Ripper first started, the cry of *murder*! meant little in the streets."

"Is there a way, perhaps, to discover if anything went on in that direct area? Or, perhaps, even in the time before the Ripper."

She smiled. "Underground London is amazing, as I'm sure I've said. I don't know of anything in particular at this moment, but I can do some research on the anthropologists and archeologists who have been here in the last years."

"I would so appreciate that."

"I can say that your theory is more than just possible. People apply to dig a cellar when they haven't had one—

and bones are discovered because the property once held catacombs. Then again," she murmured, shrugging, "as I said. The area was horrifically poor—and that meant that it could also be horrifically violent. Muggings, assaults and robberies going on, constantly. Oh! Not to say that all the people were bad, quite the contrary. Most were just struggling to get by, and maybe even find a way to make a better life for their children." She paused, frowning. "I have an idea of where to start. In the late 1700s, there were strange disappearances in the area by the church. The Metropolitan Police Act wasn't in force until 1829 and before that you had elected constables, but none paid, and as populations increased so did crime. Some of the buildings near St. Botolph's were owned by the younger son of a titled family, a man named Nathaniel Bradenton. He was thought to be somewhat of a shady character, resentful that he'd inherit just about nothing while his older brother would be set for life. His own daughter left behind a diary that is heartbreaking to read—she feared that her father was half-mad, and she didn't know what he did in the late hours of the night that so often caused him to come home disheveled and *almost foaming at the mouth, like a rabid dog*, according to her diary. I don't know if the area has been inspected or if there has been any building that would call for discovery of the underground, but I will see what I can discover."

"We will so appreciate any help that you can give us," Della told her.

"Of course! I will help in any way!"

There was little else that Della could do regarding the possible history of the underground that she needed until Lucretia had time to do her research. She smiled, thanked her and left.

Despite the kindly patrolman's offer to come running when bidden, Della decided just to call a rideshare. She thought it would be faster; it was.

But she had herself dropped off on the corner across the street from the house they had rented. They had gone into the pub, but they hadn't stopped by the candy store or the clothing shop. She wondered if she should get Edmund or Sean to join her, but she was there now and it seemed to her that time was becoming more and more important.

They had to find Jesse Miller before he struck again.

She started with the candy shop.

It was impressive; customers could watch toffee being made in one corner. In another corner, fresh nuts were salted or mixed in with honey or other additives.

There were rows and rows of every candy imaginable to man, and an impressive register area with giant candy canes as if they were the gateway to a magical kingdom.

There were employees working throughout the shop but Della headed to the young woman behind the giant candy canes. She couldn't have been more than twenty or twenty-one, blue-eyed, dark-haired and energetically cheerful.

"Hello there! How may I help you?" the woman inquired politely.

Della smiled and produced her badge, which, of course, just confused the young woman until she explained that she was part of an international unit seeking the man who had murdered a woman so brutally as a "Ripper."

"And you think he's here?" she asked in horror.

"No, no, certainly not now," Della said. "But we're looking into possible hiding places—"

"Oh, my God! No, no, we have security cameras! They're

manned through a central station where someone is always on duty," the girl informed her.

Della nodded. "Is there a cellar here?" she asked.

"A cellar?"

"Basement, cellar."

"Um, yes. We store ingredients down there and my boss, the manager, has his office down there."

"Would it be possible for me to see it?" Della asked.

The girl frowned, confused. "I—I don't know. He isn't here right now. And... I mean, you really have jurisdiction here?"

She smiled. She should have called Edmund.

"I'm not looking to arrest anyone here or cause any problem or hardship for the business. I'm just trying to see the layout of the underground."

"We would never help such a monster!" the girl protested.

"I'm not suggesting you would," Della said. "We're looking for any anomaly in the ground, in the buildings, in the size of the space beneath the ground floors."

"I, uh... I will make a phone call," she said. "Excuse me."

Della smiled and waited. She looked around the shop, fascinated. She'd been a few places where there might be one candy-making station, but this was exceptional. The walls were freshly painted, chrome and glass were everywhere. It was light and bright.

Which made her wonder about the entrance to the cellar; she couldn't see where it was.

"Miss...sorry, Miss Agent, I've spoken with Mr. MacFarland and he says that of course, I must show you anything you need to see. Let me just get Vickie to watch the register and we'll go on down."

"Thank you. And please convey my thanks to Mr. Mac-Farland."

The girl nodded and waved to a friend, explaining briefly that they needed to go below.

Della discovered where the stairs to the cellar were—behind another set of giant candy canes.

The candy canes were in fact a modern addition to the handrail that followed the stairs to the ground beneath.

The flooring here was brick. Della thought that it was brick that had been there for two centuries or more.

The manager's office was to the left and in the center and to the right were rows of shelving that contained supplies for the store. The walls appeared to be naked brick as well, even in the office. But someone did sweep and clean down here and the cellar seemed to be well ventilated.

"Well, here we are," the girl said.

Della frowned suddenly. Just as in the pub, there was a closed door toward the rear of the basement.

"What's in there?" she asked.

It was in alignment with the little room in the back of the pub. Did that mean anything? Did it just mean that the builders had liked little rooms at the back of a cellar?

"Cleaning supplies," the girl said. "We carefully keep them separate from any of our edible materials!"

"Of course," Della said. "May I?"

"I—sure."

Della walked across to the little room.

Like the supply room in the cellar of the pub, it was paneled.

She had to tell Mason and the others after one more stop. It might mean nothing.

It might mean everything.

She carefully studied the walls in the little room, but again, as in the pub, she couldn't see where a break might exist.

It was time to check out the clothing shop.

She thanked the girl and assured her that if they needed help in the future, they would go through Mr. MacFarland, the manager.

"I didn't mean to put you in an uncomfortable position," Della said.

"It's okay, really." She smiled. "I'm Liz, by the way, and I understand what you're trying to do and I greatly appreciate all your efforts—this man is terrifying! But why can't the police get him, stop him?"

"Because he's disappearing somehow, and the where and the how are what we need to know," Della said. "And we truly appreciate all the help we can get."

"Of course!" Liz was energetically sincere and Della thanked her again.

"Wait!" Liz said as Della turned away.

Della hesitated, hopeful that Liz might have thought of something she might have seen that could be helpful.

"Would you like some candy?" Liz asked. "We always have samples!"

"Um, thank you so much. Not right now. But maybe I'll be back with a few of my partners—and we'll all have a sample. Everything looks great!" Della said.

She managed to escape out to the street.

One left.

The clothing store.

And if there was a little paneled supply room at the back of the cellar there, lining up with those in the candy shop and the pub...

Was it enough to warrant them going in to knock down walls?

She wasn't sure at all.

But she was convinced that Jesse Miller had been watching them at the house—and not from afar. He had been within a hundred yards of them, night after night.

And, yes.

There had to be a way to discover just how.

It was remarkable, the way he could see them so frequently.

And irritating, of course, when they went in different directions and he didn't know where they were going or what they were doing.

But they wouldn't find him. Because no one could find him. No one had ever been privy to the information he'd discovered.

Information so very fitting.

That day, he had managed to watch. He had seen them go into the pub. Close, oh, so close, and yet so far away!

And he had seen when *she* and Tall Mister Macho Agent had driven away in a patrol car. Were they always stuck together like glue? So, so annoying.

But it didn't matter; his plan was surely foolproof. They relied so heavily on technology, and one little clip of a wire could change all that. And yet, did he even care if he was on camera? Because he was ever-changing, ever-evolving, as only a criminal who could disappear into history could be.

He was yawning, about to give it all up, when he saw her.

She was alone.

Heading into the candy shop.

He smiled to himself again.

Close, oh, so close! Yet...

No. They couldn't possibly discover the truth. Not in time. Because he'd carefully made his plans, carefully planned for every contingent.

His time with his "Mary Kelly" was coming, so much sooner than they might imagine. Sometimes, a man had to reinvent history, just a little.

And "Mary Kelly" had to be dealt with immediately.

He smiled, leaning against the building across the street from the candy store, the clothing shop and the pub. He could see her at the counter in the candy store, talking to the young woman right behind the candy canes.

She was a pretty thing, too. Naturally, a whore. Since he was doing things a bit differently, she just might suffice as his Catherine Eddowes.

But all that could come later. He had only one interest at the moment.

His Mary Kelly.

Beautiful, with those startling green eyes, sweep of soft pale brown hair. Her laughter was musical, her walk was a dance...

He couldn't wait to see her eyes, those emerald eyes, staring into his when she knew that it was all over, that nothing could help her, nothing could save her.

She was his.

Time...yes. Patience was one thing, necessary for him. But there was that time when patience was no longer necessary.

And if *she* was back, the others would return soon. They would sit and share what they had learned—none of which would help them any—and then they would order their dinner.

And he was here. Right here. None of them could see him. None of them was around to see him, to see that he was always near, so close, watching them running around, chasing their tails.

But soon…so very soon!

They would know.

CHAPTER FIFTEEN

"Quite honestly, I arrive when something has been discovered, and, of course, I'm an American, a guest here," Professor Goodridge told Mason. "I would, of course, help you in any way, and, naturally, I know about many important discoveries, but... I'm sorry. I've heard nothing about a cache of ancient bones in your area, or fragments of the Roman or medieval past. The buildings you're asking about were largely constructed after the Great Fire—not to say that there wasn't history occurring after the 1600s, that's ridiculous, of course. And not that discoveries haven't gone on forever! Most people believe that Richard III had his nephews murdered soon after his elder brother, Edward's death in 1483. Richard managed to get the princes declared illegitimate and housed them in the Tower and then...voila. They disappeared! In 1674, workmen at the tower discovered the bones of two young men or boys. Some say the princes might have escaped their uncle, some say someone other than Richard murdered them, but the bones exist and sadly, it seems likely to me that they are the bones of the murdered princes. They lay hidden for over a hundred and fifty years and finding them was almost sheer accident. That is often how the past is discovered—by sheer accident. And... Sorry, you don't much care about the princes in the Tower," Goodridge ended, appearing worried and chagrined as he looked at Mason.

"No, I imagine your lectures are fascinating," Mason assured the man. "It's just that right now—well, I'm trying to prevent other murders."

"I wish I could be of greater assistance. Of course, I will look through all my resource materials and see if I can find something, anything, that will help you. Of course, Lucretia is filled with all kinds of knowledge as well—"

"Della has gone to see her, so we're hoping, between the two of you, one of you may find something. And, of course, we thank you for your time," Mason told him.

As he walked up the embankment from the dig, he heard his phone ringing. It was Della.

He answered it more anxiously than he would have liked.

"Hey. Are you all right? Everything okay?"

"Yes, fine, I'm back by the house—"

"You called the patrolman?"

"Mason, I didn't think that a random driver would be after me. I called a rideshare and I'm by the house, safe and sound. I went to the candy shop—down in the basement, there's the exact same room. A paneled supply room."

"Did it look as if anyone had been living in it or using it to sleep?"

"No. But it's along the same line as if... Mason, I think that there might be tunneling that either connects—or at one time connected—the buildings. And if I'm right, I'll find the same in the clothing shop I'm going into now. Then I'm heading to the house and we can ask Bisset and Edmund if they can find legal maneuvering for us to get down into those rooms and explore more fully."

"Tear down walls."

"Well, yes."

"We will need both François and Edmund to assist in that."

"Where are you?" she asked.

"Just leaving."

"Did you get any help?"

"Not really but Goodridge is going to see if he can discover whether there is something historically notable about the properties that we should know."

"Lucretia Mayberry is doing the same. But she had an interesting story for me. Apparently, the buildings there were all owned by the poor younger son of a rich and titled man, and in her diary, his daughter wrote about his erratic behavior. People disappeared around him. I think his own daughter suspected him of being a murderer. But, of course, there were never any bodies."

"You think that he buried them in the basement in the wall?"

"That's possible. But I'm also thinking that he had tunnels through his buildings—and that's how he disposed of his victims."

"All right. I'm heading back and I'll be there soon. François and Edmund are heading back there now, too. Sean has decided that he's not leaving Stacey's side, and I've said that was fine—she needs protection until this over. But we'll have dinner like normal people and I agree with you—we need to pursue this line of investigation. We'll run it all by the rest of our unit—minus Sean, we'll catch him up when we can. Meet you at the house."

"See you there," Della said.

Mason ended his call and hurried on up to the road. He didn't call the patrolman, either.

Rideshare seemed faster.

And he wanted to get back as soon as possible.

The clothing shop was not pretentious. Specials were advertised and clothing was arranged with men's to the left and women's to the right. More formal wear was in the rear, while the center held the items that were on sale.

It was nice, Della thought. But she had liked the area around St. Botolph's. It offered such findings as the comfortable pub, the unique candy shop and this place where the average man and woman might shop without going into debt.

As in the other two establishments, the interior had been updated. The clothing racks were a shining silver, the walls were freshly painted, and she was greeted by a handsome young man in casual attire as she walked in and surveyed her surroundings.

Once again, she went through the routine of showing her badge and explaining her position in the United Kingdom.

He was quick to understand—shaking his head over the Jack the Ripper murder and even more so over the way the killer was taunting the media.

"Strange, of course. There were hundreds of letters sent to the police in 1888 and they believed that the majority of them were hoaxes. But when I see the news and what this horrid excuse for a human being is saying, I think that it is him. And we have created a good working man's neigh-

borhood here, a reputable place where people come, and…
Well, what can I do? What could a twenty-two-year-old
shop lad possibly do to help you?"

"Do you have a cellar?" she asked him.

"Yes."

"May I see it?"

He shrugged. "No management is in, but…it's a cellar."

"What do you keep down there?"

"We buy wholesale before we sell retail. Stock. Lots of
stock. As you can see by my name tag, Special Agent Hamilton, I'm Mark."

"Mark, thank you. In the cellar, is there a little room?
One where you might keep cleaning supplies?"

"We have a little room but we don't keep cleaning supplies in it. Mr. Woodridge has his office there."

Mark frowned suddenly. "Wait. You think this man
might be hiding in this store? I'm telling you, that's not
possible. We have cameras. There's even an alarm on Mr.
Woodridge's computer. No one could come in and out of
here. I promise. Oh, and he can be a hard case as a boss, but
he's also good to employees who work hard and—no pun
intended—meet the mark." He grinned at her. "In other
words, Mr. Woodridge isn't a crazed killer."

"We don't suspect that he is," Della said. "But I'd still
like to see his office, if it's possible. What I'm looking for is
structure."

"Um, okay. Let's head on down!"

He called to another young woman who was working,
indicating that he was going below. She frowned and then
shrugged.

The stairs were toward the rear of the shop—wooden
stairs that had probably been there for years and years.

This cellar contained row after row of clothing hanging from racks, shelves with sweaters and more still in plastic wrap, and more shelves filled with shoeboxes.

But the shop didn't lack cleaning supplies—they were just kept to the far right in a little nook.

A door led to a room…

A room placed just as the supply rooms in the candy shop and the pub.

Mark opened the door for her. Mr. Woodridge kept a neat office. His laptop was large and closed, his desk was shiny wood—and the security cameras in the room were clearly visible. There were three chairs that could be drawn up to the desk and fine wooden filing cabinets to round out the furniture.

"Just an office," Mark said.

"Yes, just an office."

An office—with the same paneling she had seen in the other shops.

But that was all she needed for now.

She thanked him sincerely, gave him her business card and told him that she might see him again.

"I do hope so!" he told her.

She smiled.

"I mean, only in a good way. I would help. I know that Mr. Woodridge would help. I mean, I'll tell him about you being here—I'm supposed to, right?"

"Yes, of course, please tell him. I believe he'll be hearing from the British authorities—they may be asking for his help. And thank you again."

Della left the shop, anxious to reach the others and tell them what she had discovered—and what she thought it might be.

No, the shop owners and managers weren't helping the killer.

They were clueless. But that long-ago murderer Lucretia Mayberry had told her about might well have paved the way for their current killer.

She headed across to the house, carefully looking around before keying in the alarm, then heading on in and resetting it.

"Hello!" she called.

No one replied. She was the first one back. Anxiously, she looked at her phone, hoping that maybe Lucretia had called her and she'd missed it. No such luck. But as she looked at it, her phone rang. She smiled. Not Lucretia.

Mason.

"I'm here, I'm fine, I'm safe—I'm in the house."

"I'm almost there. Sorry, just…"

"It's okay. I like to check up on you, too. And, of course, anyone we're working with."

"I just talked to Edmund. He's been following Rick Fields all day and Bisset has been at headquarters, going through the many, many sightings of Jesse Miller—which we were going to get after the press conference—but nothing came of that. The people who called in seemed to be well-meaning, but they saw him, and he was gone. A few of these sightings were checked out—one man turned out to be a history professor, another a plumber, both not Jesse Miller and both married with children and neighbors who vouched for him. Now, neighbors vouching for someone may not always be the truth, but…the men that were seen were not Jesse Miller."

"Well, I want to hear everyone's opinion on my belief that there's something underground near us—and not even the people who live and/or work in the buildings have any clue."

"We'll figure it out—those guys are headed there and I'm back any minute."

"Great."

Della ended the call and walked into the kitchen to heat the teakettle. She set her bag down on the counter, but, as she reached for the kettle, she turned and looked at the door to the house's basement.

The house had been utilized by Scotland Yard before their unit had moved in. Della knew that it had certainly been thoroughly checked out.

And yet, she'd been in basements all day.

Curious, she left the teakettle where it was and headed down to the basement.

CHAPTER SIXTEEN

Mason was let off directly in front of the house. But before he could enter, he saw that the ghost of Abigail Scott was standing across the street, anxiously watching for him.

He waved to her and walked over to her.

"I've seen him," she said anxiously. "I saw him today, he was lurking…just watching the house, walking around, looking different in the afternoon than from the morning, and changing again as the evening came on. But he's been watching the house, watching you…and then he's gone again! Maybe…just maybe, one of you needs to be here. I can watch…and when I see him, let you know. You don't have to worry about me getting in the house—I can manage just fine. What terrifies me so is that when he disappears—he disappears! I try to race after him, but… He's here, and then he's gone!"

"Della believes he's hiding underground somewhere— we just have to find out how he's accessing his hideout," Mason told her. "But we will. And I believe you're right—

one of us must stay at the house tomorrow. And wait. And when you see him, let us know immediately and we'll be out there and… Well, hopefully we'll manage to get him before he hides again."

"You'll be out again tonight?"

"Indeed. Yes. We'll be out there because he's out there."

"I'll be watching, too," she promised. "I'm so distraught that… I just wasn't fast enough."

"He's smart, but he's angry, Abigail. We did manage to stop him from getting to Stacey. He wrote a missive about his murder, and he couldn't carry it out so he wrote in another threat."

His phone was ringing as they spoke. He picked it up when he saw that Edmund was calling.

"Edmund, anything?"

"Well, it's nothing crucial, unless you're really hungry. We're going to order Indian food—a place that Sean knows well, though he won't be with us. Best curry in town, he tells me. That okay?"

"Indian is good with me," he said. "Best curry in town sounds fine." Mason thanked the detective inspector before hanging up.

He grimaced at Abigail and said, "We'll be back out in a few hours. He's dangerous now."

"And an officer is with that young lady—"

"Stacey, yes. Sean is concerned. He's afraid that the killer won't be dissuaded, that she'll be his target. Other officers are working, guarding her and, of course, we have the young man who lured her out under guard, too. We're afraid that Jesse Miller will go after him, too. Miller knows that we brought Rick Fields in, so…"

She nodded worriedly. "All right, please, go ahead then.

Your dinner will be coming and, as you say, we'll all be back, walking the night. Please, know that I'm here, that I'm out here, that I'm working with you."

He smiled. "I feel like Della. I wish I could hug you, though I'm not sure if that was proper in your day."

"Well, Special Agent Carter, it is your day. And I will do my best to hug you."

She came forward, her ghostly arms surrounding him. He felt the strange warmth that came with the chill and did his best to hug her back. Then, of course, he realized that he was on a public street and carefully straightened, smiling at her all the while.

She laughed. "Ah, we must take care! It will not do if the man who might stop a murderer is locked up instead!"

She turned and headed down the street. Smiling and shaking his head, Mason headed toward the house.

He came in to find that Edmund Taylor, Jeanne Lapierre and François Bisset were seated at the table, studying their laptops.

"They've now received hundreds of tips on the hotline," Edmund said, looking up when he entered the house. "Hundreds. We're looking through them, but..."

"I think we know where he is—right here somewhere, under our noses."

"Yes, I explained to Edmund and Jeanne that you went to see the archeologist and the anthropologist because you believe that he's getting underground somewhere here, near us," François said. "Or, he's simply slipping into one of the businesses. And there are flats above some of the businesses. But we've had police knocking on doors—not banging down doors, mind you, just warning the residents to be careful. There is little else that the city is talking about, and every neighbor who has a dispute with another is suggesting that the object of their animosity is the killer."

"Unfortunately, that's human nature. You can vilify just about anyone who angers you," Mason said. "But we do need to go through everything because something real could be in there along with all the panic. Then again, we can eat, give up computers for the night and do that fun thing—troll the pubs for a killer."

"Dinner should be here any minute," Edmund said. "I will be ready. I keep forgetting lunch—and it's here!"

"Dinner. Wonderfully welcome. And while we French don't have the culinary availability of the best in Indian cuisine, I have cultivated a wonderful love for curry!" Jeanne said.

Edmund headed to the door to get their delivery. As always, he walked a few feet behind, ready to draw his Glock should the delivery not be what was ordered.

But Edmund accepted the bags, thanking the delivery-woman, and assuring her that her tip was on the app. The young woman delivering the food was attractive and seemed to find Edmund to be so, too. She smiled, thanked him and said that she'd be delighted to be their delivery-girl again.

Edmund grinned as he closed and locked the door.

"Our young *ami* has a conquest!" Jeanne teased

"The lass was lovely. Maybe one day when we're not so hot on a killer…"

"Ah, *mais oui*!" Jeanne commiserated.

"Need help with those bags?" Mason asked, grimacing.

Edmund laughed. "I only need to make it to the dining room table. But you can help me open the bags."

"I will get napkins and silver," François offered.

"And I am famished—I will open the boxes as Mason sets them out."

Mason distributed the food out, thinking that Della would come down while he helped, but she didn't.

Mason smiled and looked up the stairs. "Is Della up in the room?" he asked.

Edmund looked at him and frowned. "She must be here somewhere. She'd been about to put the kettle on. She must have run upstairs for something—I haven't seen her yet."

"But she's here somewhere—I checked the cameras as we were arriving and I saw her return to the house," François assured him.

Mason frowned, wishing he didn't feel a sense of unease so instantly.

He needed to behave like a normal person!

He managed to nod to Edmund and say, "I'll check upstairs."

"Wonder if she fell asleep!" Jeanne mused. "I wouldn't blame her! But wait!" Jeanne already had all the boxes of food open and he'd dished out yellow rice onto a plate. "Wait, seriously, taste this. You will then lure her down quickly for a delicious dinner among coworkers and friends."

Mason wasn't sure that he felt hungry himself, but in the vein of diplomacy, he accepted a bite of the rice.

It was good. He wasn't that big a curry fan, but the rice was excellent.

"I'll go lure her down," Mason said.

"Maybe. If she fell asleep, I'd leave her. Sleep has become such a precious commodity," Edmund said.

"Trust me, she's not asleep. I'll run up."

"Good timing," Edmund said, looking at his phone. "The food is delicious and—"

"We should politely wait for Della," François announced.

Seeing the stricken look on François's face, Mason laughed. "I know Della and she will not mind in the least if you get started. You eat—and I'll go get Special Agent Hamilton."

"Now there's a plan we can carry out," Jeanne said lightly.

But Mason moved up the stairs quickly.

Della was not in the bedroom. And while he respected her talents and her abilities and knew that she was a damned good agent and an amazing shot, he felt an unease he couldn't tamp down seeping into his system.

Something was wrong. Something was happening tonight.

The basement in the house was finished nicely. It had painted walls, a water heater, storage containers and shelving—and sofas, a TV screen and a Ping-Pong table.

Nice! Since the police department so often booked the property, it was natural that they'd supplied entertainment for whatever officers—for whatever reason—might be doing a stakeout or other reconnaissance in the area.

But it also had a closed "utility" area—just like the candy and clothing shops across the street and the pub.

She was startled when her phone rang but she answered it quickly, expecting it to be Mason. But to her surprise, her, "Hello," was quickly answered by a woman saying, "It's Dr. Lucretia Mayberry. Special Agent Hamilton?"

"Yes, yes, it's me, thank you. Did you find something out?"

"I'm not sure. But I told you about the owner of the property in that area, how his own daughter thought that he'd gone crazy and was doing terrible things?"

"Yes, yes, of course."

"Well, there was never a *dig* so to say, in the area. But a water heater was being replaced—and right in what they call the Prince Edward house—he supposedly visited there, you know, the poor prince had a horrible reputation. Anyway—"

"A house near the church?" Della asked.

"Yes, quite near. And right across from a candy shop now, I believe. Anyway, in 1935, when the owner was doing some repair work after a leak in the basement, he discovered that there was a tunnel leading from the house. Personally, I think it should have gone farther, but it solved, I believe, one of the mysteries that came before. The owner was horrified—bones were discovered in some of the brick-work. Of course, he quickly had them removed, and sealed the door and… I don't know what was going on in 1935, but there wasn't much of an investigation. I suppose they knew that the bones had been there over fifty years—there should have been an anthropologist called in—the killer was dead, and they chalked it up to Mr. Nathaniel Bra-denton, but, of course, he was dead, his family had sold all their property and immigrated to the United States, so…"

"But if there was a tunnel under the house, it led some-where, right?"

"Quite possibly. There are areas where we do find his-toric treasures, graveyards, medieval settlements and Roman settlements, often one on top of another. From Roman to medieval times, there might have been anything. Layers of history. I'm assuming that your coworkers can contact the high-ranking British powers that be and get permis-sion to explore further. We have technical equipment that can help make sure we don't destroy property, but most people would be eager to find something historical and…

Well, this may help you find a hideout and give something to posterity! I would be more helpful, but I think that most people will listen to someone in law enforcement rather than go on a hunch by an anthropologist."

"Thank you, Lucretia," she said. "Thank you so much. If you learn anything else, please tell me, and I promise, we'll keep you apprised of everything that's going on."

"Terrific!"

They ended the call and Della paused, looking around the basement again. London was old. Not with the depth of years as Africa or the Middle East, but...

The present often lived over the ashes of the past.

And while she couldn't be sure, their current residence could very well be what was once referred to as the "Prince Edward" house.

She walked to the back where the brickwork appeared to be comparatively new. She could imagine the owner in 1935, discovering that his basement led to a burial place. So, yes, he'd had that area bricked in—he wouldn't want to continue thinking about the bones that had greeted his workmen. But still...

Maybe she had watched too many detective movies as a kid. The kind where you twisted a bust of William Shakespeare and a fireplace revolved to allow entrance into a secret room.

And maybe it was logic.

She didn't believe that the killer had been in the house; there were six of them living here, always with someone on guard. There were cameras and alarms. No, the killer hadn't been here, but...

If there was a tunnel behind the brick, it could lead the

way to the place where Jesse Miller had been hiding, slipping underground and appearing to disappear into thin air.

The question was...

Just how thorough had the workmen been in 1935?

She began to go over every brick, every nook, every cranny. It occurred to her to think about geography. Where would a tunnel correspond to something that could lead beneath the ground and across the street?

In the back, in the little room corresponding with those where one man had kept an office and others had kept supplies, she found a wooden bookcase flush against the wall. It was filled with old volumes—and new ones. Nonfiction and fiction, reading materials perhaps for the officers who had taken their rest alone and weren't into streaming the latest series or playing Ping-Pong.

She frowned, noting a slight break in the brick behind it.

The thing was heavy. She was strong—hours in the gym with other agents—but she didn't know if she was strong enough. That was all right. She could get Mason and the others if...

She managed to budge it, inch by inch, pulling it away. There was the slightest crevice in the brickwork, but...

The brickwork was old and hastily constructed. She sought for something to work against it and found a bottle opener out by one of the couches.

She used the metal against it and a brick fell to pieces and when it did, she was stunned to see the others in a two-foot area crumble and fall. Only a little light filtered into the darkness beyond, but she had to step through, just a few feet, to see if she had, indeed, found a tunnel.

She was right, thanks to Lucretia! This tunnel led somewhere, and that somewhere would be where Jesse Miller was hiding, dropping into the earth…

Disappearing for all intents and purposes.

She turned to head out, to hope that Mason had made it back.

She couldn't wait to explore the realm of darkness that beckoned beyond!

Mason had reached the first step to head back downstairs when a physical occurrence added to his gut feeling of apprehension.

The house fell into stygian darkness.

He was tempted to call out quickly to Edmund and the others; he didn't. Instead, he carefully and quietly made his way down.

He felt a moment's dizziness as he did so. He gave his head a serious shake. He moved forward again, his hand automatically falling to the Glock in the holster at his waist. He was fine for another few steps, then the wave hit him again.

It was almost as if he'd been…drugged.

Impossible. He hadn't had anything to eat or drink in ages except for the bite of yellow rice.

The yellow rice.

He fought the dizziness, telling his physical self to get over it—he'd had one bite. But when he reached the foot of the staircase, he had to carefully make his way to the table.

He couldn't see, but he could feel. Mentally seeing the layout of a table, he found the chairs and his hand fell on a head; *Edmund's*, he thought. He quickly sought a pulse at the man's throat. Edmund was alive, just out. Moving around the table, he found François and Jeanne—both in the same condition, out cold, but having a pulse.

Drugged. They'd made a major mistake. They'd ordered out. Jesse Miller had watched the house; they knew that. And he was quite capable of charming people, paying them to do his bidding. There was no telling what he'd managed to tell the pretty delivery-girl. But he had managed to get his hands on their food. God knew what was in it. He needed help for the men, and he knew that he desperately needed to find Della.

Find her, or get help first?

He never answered himself. He felt a presence at his side. Abigail Scott.

"He's in here!" she whispered. "I never know what he I s doing sometimes, I thought he was wandering...whatever, but he's managed to cut the lights to the entire block and I don't know what else, but it's cut the cameras and the security at the door. Dear Lord! These men... But I don't think they're meant to die."

"Just Della. With none of us stopping him," Mason said.

And the dizziness was gone. He felt a horrible fury seize him and he knew that he had to fight it as well.

"She's not upstairs," Mason said. "But you know she's in the house."

"I saw her come in. She didn't leave."

"Then check the bedrooms upstairs. I'm going to try the basement."

"Of course!" Abigail said. "And I will be with you shortly!"

He felt her leave him and he carefully made his way through the house to the kitchen. He had his penlight on him, but he didn't want to attract the attention of the killer.

Not until he found Della.

He made his way blindly through the kitchen to the doorway and the steps to the basement.

Determined to be silent, he made his way down through the abyss.

"Come out, come out, wherever you are!"

The whisper was close, coming just seconds after it seemed that the entire world had turned black as pitch.

For a split second, it caused Della to freeze. She was still in the hole in the bricks, but since they were in a tumble before and around her, light would quickly show her whereabouts.

Unless she moved more deeply into the darkness of the tunnel.

Still, he would follow her.

She had barely moved when she felt him behind her and then an arm swept around her and she felt the steel of a blade at her throat. She'd left her bag with her Glock upstairs, but she had her Baby Browning in the holster at her ankle.

But with the blade at her throat...

"So, you have been hiding down here," she said.

What had happened to the others? Had they even returned to the house? If not, they'd be on their way. She just had to keep him talking.

"No, not here," he said. "But what a delight that you discovered this! I didn't know the tunnels came this far. I watched you, of course, pretty, pretty, Special Agent Hamilton! I knew that you'd figure it out soon. No, I haven't used the shops—none of your respectable store owners are involved." He paused to laugh. "There's an entrance through the sewer line, but once you discovered the entrances through the stores, well, it was only a matter of time. But...you're out of time."

"I don't think so," she told him.

"You don't think so? I have a knife at your throat."

"The others are here or will be," she assured him.

"But they ate the curry!"

"They ate the curry? I wouldn't count on that," Della said. "I mean, I'm supposed to be your Mary Kelly, right? That means you need a lot of time. I don't think you're going to have it."

"I'm telling you, they ate the curry. Hey, not even I can see so completely in the darkness, but your big strong men were crashed into the table."

"All of them? Did you count?"

"Well, you're down a few. You for one. You're here with me!" he said, whispering in her ear. "And that local fellow, Inspector Detective Sean Johnstone. He's following Stacey around like a puppy dog. Poor lad. He is so smitten! I will get to Stacey, but you've forced my hand, I've had to change my order."

His whisper against her ear was fetid. She was surprised to realize she felt an even greater fear for the others.

She knew to be afraid, to be seeking any chance...

The curry. They'd been drugged.

"Some people don't like curry," Della insisted.

"Ah, but you are all so polite! Ready to dine on whatever others want. So...there is no help, Della. Think of it this way. You will go down in history! Historians and researchers and armchair detectives will know you were the second victim of the King of Rippers, that you were the most desired, the most wanted...the most tenderly given time and care! No, of course, you are Special Agent Della Hamilton, so I'm wary of you! We will move out of the tunnel here, out of the room and to the couches. There, we will have our fun."

She wondered at what stage she might dare escape him to reach for her Baby Browning. But, of course, he was wary...

Wary of her, but he didn't know that she carried the Baby Browning. He believed that her bag was where she'd left it in the kitchen, her Glock with it.

"Fine. Let's move out."

"My knife will stay at your throat."

"If I ask you to move it, will you?"

He laughed. "No. And I'm not sure why you're not saying, *hey! If you're going to kill me, do it now, do it here. Oh, wait. You've got your knife at my throat, I'm not going to let you be perfect—you kill me right here and now.* Oh, but wait. Everyone clings to hope, right? You can hope people didn't eat the curry, but they did. And I saw Special Agent Mason Carter enter the house, too—before the curry! But, okay, you go ahead, live on hope!"

"I can live on hope. But you're not supposed to use that knife against me. It's believed that the Ripper strangled his victims first, so you'll be screwing that one all to hell."

She felt the blade press tighter for a second; she'd angered him.

"You already caused me to change things up!"

"You started by changing things up! You didn't kill down-and-out prostitutes, some so sad and desperate they became alcoholics—"

"All women are whores!"

"Ouch! Wow, someone sure hurt you. Or was it your pride and dignity that they hurt. Oh, and you couldn't be the Vampire King—that's Stephan Dante. So, pathetically, you already had to change that up, too."

"I am going to have so much fun with you!" he hissed. She winced, feeling the spittle that sprayed from his mouth with his anger.

But it was then that she felt something else. A strange sense of cold that was also oddly...warm.

Abigail.

And the ghost whispered to her, "Keep him talking. Mason is here!"

Those words gave her greater strength and hope than she might have ever imagined. And to her surprise, Jesse Miller waved his free hand around, as if trying to rid himself of a fly.

"Damned cold basement!" he muttered.

"Oh, it's not the basement, it's a ghost," she said.

"There's no such thing."

"Oh, but there is."

"One of the Ripper's victims, right?" he said.

"Lie!" Abigail said.

"It's Mary Kelly," Della lied. "She's stroking your arm right now. And she'd going to haunt you from here to eternity. Feel her?" she asked in a hoarse whisper.

He wrenched her arm behind her back with his free hand, keeping the knife tight on her throat. They were halfway out to the center of the basement, rounding the picnic table, she thought, though even shapes of things were almost impossible to see.

Abigail stroked his arm, just as Della had suggested.

He almost jumped; he still had the knife tightly set to her throat.

"To the couch."

"Feel her, feel Mary, feel her anger..."

They were getting closer and closer to the couch. Time was running out and she knew it, but she also knew that Mason needed the sound of her voice.

She knew he couldn't shoot blindly in the darkness; he could hit her.

"Stop it!" he shrieked.

"You think that she's something. When I'm a ghost, I am going to make your life an absolute living hell!" Della promised.

And that was it; he shoved her so hard that she flew away from him, crashing back heavily on the couch.

But it gave her the opportunity to reach for the Baby Browning.

She never had to use it. She heard Mason's voice in the darkness as he spoke to Jesse Miller.

"No ghost, Mr. Miller. Special Agent Mason Carter right behind you. And that thing protruding into your back is a special issue Glock. One move and we'll be giving you the opportunity to haunt us as a ghost."

She thought that Miller froze. Mason flicked on his penlight with his free hand and she saw that Jesse Miller didn't want to die himself.

"Drop the knife," Mason ordered.

Something in Miller changed. He had wanted immortality. Maybe he thought he still might achieve it with the murder of an FBI agent.

He didn't drop the knife; he lifted it to hurtle it at Della. She and Mason both fired.

Jesse Miller went down and, thankfully, the knife flew into the couch, killing nothing but the upholstery.

The would-be Ripper on the floor moaned. Della leaped to her feet to join Mason.

"I was afraid I'd hit you," Della said. "I aimed for his knees."

"I think it's a through and through. Depending on whether I hit vital organs or not," Mason said. "And Sean Johnstone's crew will be pouring in any minute—I texted them on my way down the stairs. And…"

He stopped speaking, pulling her into his arms.

They held there together for seconds that were also timeless.

Then a floodlight filled the basement as officers came hurrying down the stairs, someone assuring Mason that the men upstairs would be all right, reaching for Jesse Miller who was so injured that he'd lost all fight.

With the light now flooding the basement, Della could see the ghost of Abigail Scott, standing just to the side.

Della inclined her ear to her. "Thank you!" she mouthed.

Abigail nodded grimly and they all watched the action now taking place.

Medics came rushing down, too. Jesse received the attention needed to save his life.

His eyes were open and he stared balefully at Della.

Mason walked over and looked down. "Hey, you should have listened to her. Not everyone likes curry!"

EPILOGUE

François Bisset, Jeanne Lapierre and Edmund Taylor were mortified. No matter how many times both Della and Mason tried to tell them that it might happened to anyone, they couldn't believe that they had been taken down so easily.

Of course, they found the young woman who had delivered the food. And she was horrified and in tears when she found out that she'd been taken. Jesse Miller had charmed her, telling her that his best friends were staying in the house and he just wanted to slip a little note in with the food. He'd tried to pay her, but she'd believed him that he was just trying to reach his friends in a new, fun way, and she had thanked him when he'd held the bags for her so that she could quickly answer a phone call.

They decided not to press charges; some people were capable of punishing themselves and Mason believed that she was one of them. And it might have been a good lesson in life learned as well. She would be careful of the men she allowed to charm her in the future.

"That's the scary thing, right?" Edmund said quietly to Della as she was escorted from headquarters. "People think that killers are monsters. That they're going to behave or look like monsters. Some do. But…the scariest killers are those who appear to be angels on earth."

Della nodded.

They'd been thanked for their work by their superiors in England, the United States and France, but it had been Jackson Crow who had talked to them. They needed to be briefed back at Quantico, and with their international agreement, that meant all of them.

Blackbird would continue to fly.

The media, of course, had wanted everything. She and Mason managed to get Edmund and his superiors to deal with the frenzy.

Because they had a few days.

In that time, Lucretia Mayberry was given the necessary permits to begin a historical search, along with an archeological team, on the tunnels beneath the streets that Nathaniel Bradenton had created when he'd owned the whole lot of properties—a place to dispose of those who had disappeared during his particular reign of terror.

Sean no longer needed to guard Stacey, but they quickly learned that he wasn't leaving her side, anyway.

The attraction that had begun was growing.

And who knew where it would lead?

François and Jeanne hopped the Chunnel for a few days at home.

Mason and Della went on the London Eye, or the Millennium Wheel, where he teased her, wondering how such a tough agent could get nervous at heights.

The view was spectacular.

They visited the original Madame Tussauds.

They acted like tourists.

They left what had, indeed, once been called the "Prince Edward" house and spent their few nights in a beautiful hotel right by Buckingham Palace.

And when they finished being tourists, they came back to their room and played some more.

Entering their room on their last night, Mason set his arms around Della's waist and whispered from behind, "Take it off, take it off!"

"Oh!" she teased, spinning around in his arms. "I can do that!"

She grinned and did a sensuous body twist—and slid her Glock from the holster at the small of her back.

They might have been tourists, but they were still Blackbird.

He grinned at her.

"Now you!" she teased.

"Well, I don't do it quite so well..."

"Anyone can learn."

His Glock went down on the bedside table.

He cleared his throat.

"I meant more than that."

"Oh!"

Once again, she grinned, twisted and writhed, and the Baby Browning came out from her ankle.

"Nice, but... I guess I'm just going to have to show you!

She laughed, flying into his arms.

He showed her every move he could think of, and those

that grew from within. There would be another case soon. There would be other nights, but this one…

This one ran beautifully late.

And when they slept, it was deeply.

Still, the sun had barely risen when Mason heard his phone ringing. He reached over to the bedside table and answered it sleepily, not looking at the caller ID.

He was startled by the hoarse, mechanically altered voice that came to his ears, speaking three words, and three words only.

"Vampires are real!"

"What is it?" Della asked.

He shook his head, frowning. "I'm not sure…"

He saw that his phone was ringing again. This time, he looked at the caller ID.

It was Jackson Crow.

"I don't know," he told her. "But I think I'm about to find out."

★ ★ ★ ★ ★

New York Times *bestselling author
Heather Graham has Blackbird confront
their past when the murderer behind
their first case breaks loose!*

Read on for a sneak peek of
Cursed at Dawn

PROLOGUE

Yes, he was bleeding.

No, he didn't care.

He'd replace the blood soon enough. Because for now...

They were rushing to make sure the bleeding had stopped. He lay with his eyes closed, waiting. The right moment would come. They checked his heart; they monitored his breathing...

The medical profession offered people who were rather pathetic. They took their Hippocratic oath, and then they were bound to save every man. Of course, many of them tended to think they were gods and had the power of life and death. Arrogant gods. But even gods could fall. Like Dr. Henson. All around him, people were rushing to save the life of the prisoner who had been plugged with a shiv in the dining room.

Rather foolish! That prisoner might well get the death penalty from either the federal government or the state of Louisiana, not to mention the other places he faced charges.

But of course, his intent was to live.

And he had faked the riot in the cafeteria with a little help from his friends.

He was good at making friends. He was such a nice guy.

"Steady," the nurse said, issuing a sigh of relief. "His blood pressure was so low...but it's climbing. A hundred and ten over seventy. I think we've got the bleeding stopped."

"I guess whoever hates this guy hasn't got the best aim in the world," the doctor said, shrugging. "Well, I guess he'll make trial. Or trials. I understand the charges against him are massive, and a lot of people want a piece of him. We have provided the whole so they can all have their pieces. Sometimes...yeah, well, we're here to save lives, right? Even if they don't deserve to be saved. Yep. We save lives. I'm going to get the guards to get back in here—we'll keep him in the infirmary, but I want him cuffed to the bed."

"He may not make it yet, Doctor," the nurse murmured. "I saw the floor where he was lying when they dug him out the pile of prisoners. He's lost so much blood. I hope the transfusions are enough—"

"I want him cuffed. Hold tight."

It was going just the way that he wanted—the way the axe murderer, Justin Miles, had said it would. So much for high security! Guards outside? But then he'd been a dying man, and they'd worried so to save his life; it wasn't good for prisoners to die in the penal system.

The doctor went out. And it was a piece of cake.

A stab of the needle into the nurse who was so shocked she never let out a peep. Then a very brief wait for the doctor. He waited behind the door, seizing the man in a neck lock the minute he walked back in, cutting off his breath...

Cutting off any chance of him screaming.

High security, right. Men running around, armed, all ready to keep prisoners under control.

When the first two guards walked in, they naturally assumed that he was the doctor and then…well, then they were easily dispatched—dead or dying, he wasn't sure. He arranged the room so that the bodies couldn't be found quickly and the stage was set. The nurse was out of the way in the closet. The doctor was on the table in prison garb, ready for a transfusion because of the massive amount of blood found with Dante's fallen body.

Except, of course, there was no chance that any amount of blood would help the man.

With the doctor's wallet, keys and clothing, the rest was easy.

Accused of so many horrendous murders! Expected to receive the death penalty.

And there he was, smiling and waving as he walked out into the sunshine. And freedom.

He could already envision his next…transformation. A beauty, of course, sleeping in eternal peace and immortal in beauty.

He could almost see it.

He could almost *taste* it.

He truly was king.

CHAPTER ONE

"I still don't see how it was possible," FBI Special Agent Della Hamilton said with frustration. Their new "special" FBI unit had worked so hard and taken such risks to arrest and incarcerate Stephan Dante, the self-proclaimed King of the Vampires, that it was unimaginable he had managed to escape while awaiting trial.

Della and her partner were headed back to the United States ready to meet with the horrified warden of the jail where Dante had been awaiting trial. They were both exhausted but wired because they hadn't slept since they'd heard the news the man was back on the streets.

Just days after they'd finally caught up with one of his protégés who had shed the concept of competing in the vampire field to become King of the Rippers, they had learned Stephan Dante had somehow managed a miraculous escape. He had killed the doctor who was desperately trying to save his life, had sent the nurse to intensive care where she remained and had killed one guard and seriously wounded another on his way out. He'd walked easily into the sunlight after having taken the doctor's clothing, identification and keys—and had simply driven away. The most bizarre thing seemed to be that it was on tape, though Dante had managed—through a tech friend he'd met while incarcerated, Della believed—to create false images of the infirmary while he had carried out his attacks with a scalpel.

They hadn't been "vampire" assaults and kills.

They had just been murders and attacks that had been expedient. He had a way of killing he considered to be unique and special. But he was also a cold-blooded killer who would rid himself of anyone who got in his way by any means necessary.

"Dante continues to carry out the impossible." Mason Carter, seated at her side in the FBI's Blackbird plane that was rushing them back to the States, shook his head and stared straight ahead as he spoke. "He manages to befriend every criminal who can do something he wants done or provide something he needs. I've never seen a criminal as capable of accruing funds and forged documents in the way he has managed." He let out a sigh. "I've been conflicted on the death penalty all my life. You execute the wrong man—or woman—and you can't fix it if you're proved wrong later. You let a man like Dante live and...others have already paid the price."

"He never made it to trial, Mason," Della reminded him. "This is horrible, but it isn't on us. And we will—"

"Get him again," Mason said.

He was still staring straight ahead. She wasn't worried about Mason as her partner—no inner conflict would interfere with his abilities as an investigator—or as a man to have at her back. He was adept at numerous martial arts, proficient with a knife and also a crack shot who could move with incredible dexterity, speed and quiet when necessary. He had blue eyes that could appear as dark as the deep blue sea—or as piercing and cold as shafts of ice. It didn't hurt that he was a dark-haired man who stood at a good six-foot-four. But, as they all knew, a bullet or an explosive could kill, no matter your size or expertise.

He had told her once that a good agent's mind was the greatest weapon they could carry.

She just worried about whatever torture he might be putting himself through. He'd been military before the FBI and had been responsible for the apprehension of some of the country's most heinous killers. He had seen his last partner gunned down before him. He had grown weary of killing. He'd been working solo until he and Della had met on a case in a Louisiana bayou, taking down a serial killer there before becoming the first chosen agents for Blackbird, a unique unit created to help when the very specialized assistance the Krewe of Hunters could give was needed in Europe.

They had worked with local law enforcement from Norway, Scotland, Ireland and France. Interpol liaison François Bisset, French detective Jeanne LaPierre, English detective inspector Edmund Taylor and Norseman detective Jon Wilhelm would be joining them the next day.

Their sixsome had followed Dante, in one way or another, through France, Britain and Norway, then back to the States.

They'd all expected to be here. Adam Harrison and Jackson Crow had set up two meetings for the group of them at Quantico—one to debrief and the other for a chance to discuss the future of their new unit within the Krewe of Hunters.

Della wondered if Jackson and Adam knew things about their team that they didn't know themselves. They had discovered that Edmund, a striking and formidable-looking man in his thirties, could converse with the dead. As always, very few among the spirit world chose to communicate with the living for their own reasons. But she didn't know about Wilhelm, Bisset or LaPierre. Law enforcement might often speak about protocol, especially within different countries, but in meeting people one seldom just asked bluntly if their fellows could see the dead.

They were back in the States, but with Stephan Dante on the loose, they could be heading anywhere in the world in the days to come.

"Mason, we can't second-guess anything," she said quietly. "We take oaths. You and I both believe in standing up and honoring them. We follow the law," she reminded him.

He smiled and turned to her. "Of course. I just... I just thought we were done worrying about him. And seriously? It was nice being tourists in London. For what? All of three days."

She grinned back at him. "They were good days, though, right? They had to end because we were due back here anyway. And I talked to Jackson earlier. When we get Dante locked up again, we get a month. He promised."

"Right. Unless something else happens," Mason said.

She shook her head. "I know Jackson and Adam. They're busy building up Blackbird, and in time we won't be the only American representatives."

He nodded and turned on his tablet. "Not sure if all this is the order in which it occurred, but this is still just... I don't see how…all right, according to the reports, Dante was bleeding out so badly it was assumed he wouldn't make it. He wasn't cuffed to the bed because everyone thought he was all but dead. He grabbed the scalpel when the doctor and the nurse were urging quick care and ordering blood for transfusions. People ran out of the infirmary, he downed the nurse and then the doctor, and stole the doctor's clothing, wallet and keys. Two guards walked in and he took care of them. He had apparently already gotten someone to somehow get him a fake MD's identification and all the right certifications to slip into the doctor's wallet. How the hell did he go from bleeding to death to slashing others and escaping in the blink of an eye?"

"Well, he isn't a vampire," Della said flatly. "The problem with Dante is he doesn't use force as much as he uses charm and wiles. He is an extremely clever, intelligent man. I believe he's one of those people who constantly studies online. And as we've known, he's great at making friends among the killer elite."

"Killers, forgers, bank robbers… I doubt he bothers to befriend those who can't do anything for him. I just don't understand. Then again, I still don't understand how Jim Jones got nearly a thousand people to drink poisoned Kool-Aid. The power of the mind is incredible," Mason said.

"Beyond a doubt. We've said it before—people believe because they want to believe. They grasp onto concepts and ideas that work for them because they're down and out, because they're bitter or because they're in pain. Some are too smart to be swayed, but I believe our Mr. Dante recognizes those he can control and those he can't—and he wastes no time on those who aren't going to fulfill any of his needs."

"That's true."

"The power of the mind," Della murmured. "I spoke with our friend and colleague, Special Agent—Doctor— Patrick Law. He warned everyone Dante might pull something. They believed they had him in control because they had so much security he couldn't possibly escape."

"They tried to save his life," Mason muttered.

"They're bound by their oaths, too, Mason—oaths similar to those we took as law enforcement."

"I know. I know. The Hippocratic oath," Mason said.

"No choice," she reminded him.

"So, we know he's out. We will learn more on the particulars of how he did it. But he *is* out—so his escape isn't the question."

Della nodded and looked out the window. They would be landing soon. She rested her head back against the comfort of her chair wishing they'd managed to sleep.

Smiling grimly, she turned to Mason.

"He has escaped but the main question remains," she said quietly, "just where will he strike next?"

When a high-risk prisoner manages to escape, he had to have had help, Mason believed.

While Della headed to the intensive care unit at the hospital to interview the nurse who had a slim chance of surviving the assault, he worked with the warden, a man named Roger Sewell, who was still in disbelief that such a thing could have happened.

"I'm sure you have already heard the particulars, but I'll go over them again," Sewell told him as they walked along the aisle where prisoners spent short incarcerations or awaited trial.

"It started in the cafeteria with the riot. Ridiculous thing, of course. No matter how hard anyone tries, there's always a pecking order in a facility like this. You wind up with rival gangs within the walls themselves. Someone hit someone else in the face with a spoonful of grits. Then all hell broke out with food flying back and forth. Crowd insanity followed, several guards were injured and Stephan Dante was found on the bottom of a pile of men with a blood pool the size of Texas under him. Naturally, we rushed him straight to the infirmary, calling the doctor, warning that the prisoner might exsanguinate within minutes."

"You found him in a pool of blood," Mason said. He imagined the scene—and why guards and a smart man might be fooled.

"With a toothbrush shank still in him."

Warden Sewell was a serious man, known for having handled the facility in his charge with diligence. He ran a tight ship while respecting human rights as recognized in the country and the state. His guards respected him. There had never been such a serious incident during his tenure. He continued disgustedly with, "Food fights happen. Gang members *gang* up on a target and break his nose. But this food fight—ridiculous food fight—escalated into disaster."

"It wasn't a ridiculous food fight," Mason told him, pausing along with the warden at the cell where Dante had so recently resided. "It was planned. And that pool of blood didn't all belong to Dante—some of the blood, sure. But you're going to find you have one or more other inmates who lost *pools* of blood in that fight."

"Wait, you're trying to tell me Dante planned a food fight to escape? But he didn't attack any of the guards. He didn't—"

"He planned to get to the infirmary," Mason told him.

"Just as he found someone—someone here on a more minor charge—to rig it so Dante's assaults on the staff weren't seen on the cameras. One of your prisoners is a damned good tech guy who breached the system."

"No. That's not possible—"

"Warden, I'm not throwing any stones here, trust me. This man has taken all of us in one way or another. But I doubt your guards were all asleep at the wheel. And when the police ran the security tapes, they saw nothing but a nurse moving back and forth across the infirmary. We know Dante assaulted his caretakers. And the guards who then tried to stop him. And then—caught on camera—he used the dead doctor's identity and clothing to escape. Oh, yes, Dante was shanked. But he's a man who made sure he drew blood without hitting any of his vital organs—"

"You think he shanked himself?"

"I do. Or he had a friend hit him in just the right place in just the right way."

"But the blood—"

"The 'pool the size of Texas' belonged to one or more other men. And a forensic crew would find DNA so mixed it would be worthless. But trust me, the entire escape was planned from the time the first spoonful of grits went flying," Mason told him grimly.

"What do you need from me now?" Sewell asked him. "What the hell can I do now to help?"

"Interviews. I need to speak with anyone who was close to or friendly with Dante in any way."

Sewell nodded. "Start with his cellmate?"

Mason nodded. "Have him brought to an interview room. I'll observe him for a few minutes before going in. What's the man's name and what is he in for?"

"Terry Donavan. His third DUI in a month involved a vehicular manslaughter charge."

"Sound like an alcoholic and not a cold-blooded killer. Interesting that he was in with Dante."

"Overcrowding in the system, I'm afraid. Special Agent Patrick Law had suggested we keep Dante in solitary, and we were planning on moving Dante to follow the suggestion." Sewell paused, winced and shook his head. "We were planning to do the right thing—just waiting on the move. We have some hardened folks here, awaiting their days in court. One man is accused of killing his entire family for the life insurance payouts. Another in here is presumed guilty of five robbery invasion homicides. Sometimes it's hard as hell to see the forest for the trees."

"Gotcha," Mason assured him.

"Observation here," Sewell said, stopping by a door. "Entry to the interrogation room just down a few steps."

"All right. Tell the guards not to shackle the man. I'm going to have to build up some trust—get past whatever blind faith he might have in believing whatever lies Dante might have told him."

"You think Terry Donavan might be involved? He's… in my mind, the man is a pathetic waste of what he could have been. In here, he's polite, agreeable and, as it appears, truly remorseful for what happened. Went through hell when he first came in—in fact, the doctor Dante killed helped get Terry through the worst of withdrawal when he came in here. If the kid—"

"Kid?"

"Sorry. He's just twenty-three," Sewell said.

"Right. If he'd had help and embraced it, he wouldn't be where he is," Mason said.

Sewell nodded. "Step on in. I'll get Terry in there," he said, pointing to the stark interrogation room.

"Would you mind seeing if you can arrange coffee and water for us both? Sounds like he's the type who just might help if I can reach him."

Sewell nodded. Mason stepped into the observation room, looked through the glass at the room with its simple table—equipped with attachments for shackles when necessary—and gray walls and flooring. That was it. The table, the walls, the floor. Planned for focus.

A minute later, he saw a guard bringing Terry Donavan in to sit. The man sat. But he wasn't shackled and after he'd been left alone a few minutes, he began to pace the floor.

He did look like a kid. Short hair still showing something of a rakish and shaggy appearance, movements nervous, eyes caught in a concerned face as he walked the few feet within the room.

The guard returned with two cups of water and two cups of coffee. That seemed to perplex the young man even further.

Mason waited another few minutes. Then Terry Donavan sat again, looking suspiciously at his cup of coffee before sipping at it, then letting out a sigh as he apparently decided it hadn't been laced with any kind of poison.

Mason stepped out of the observation room, nodded to the guard, thanked him and headed on in. He took the seat across from Terry Donavan.

Donavan looked at him nervously.

"Who are you? Why are you here?"

"My name is Mason Carter," Mason told him. "Special Agent Mason Carter. And I need your help."

"You need help—from me?" Donavan asked nervously.

He looked around the room as if afraid someone might be watching him, might see him.

Guards were watching. But Donavan wasn't afraid of the guards. He was afraid of the possibility another prisoner might hear him.

Or maybe even Stephan Dante himself.

Mason nodded, leaning toward him, deciding to first use what he knew. "You know your doctor is dead, right?" he asked quietly.

He saw the young man look down quickly and wince. The doctor had meant something to him. He had helped him.

"That had to be…an accident. I mean—"

"Terry, I know you were in a cell with Stephan Dante. I know how mesmerizing and hypnotic the man is capable of being."

"He never hypnotized me!" Donavan protested.

"Dante doesn't sit you down in a chair and tell you to count backwards while concentrating on a point," Mason told him. "He charms you—the same way a dad might charm his child while telling a bedtime story. He talks and creates a new world. And it's all right—trust me. Plenty of men and women have fallen for his stories, so well told. And you fell for him, too. If you help me, I can talk to the district attorney. It will help."

"I never meant to hurt anyone—"

"I believe you. Addiction is as terrible disease. And the doctor who gave up his life is the man who helped you through the agony and suffering of withdrawal."

Donavan looked down again, not wanting to face him.

"Why?" Mason asked very softly. "Did Dante promise no one was going to be killed as he planned his escape?"

"If someone died, it was an accident—"

"It's not an *if*. People died. And it wasn't by accident, Terry. Stephan Dante killed the doctor and took his clothing and his wallet and car to escape. Hard to do that if—"

"He was just going to knock him out. You know. Drugs. It's an infirmary. They sedate people all the time—I mean, seriously, our infirmary is like a hospital setting!"

"You don't sedate a man with a scalpel," Mason said quietly.

Donavan looked down for a long moment, his thumbs moving nervously as his hands lay on the table. He shook his head.

"Terry!" Mason said. "Hey, I can tell. You are not a bad guy. You didn't want to hurt anyone. Alcoholism is a disease, and it can take a hell of a lot to cure it. The doctor who finally led you on a path to relief—"

"Hey, I'm locked up awaiting trial where they'll want to put me away forever," Donavan said bleakly. "Had to get cured in here."

"But it could have been a cruel cure. In fact, if withdrawal isn't handled correctly at the level you were drinking, you could have been left to rot and die. But they did things here by the law—even using compassion where it fit. Dante killed the man who offered you every kindness and every ounce of compassion. How the hell can you still stand up for him?"

"I—I—I never thought the doctor would die! The doctor or anyone else. And you don't understand," Donavan told Mason, shaking his head. "And you must be blind. Don't you see it? Stephan Dante tells the truth. He said he'd be out. He said it was easy to play the authorities when we all played together. He did it. And he's coming back for me."

"He's coming back for you?" Mason asked.

"Yes! He will regain his power and all that was taken from him. And when he does have his power again, he'll come back. And he'll find us, wherever we are. He'll come in glory, and he'll sweep us away to his place where his believers become immortal—"

"Oh, good God, Terry! You've had trouble, yes, but you're don't seem to be a stupid man. Seriously, you believe that?"

"He has already done what he said he'd do!" Donavan reminded Mason.

Mason shook his head. "I just don't understand why you're falling for a ridiculous theory. Do you believe the Heaven's Gate suicides jumped on spaceships to travel to a heavenly astral plane? You do believe that the earth is round, right?"

"Of course!"

"Terry, Terry, do you want to believe in something solid and real? I'm solid and real and right here, and the FBI does have sway with the Justice Department. Let me show you something else that's real." He pulled out his phone and flipped to pictures of Dante's victims. "They look beautiful, right? But I don't believe you meant to hurt anyone. And when Dante steals all their blood, Terry, they die. They are the beautiful dead who—as all living creatures—will now rot and decay. They are not buying anyone a ticket to vampire immortality. I can help you, Terry. Trust me. Stephan Dante has gotten what he wants from you. Oh, he's not going to turn into an immortal and he knows it. By the way, he trained Jesse Miller who is no longer with us—having been tutored by Dante, but deciding to heck with vampires, he'd just become Jack the Ripper. An honest thing at least—he just liked the power of stealing life from others. That's not you, Terry. Accept this—Dante is not coming back for you. He can't help you, and if he could, he wouldn't. You can't offer him anything more that he needs. I know you're not a cold-blooded killer. So does he. You've no history of forging and to the best of my knowledge, you're not sitting on a multimillion-dollar haul anywhere. Help me—and I will help you."

Donavan stared at him a long time and then lowered his head. "I…he didn't say I had to kill anyone. He said my work here would be enough for me to gain my place with him."

"He lied. He gave you a bold, all-out lie, Terry. And somewhere inside you, you know it. You wanted to believe in him. You wanted it so badly because it was better than the prospect of twenty years to life behind bars. Anything was better than that. You know, sometimes, it starts with someone promising all good things. A truly equal society. That's pretty much what Jim Jones promised his followers—social justice. But what turned him on, what kept him moving forward at all times, was a desire for power. Dante doesn't believe in the least that he's going to be immortal. What he loves, what he craves, is power. He also loves the act of playing God—he loves killing. Terry, this is your chance help me out."

"Yes!" Donavan said, suddenly looking up at him. The man had tears in his eyes. "Yes, I will help you. I am so sorry. I—I was a wretched alcoholic. I didn't want to kill anyone, but when I didn't drink, the shaking and the headaches got so bad. Up until I was in here…up until the doctor… I…" He stopped speaking and looked Mason in the eye. "I will help you. I don't know everything, but I will help you."

★ ★ ★

"Libby Larson has two small children," Alexandra—
Alex—Beaufort told Della. "Her poor husband—he's beside himself. I don't think that Libby will be returning to
work with prisoners, not after this! In this unpredictable
day and age, the woman has a beautiful home life, people
who truly love her, and now this..."

"She's still touch and go?" Della asked.

"The doctors believe she will make it. We were just
fighting different situations. He hit her with a needle filled
with sedation, stabbed her in the side—luckily missing
major organs—and knocked her on the head with something...no one was even sure what he grabbed. But we've
been giving her constant transfusions and done everything
possible to clean out her system from the overdose of mor-
phine. Such a good person!"

Della smiled and nodded at the young nurse speaking
with her. "Did you know her before she came in after the
attack?"

"I did. We went to nursing school together. She believed
everyone deserved a second chance. That human beings
were basically good, and that..."

Her words trailed.

"I still believe, just like Libby, that most people are
good," Della told her ruefully. "It's like anything—we hear
the most about the bad. And sometimes we're unfortunate
enough to see it. But I've been at this a while, and I can
tell you most people are good and want to help when help
is needed. We know about the bad—which I believe is the
fringe—because the bad is always loud and makes us question all else. Anyway, sorry, I understand her—and understand if she doesn't go back to work at the facility. I didn't

come to cause further problems. I don't want to upset her anymore. But if possible, I would like to talk to her."

"She wants to see you," Alex said. "She heard the FBI had brought him in, and she wants to help catch him again. Still...for her safety and well-being, five minutes?" Alex asked.

"Five minutes," Della promised.

Libby Larson was in a private room. An IV ran fluids into her arm while the tubes in her nostrils provided oxygen.

Even in a hospital bed with wires all around her, Libby was a beautiful young woman. Her eyes were closed when Della entered the room, and she couldn't help but wonder if Dante had been furious he couldn't tend to her as he did his victims—dressing her up to lie in "sleep" like a fairy-tale princess just waiting for true love's kiss.

Her hair was dark black and swept across the whiteness of the hospital sheets. When she opened her eyes, they were an incredible deep brown.

"FBI?" she whispered.

Della nodded, smiling, drawing up a chair. "And so grateful to see you alive and on your way to recovery."

"I knew who he was. And still...we thought he was going to die. The doctor...oh, God, we were even discussing the fact that we were compelled to do everything we could to save his life. He should have been dead! I was one of the medical personnel who rushed into the cafeteria when the guards had it under control, and I saw the blood... He shouldn't be alive! But he is, and Dr. Henson is dead and others and... I'm so sorry!"

"What happened?" Della asked. "Do you remember anything at all?"

"Yes. When Dante came in, naturally, he wasn't cuffed.

I don't remember exactly, but one of us figured he needed to be restrained and the doctor went out to see the guards. Then I felt a stab, a little prick, and I was bleeding and confused and then I think something hit me on the head but I barely even felt it… He was so fast. I—I don't remember more!"

"Did he say anything at all?" Della asked. "We're trying to ascertain where he might be heading."

"No. Not a word. But…"

"But?"

"I'd seen him before," she said softly. "Prisoners get vaccines, checkups. He was always so polite, friendly to those around him. And prisoners…talk. When they don't think others can hear them. He made friends with everyone in here—the worst of the worst." She paused, wincing. "The only hard-core people he seemed to ignore were pedophiles— he had no interest in them."

"To the best of my knowledge, he doesn't kill children," Della said.

"How can a man appear to be so decent, polite—even charming—and be such a monster? And I can't help but feel it's partially my fault—"

"Never think that. Never. Saving lives is a beautiful thing. Trust me. Stephan Dante has fooled just about everyone he's ever met. Don't let him succeed. Don't let him change you," Della said softly.

"He whistled sometimes."

"What did he whistle?"

"I can't quite put my finger on the tune, but…"

"Yes?"

"It seemed as if he was taunting people with it. A lot of what I'm saying is hearsay. I only saw him a few times while he was incarcerated, I just..." Tears stung her eyes. "The doctor is dead. A guard... That man is a monster!"

"Thank you," Della told her. "Thank you. And get better! You need to rest and recuperate."

"I will. I have children and the dearest husband in the world. Do you have children?"

"No, I don't. But I've heard yours are wonderful."

"Little boy and little girl. And my husband! Are you married?"

"No."

"I'm sorry. That was rude—"

"No, it's okay. There are people in my life who make it very precious, too."

"Hold them close. Because we never know. We just never know." She smiled weakly. "Ah, no children, but there is someone you love. I mean, besides your family."

"Yes," Della said, smiling in return. "There is someone very important in my life."

"Make sure they know! There were moments when I was semiconscious when I thought I might die, and I wondered what my last words were to my husband. And I was so glad...we'd been on the phone. He'd told me he could pick up the kids, and I thanked him and I told him I loved him. I was so glad to realize that! Well, happier that they think I'm going to be okay, but...tell people that you love them. Because none of us knows what our last words to anyone will be."

"I will. I will remember your words. And thank you. Thank you again. I'm going to leave my card on your bedside table. If you think of anything else that might be helpful, will you have someone call me for you?"

"Of course, yes. And I'm going to work on my memory—and my whistle."

As Della rose to leave, Libby Larson indeed began trying to whistle, trying to replicate what she had heard.

Despite her condition, she found a tune.

And as she walked out, Della went still. At first, the whisper of a whistle just teased at her memory as well.

Then she thought she recognized the tune—and yes, it had been meant to tease and taunt.

And knowing Dante, she thought bitterly, it was almost an invitation. He wanted them to run around trying to follow him.

He didn't want them missing any of his handiwork.

Don't miss
Cursed at Dawn
from New York Times *bestselling*
author Heather Graham,
available August 2023 wherever
MIRA books are sold!